THE SENIOR YEAR

Joseph S. Nettles

iUniverse, Inc.

New York Lincoln Shanghai

The Senior Year

iUniverse, Inc.

For information address:
iUniverse, Inc.
2021 Pine Lake Road, Suite 100
Lincoln, NE 68512
www.iuniverse.com

Front Cover Illustrated by
Jo and Curtis Chapline

ISBN: 0-595-31097-4

Printed in the United States of America

For Lisa, Josie, Linda, Iris, Anthony, Mustafa, Frank, Bob, Joe, John and Gene for their proofreading and/or comments, and especially Roseann for letting me interrupt her at all the wrong times to help me navigate through the grammatical mire, thorns and bumps in the night, that plague a creature, such as myself, trying to tell a story. And to a special friend, George, whom I've never met that works with me on a mutually inspired project.

Foreword

This story is pure fiction. Any resemblance to persons, living or dead is purely coincidental. Some of the medical terminology used in this novel is strictly from the imagination of the author and is not meant to infringe on words from a valid medical vocabulary. The town, Waynesford, Indiana is made up to accommodate other aspects of this story. While there are hints of time frames mentioned in this novel; i.e., the 1940's/50's, the author believes this work is compatible with most time periods and feels the readers enjoyment will be enriched by cloning their own experiences to the era represented.

PART I

CHAPTER 1

▼

Evanston. Illinois

The doctor extended a hand of congratulations to the new father, Bernard Kreppe. He had been waiting in the expectant father's lounge for what seemed like an eternity. His wife endured a long and arduous labor before finally giving birth to their healthy new son. He viewed his newborn through the nursery window. The proud father watched as a nurse took the infant from his crib and disappeared through the rear door of the nursery. Momentarily another nurse appeared and directed Mister Kreppe to his wife Maggie's room. She was holding their son when he entered.

"Little man, meet your father," Maggie said, pridefully. "Isn't he beautiful?" she appealed to her husband.

"We did well," Bernard said. "He looks just like you, dear."

"Oh, that's not so," she said modestly. "He looks like his father. Look at those eyes." She hesitated and turned inward for a brief moment, thinking how best to approach her husband with a personal problem she was having regarding the baby's name. There was no good way. Just bring it up and hope for the best. "Sweetheart—I've been thinking; I know how much the name Nostradamus means to you, but couldn't we give our son a more contemporary or casual name like William or Robert?"

"Maggie, dear, this name question has already been discussed and settled. We agreed to name our child Nostradamus if it was a boy, remember? Nostradamus is a man's name, strong in character. It signifies the intellect of the fifteenth century French physician and astrologer. The boy will grow up reflecting the spirit of his namesake. No, dear. This has been my dream. The boy must be named Nostradamus."

"Yes, but—"

"Now, now, dear. We'll compromise," the father said. "His middle name can be your maiden name? How about that?"

"Fuller?" she asked, knowingly.

"Why not?" Bernard said. "This way we share the credit for naming our son."

Maggie tried not to show her disappointment, but she knew this was the best she was going to get from her strong-willed husband. She raised her son up to an almost vertical position to introduce him to the world. "World," she said. "Meet Nostradamus Fuller Kreppe."

The Stevens Hotel, Chicago
Two Weeks Later

The easel at the entrance to the main ballroom hosted a framed poster featuring "Martin Munroe and His Celebrated Orchestra". The ballroom was filled to capacity with little or no room on the dance floor. The reckless dancers ricocheted off one another to the bouncy rhythms of the Charleston.

A bellman waited patiently next to the stage while Martin Munroe finished his trumpet solo. Martin anchored his horn on a stand for that purpose, then retrieved his baton and assumed position as director of his orchestra. The bellman stepped forward and interrupted with a message from a nearby hospital. Martin's wife was about to give birth. "They said if you hurry you can make it."

Martin signaled Cully Tujaque, his relief from the orchestra's front line, to take over while he went to be with his wife. Cully was one of those rare musicians that could double on most any instrument. His primary job was playing first trumpet with the Chicago Symphony Orchestra, but he played with his friend, Martin Munroe, when the symphony had a lull in their schedule. He was prepared to take over if and when word came of the impending delivery.

Martin looked at his watch. It was ten thirty. He hurried to the Michigan Avenue exit and departed the building into a blinding snowstorm. The crystal white flurry banked against the windshields of parked cars and sloped against buildings and crossed icy sidewalks. The only traffic navigating the slippery streets was a string of taxi cabs. Martin flagged the first empty cab and instructed the driver to take him to the West Side Hospital "and step on it," quickly realizing the condition of the streets wouldn't allow for excessive acceleration.

As Martin entered the hospital, his nostrils were charged with the sanitation of Lysol. The halls of the aged building were orderly spaced with religious statues in ornate niches. They stood on marble floors beneath high arched ceilings. The intersections were mitered and resembled Vatican-like architecture minus the frescoes on the ceiling.

Martin wasted no time finding his way to the nursery. A nurse greeted him with congratulations on being the father of a healthy eight pound baby boy. He felt terrible having missed the birth of his son and not being with his wife at the crucial time of delivery. The nurse directed him to his wife's room where he paused outside for a moment, composing himself and settling down from his rush to get there.

Martin quietly opened the door and peeked in. His wife, Minette, heard the door squeak and turned her head in his direction.

"Oh, Martin, it's you," she said. "Thank God. I am so glad you are here. Congratulations, daddy."

"Congratulations to you, sweetheart," he said upon entering the room. "It's a boy."

"I know," she said. "I was there, remember? I'm disappointed I wasn't the first to tell you."

"Keep still and rest." Martin insisted. He bent over the bed and kissed his wife on the forehead.

"They're going to bring the baby to me in a moment. You sit here by me," she said, patting the bed next to her. "I want you by my side."

He squeezed her hand in acknowledgment of her request.

The door opened again; this time a nurse entered carrying their infant son.

"Here's my handsome fellow now," she said, reaching out to take her baby.

"He looks just like his father," the nurse said.

"He's better looking than his father," Martin advanced proudly.

"You need to call Elaine and tell her the good news," Minette suggested to her husband.

"I will, dear. She'll be happy to know she has a baby brother," Martin said of their ten year old daughter. "Her wish finally came true."

"Now—What are we going to name our little trumpet player?" Minette smiled as she faced her husband.

"You said once you liked the name Milo if it was a boy," Martin answered.

"What do you think, darling?" Minette asked, passing the final decision back to her husband.

"Well—Milo is not your everyday Joe or Bill. I like it," Martin said.

"Then Milo it is," Minette closed the question.

"It's time to take little Milo back to the nursery," one of the nurses interrupted. "I'll bring him to you again when it's feeding time and you can do the honors."

"I'll go so you can get some rest," Martin said, "and swing by in the morning." He kissed Minette goodnight and left.

CHAPTER 2

▼

Evanston
Four Years Later

Bernard was at the kitchen table watching Nostradamus finish up his evening reading lesson.

"What's this word?" he asked his son.

"Push–me–pull–ya," Nostradamus answered proudly, emitting a snicker brought on by the length and sound of the catchy name.

"What are you going to read when you finish *Doctor Dolittle*," his mother asked.

"There are lots of books in the library, Mommie. You pick me one."

"We will find you a good one to read," Maggie said. "I promise. Come on little one, lets pack em' in for the night. It's past your bed time."

"Please Mommy, let me read one more chapter."

"Oh—kay, just one more," his mother said, giving in to her persistent son's plea. "One more chapter, then it's off to bed you go."

"I promise," Nostradamus said.

There was a knock on the front door. "I wonder who that could be?" Maggie questioned. She looked at the wall clock. It read a little after eight.

"I'll see who it is," Bernard said as he pushed himself up from the table and moved in the direction of the front door.

Their neighbor sent an apple pie by her son, Tyrone. Tyrone was Nostradamus' playmate. He was a little black boy the same age as Nostradamus. The whites of his eyes were contrasted to the chocolate velvety texture of his skin. With his bright eyes and flashing white teeth he could be the spokesperson for either Murine or an Ipana toothpaste advertisement or both.

"Hi, Nostradamus," Tyrone beamed a greeting to his friend.

"Hi, Tyrone."

Turning to Mrs Kreppe, Tyrone announced, "My momma said she baked this pie especially for the Kreppe family."

"Well—isn't that sweet," Maggie said accepting the pie from Tyrone's hands to hers.

"Are you going to eat it now?" Tyrone asked, hinting for an invitation.

"That depends," Maggie stated, stringing Tyrone along regarding his cute question.

"Depends on what?" Tyrone asked hungering for a piece of pie.

"On whether or not you think it will keep until tomorrow."

"No Mam. I don't think it will keep that long."

"Then what should we do with it?"

"If you ask me, I think you should eat it now and I can hang around in case you need some help," Tyrone responded, flashing his signature smile. The whites of his headlight eyes beamed steadily at Maggie as his taste buds foamed in anticipation of getting his own slice of apple pie.

"I think it will keep until tomorrow," Maggie said, deciding to end Tyrone's suspense.

"Could you save me some if I came back tomorrow?" Tyrone begged of Maggie.

"You come by tomorrow and we'll have apple pie a la mode. How does that sound?"

"Sounds okay to me, but what about Nostradamus?" Tyrone asked brandishing his smile, not wanting his friend to be left out.

"Don't I get some too?" asked Nostradamus, protecting his domain.

"You too," his mother said. "We can't have pie unless everyone is included. You're safe for tomorrow."

Bernard admired Tyrone's bright smile and buoyant attitude. It prompted him to ask, "Tyrone, what do you want to be when you grow up?"

Tyrone beamed from ear to ear, exhibiting his brilliant toothpaste smile again. "Why I wants to be a gabage man," he related his aspiration proudly.

Not wanting to be outdone, Nostradamus said, "That's what I want to be too—when I grow up."

Downtown Chicago

Martin, Minette and Cully Tujaque were attending the annual ceremonial dinner sponsored by the Instrument Manufacturers Association of Elkhart, Indiana. After dining, crafty sales pitches were given by various companies followed by award presentations of new instruments to their stable of celebrity musicians. This act of kindness granted them fodder for their advertising machinery and guaranteed bragging rights that *so and so* of *such and such* fame preferred to play their instruments over comparable models from the competition.

Ballard, the maker of Martin's trumpet, presented him a gold plated edition with his name etched amongst elaborate scroll work engravings on the bell. Each year, Martin would sell his old horn to a fan, but this year was different. He was going to give last years Ballard to Milo, judging he was old enough to start taking lessons. Cully was close enough to the family to be offended if he weren't allowed the honor of teaching young Milo to play his new instrument.

The next morning as Minette prepared breakfast, Martin came into the kitchen. Milo was playing with the cereal in his bowl.

Milo," Martin said, addressing his son. "I have something very special for you; something that will make you very proud to own. Daddy has to go out, but I will be back before I go to work and give it to you then."

"Why, Daddy. Let me have it, let me have it, let me have it now—pul-lease," Milo begged.

"Martin, why do you do the child this way?" Minette chastised her husband. "You knew he would be unhappy if he had to wait for his present."

"Milo will have something to look forward to when I return this afternoon," Martin said.

By now, Milo was slouching sideways in his chair with his elbow on the table and his cheek mashed against his fist in a show of disappointment.

Sensing Milo's let down, Martin walked over to his son and rested his hand on the lad's shoulder. "We have to wait for Uncle Cully," Martin said. "It is so very special, it'll be worth the wait. You'll see."

Milo spent a restless day waiting for his dad's return. He went grocery shopping with his mother. She took him to a toy store to help pass the time and they stopped for ice cream. Finally, it was early afternoon and Martin was due to show up at the house. Milo's anxiety had worn him down and he had fallen asleep in a chair trying to hold out for his dad's promise to be home early. Minette picked her son up and managed the stairs, holding him in her arms. When she reached his room, she placed him lightly on his bed and covered him with a blanket.

Martin arrived home shortly thereafter accompanied by Cully Tujaque.

"Where is Milo?" Martin asked Minette.

"He was so excited waiting for you, he wore himself out and fell asleep. I took him upstairs to his room so he could take a nap."

Martin went to the closet and extracted the trumpet he was going to give Milo. Very carefully he opened the case for what was to be the last time and removed the horn with tender affection. He inserted the mouthpiece into the open shank and taking a deep breath, put his retiring trumpet to his lips. He began to play, very sweetly, Milo's favorite song, *What a Friend We Have in Jesus.*

Milo was startled by the sounds coming from his father's horn. He opened his eyes and stared at the ceiling while he constructed his whereabouts. Hearing the sounds of the horn, he knew his father was home and he was in his room having just awakened from a nap.

"Daddy," Milo let out a scream at the top of his voice, shrieking throughout the house. "Daddy," he screamed again. He scampered from his bed, down the stairs and into the living room with outstretched arms. "Daddy—Where is my special present? Give it to me. Give it to me. Please—give it to me now."

"Aren't you going to say hi to your Uncle Cully?"

Milo looked around the room and found Cully sitting in a rocking chair. He ran over, jumped in his lap and wrapped his arms around Cully's neck.

Cully pointed to his cheek where he wanted Milo to plant a kiss. "Give me a Yankee Dime," he said to Milo. The youngster kissed Cully as instructed then slid off his lap and rushed back to his father.

"Can I have my present now, please?"

"Sure, why not." Martin said. He took a polishing cloth and wiped the fingerprints from the horn and placed it lovingly in Milo's small hands.

"This was my favorite trumpet, Milo," Martin said, "and now it's yours. I waited for Uncle Cully before giving it to you. He wants to tell you something."

Cully made a motion for Milo to come sit in his lap. Milo went back to Uncle Cully as signaled, taking the trumpet his daddy had just given him. "I'm going to give you lessons Milo, and pretty soon you will be able to play better than me or your dad."

Milo didn't know what to think. The trumpet was a real prize compared to the plastic toys he had to play with. He knew it had been his daddy's trumpet and that neither his dad nor his mom would let him play with it, and now it was all his. He wrapped his lips around the mouthpiece and blew. A whistling sound came rushing through the tubing and out the bell.

"Don't you worry, Milo," Martin said? "When Uncle Cully finishes teaching you, you will be a real trumpet player. What do you have to say to that?

"Thank you, Daddy. I'll play just like you and Uncle Culley."

CHAPTER 3

▼

First Grade, Evanston
Two Years Later

Maggie and Bernard came to the realization that the name Nostradamus was a mouthful and too burdensome for everyday use. They mutually agreed to shorten Nostradamus to N.D. over N.D.'s objection. As a youngster, he didn't understand his parents were being considerate of him. He liked the name Nostradamus.

N.D. went with his mother the next day to the library to return an array of overdue books and check out new ones. While there, he spotted one with the name Nostradamus in the title. "Mom," he was excited. "Look at this. It has my name on it. Let me check this one out."

"Honey," Maggie said, "you are a little young for this book. Let's wait until you are older so you can appreciate it."

"No!" N.D. shouted. "It's got my name on it and I want it NOW!—Pul-lease."

"Well, if you are going to make a scene, I suppose we can get it."

"Thank you, Mom. Thank you. Thank you. I'll read it first, I promise."

Nostradamus stories was the beginning. Books on Socrates, Plato and Aristotle followed in rapid succession. Naturally, at first, N.D. had problems with this heavy reading material. What he didn't comprehend, his father explained to him in terms he could understand. Reading and comprehension soon became a game as he dug deeper into ancient literature. Right or wrong he would draw conclusions to the materials he read, then apply his own logic based on his interpretation of the sequence of events. Greek History fascinated N.D. and he became addicted to one of the earliest testaments to mankind. His interest emerged from the variance in Greek civilizations beginning with the archeological finds of the

Minoan Society on Crete. Greek history was followed by Greek Mythology, succeeded by Tolstoy's War and peace, the American Civil War and eventually the challenge of Shakespeare. His parents let him ramble through the books and made no attempt to hold him back.

*　　　*　　　*　　　*

Maggie had enrolled N.D. in the first grade and was getting him ready for his first day at school. "You be a little gentleman," she warned, "and don't brag to your school mates about how smart you are. It is wise to let them find out for themselves."

"I got it, Mom. I'm too intellectual to be around ordinary kids. Is that it?"

"No, darling," Maggie corrected her son. "You're not any smarter than anyone else. You may have read more and think you are."

"But you and Daddy say I'm smart."

"All parents say that about their children. Go to school and see for yourself, then come home and tell me all about it."

"Oh—okay," N.D. said. "Do they give you a girlfriend your first day at school?"

"No Sweetie," his mother said as she straightened the knot on his necktie. "If you want a girlfriend, you'll have to find one on your own. That's the way it works, then you get the one you want."

N.D. didn't know why he brought up the subject of girls. He didn't like them to begin with. For some unknown reason, he duped himself into thinking that having a girlfriend was a necessary part of going to school.

*　　　*　　　*　　　*

At the school house, Maggie accompanied her son to his assigned room and left after small talk with the teacher.

"I'm Miss Dowdy," the teacher said, introducing herself to her pupils. "I want each of you to stand up and tell the class your name, starting over here." She pointed to the pupil she wanted to begin the process.

When it was N.D.'s turn, he stood up and announced to the class that his name was "N.D. Kreppe."

Miss Dowdy asked him what the N.D. stood for and he threw out his chest and proudly announced, "none of your bees wax."

The startled teacher objected strongly to his answer and warned the rest of the class about their outburst of laughter.

"N.D. You will have to tell the class what your initials stand for or you will have to put on the dunce cap and stand in the corner of the room." She held the dunce cap up for all to see.

N.D. was intimidated by Miss Dowdy's threats and took a deep breath and started over again. "My name is Nostradamus Fuller Kreppe," he said with enthusiasm.

Muffled giggles spread throughout the classroom. The bully crowd, bunched together in the rear of the room, outright guffawed.

Miss Dowdy rapped the top of her desk with a ruler. "Let's have some order in the classroom," she demanded. "It is not polite to laugh at another person's name."

She admonished the bullies outright, whose grins morphed into straight faces and giggles modulated downward to silence. "That's better. Now let's move on," Miss Dowdy said, taking back control of her class. "All together now. Let's tell N.D. we are sorry. Ready?"

Thirty little voices came together in unison. "We're sor-ree." It was the sound of innocence. The usual trouble makers heeded under duress of Miss Dowdy threats.

As the class continued with their introductions, N.D. became introspective and decided then and there that he wanted to be called by his middle name, Fuller. It was more standard in sound and non-humiliating. Besides, he would never have to explain what the N.D. stood for, ever again.

The recess bell rang and N.D. made a beeline to his mother's house.

"What are you doing home, dear?" his mother, asked, surprised to see him.

"The bell rang so I came home for lunch," he said, searching for the food.

"Honey, it's too early for lunch. Recess maybe—?"

"I'm hungry now, Mom."

"Let's get you back to school and keep you out of trouble," Maggie said. "Okay?"

"Oh-kay," N.D. stretched his words, obviously disappointed.

His mom drove him back to school. The school yard was empty of students indicating that recess was over. His little mind focused on being in *dutch* with the teacher. He wanted to get along and be accepted as a serious student despite the deceptive trail of mess-ups he was leaving behind.

When he straggled into Miss Dowdy's room, she asked, "where have you been, N.D.?"

"I thought it was lunch time," he answered. "I went home for lunch."

Snickers and giggles followed N.D.'s honesty and labeled him as the first grade screw up. Neither the teacher or the class knew he had ingested reading material on Nostradamus, and down the line through the American Civil War and Shakespeare. His achievements were astounding and were the results of his father teaching him to read several years prior to his invasion on the public school system. His reading was now an insatiable habit. By all standards, he was the most intellectual person in the school, including Miss Dowdy, but his immaturity was working in the background, against him. His classmates laughed with almost every word he spoke and everything he did. What they considered funny, he considered insulting to his pride. He knew he was better than the way he was being treated and decided he probably wasn't going to like school.

When the first day of school was finally over, N.D. walked out of the building into the fresh air and was happy he was headed homeward when the bully squad from his class filed out from behind a building and encircled him.

"What did you say your name was," asked the leader?

"That's for me to know and you to find out," N.D. salvoed back with indignation.

"We know what it is," one of the boys came forward. "It's Nostra-dumb-ass?"

"That ain't so," another boy said. "It's full-er-crap."

The gang started a cackle that transposed to more abusive ridicule. Everyone was having fun at N.D.'s expense except N.D. One of the molesters crouched behind him on all fours and the one with the big mouth pushed. N.D. spilled over the guy hunkered down behind him, landed on his shoulders and dirtied his head in the mud. Huge tears welled in his eyes as the challengers started laughing again and pointing to him.

"You are all a bunch of cowards," N.D. yelled as he regained his footing and stood up to his assailants.

"Who you calling a coward?" one of the boys charged sarcastically as he shoved N.D. backward.

"You are all cowards," N.D. managed to shout, holding back tears.

"You think so," this one guy said pointing to his chin. "Come on and hit me. Let's see what you got." He was trying to provoke N.D. into starting a fight. "Give it your best shot," he said, "then I'll show you who's a coward."

"NO! I'm not going to hit you. I'm going home," N.D. said.

"Not before you defend yourself for calling us cowards," one of the antagonist said as he worked up a mouth full of saliva and discharged it on N.D. Another guy spat on him which started a chain reaction. Before it was over N.D. had been bathed in spit and individually spat upon, at least once by every member of the gang. He started crying and swinging wildly as the band of uncontrolled hoodlums attacked him. When they finished beating up on N.D., he was warned not to squeal on them to anybody or the next time he might not be so lucky. He believed their threat out of fear of reprisal.

N.D. was sniffling when he walked into the house. His mother's instincts warned her of N.D.'s distress. She came running to see what was wrong with her young son. What she saw was horrifying. N.D.'s clothes were torn and tattered. His bare skin was scratched in visible areas and skid burns were acutely red on his knees and elbows. His nose was dripping blood and he had a shiner on his right eye.

"My baby," Maggie cried. "What happened to my baby?" she stooped, taking her son in her arms, holding him close. N.D. started to sob out loud as his mother comforted him.

"Who did this to you?" Maggie asked.

"Nobody," N.D, answered, still sobbing and trying to protect his assailants.

His mother knew better, but wasn't sure how to handle the situation. She decided to let her husband deal with it when he came home. When confronted, his father's remarks to his wife were to leave the lad alone. Hassles were part of growing up. Maggie didn't buy it. Bernard hadn't seen the condition N.D. was in when he walked into the house.

That evening at the dinner table, Bernard saw N.D.'s scratches and bruises more clearly under the dinning room light. He was angry his son had been tormented and there didn't seem to be anything immediately he could do about it, except confront the principal, and he deemed that would cause more trouble for N.D. He decided to leave it alone unless it happened again.

"Daddy?" N.D. appeal to his father. "I don't want to be called N.D. anymore."

"May I ask why?" his father inquired.

"When the kids at school found out what N.D. stood for, they laughed at me."

N.D.'s request left little room for argument. Recollecting that boys will be boys, Bernard knew right away that Nostradamus was teasing fodder for the cliques and bullies around the school yard. "Sounds good to me," his father said, giving in to ease N.D.'s pain. "Everyone has a name. What would you like yours to be?"

"I like Fuller," N.D. said.

"Fine," his father said. "After all, Fuller *is* your name. From this moment forward, we shall refer to you as Fuller, but don't forget your first name is Nostradamus. Someday, when you are older, you'll be proud to be called Nostradamus and you'll thank your mother and me for having the presence of mind to give you such a strong name. You'll be the better man because of it."

"Thank you father," Fuller said, going over to his dad and giving him a hug.

West Side

Uncle Cully was giving Milo his latest lesson in trumpet technique and intonation. "You've come a long way, Milo. You take to your trumpet like a duck takes to water. I'm proud of you, little fellow" he said, "as I know your mother and father must be. I've got an idea. How would you like to play Christmas Carols with the Salvation Army Band?"

"Really Uncle Cully? Please tell me it's so."

"I can't do that, Milo, but I'll work on it for you. I will ask Major Stiles for his support of the idea and see what he thinks."

"Mom! Mommy!" Milo summoned his mother. "Guess What? I'm going to play Christmas Carols with the Salvation Army Band. Uncle Cully says I can."

"That's nice, dear," Minette said, turning her focus on Cully, giving him a questionable eye.

"We'll see," Cully said to Milo. "We'll have to see what kind of interest we can drum up."

*   *   *   *

A light layer of snow blanketed the Chicago Loop. The wind off of Lake Michigan caused a canyon effect between the tall buildings making little swirls that resembled miniature tornados spawned by the wind velocity and loose snow flakes. On State Street near the entrance to Marshall Fields, a Salvation Army lady with her red bucket and tripod, rang her little bell soliciting donations. Next to her was the Salvation Army Band playing Christmas Carols with little Milo Munroe playing his trumpet in perfect time to the music. He seemed to be a bigger draw than any of the adults on his team. His cap was too big for his head and fit over his ears. Little snow banks were accumulating on his shoulders and snow flakes stuck to his eye lashes momentarily before thawing. He played the written music attached to the lyre on his horn. His tone was clear, steady and pleasing to the ear, thanks to Uncle Cully's meticulous teaching and disciplining. People approaching the band heard Milo's trumpet before they heard any of the other instruments which was a testament to his musical craftsmanship.

Milo was so enamored of his role with the band that he played through lunch. He played with great intensity of feeling and drew a loyal crowd that was captivated by the beautiful sounds emerging from the horn of a six year old. When the team returned from lunch, the crowd he had gathered dispersed. He was so into his job, that he felt let down and lonesome for the Christmas season when it finally ended.

CHAPTER 4

▼

Evanston
Three Years Later

Members of the faculty had been noticing how peculiarly brilliant Fuller's diction was developing and were overwhelmed by his overall intelligence leaking through his everyday involvement at school. No one in the system knew of his reading habits. The only clues were his rise to shine in all of his school assignments and examinations. His intellectual acceleration and articulate delivery was far beyond the bounds of the fourth grade curriculum he was mired in with lessor students. His scholastic bent was over the heads of his peer group. The school authorities were slowly accepting the fact they had a genius on their hands. He knew he was blessed with prevailing intelligence and was smarter than most, but was never told he was special.

His fourth grade teacher, Mrs. Sissie, had an exercise for her students whereby they were to stand before the class and give a short talk on someone they considered to be their special hero and why. A little girl was chosen first to come forward to the head of the class and reveal her hero.

"My name is Elizabeth and my hero is Dale Evans because she is married to her husband who is, Roy Rogers. He shoots the bad men and then tells her about it at supper time and they kiss and make up."

"Thank you for sharing that with us, Elizabeth," Mrs. Sissie said. "A big hand, class, for Elizabeth."

Next was a little boy: "My name is Randy," he said. "My favorite hero is Davy Crockett becuz he helped fight the Mexicans when they came over the wall at the Alamo and kilt him."

When it was Fuller's time, he went to the head of the class and said, "My name is Fuller. My hero is Socrates. He was born in the year 470 B.C. and died in 399 B.C. He is my hero for two reasons. First, he taught Plato what he knew and Plato wrote *The Republic*. In it, he defines his insight of an ideal state. He also wrote laws in which Socrates is the number one participant. Secondly, Socrates contributed to western thought by his method of inquiry, known as the method of *elenchos* which is the foundation for a good portion of western philosophy. During Socrates lifetime, the Athenian Empire was defeated by Sparta, the bad guys. Socrates was often resented by influential figures of the day because their reputations for wisdom and virtue were debunked by his questions. An Athenian public court tried Socrates for impiety and corrupting the young. They found him guilty as charged and executed him by making him drink hemlock which is a poison. Of course he wasn't guilty and that is why he is my hero. Ta-daaah—" Fuller trumpeted out loud ending his story.

Some members of the class went *duh* as their jaws fell open, wondering what that was all about. Others went *huh*? They were blind sided by Fuller's spouting and had no idea what he was alluding to.

Fuller sat down at his desk, especially pleased with himself.

Mrs. Sissie, impressed, asked Fuller, "what else do you know about Socrates?"

"I know a lot," Fuller said, "First he—"

"That'll do for now," Mrs. Sissie interrupted. "How much do you know about Plato?"

"Oh, I know a lot about him too," Mrs. Sissie.

"We will talk about that another time also," Mrs. Sissie said, intruding on Fuller's willingness to share more of his achievements.

"I've also read War and Peace," Fuller volunteered proudly.

"We'll talk about that too, at another time," Mrs. Sissie asserted.

Mrs. Sissie wasted no time in confronting the principal about Fuller. She went straight to the school office when her class was over.

"I knew we had a genius on our hands," the principal explained to her. "I just didn't know on what level to place him."

"What do we do with him?" asked Mrs. Sissie.

"Just keep an eye on him," the principal said. "These types tend to be over-confident and sometimes need to be disciplined."

"To tell you the truth," Mrs. Sissie informed the principal, "Sometimes I feel inferior to him and other times, downright afraid."

"Don't be," the principal advised. "What he has acquired in knowledge, he lacks in maturity. Always let him know you're in charge."

"I will," said Mrs. Sissie, feeling somewhat relieved they had cornered Fuller's intellect into a manageable perspective. "Thank you for your confidence in me," she said to the principal as she readied herself to leave the office.

West Side

Cully Tujaques was at the Munroe household to work through a musical routine with two other members of Martin's orchestra; Pete Scalibib, the lead sax man and Joey Crabtree from the trombone section. They were there to work with Martin and Cully on perfecting the entrance to one of their new musical numbers. Milo was running scales when they arrived, but put his practice on hold to watch the professionals wrestle with their problem.

"You sounded great, maestro," Cully said to Milo as he entered the room. "You're the only student I ever had that surpassed me on the trumpet." He was teasing, of course, but had an affectionate feeling he was creating a trumpet monster.

"I know that's a lie," Milo teased back. "I couldn't do it if you hadn't shown me how."

Milo had reached a point in his musical training where he was developing a broad technical ability and couldn't get enough practice to satisfy his enormous passion to excel on the trumpet. His efforts were self satisfying as well as pleasing to his dad.

"Pretty soon you'll be after my job," Pete said, clowning around.

"I can't play the saxophone, Mr. Scalibib, you know that," Milo said, flattered by Pete's remark, "but I'll learn if you teach me."

"Not a chance," said Pete. "I don't need the competition."

"I look to the time we can play together," Joey said. "You sound like a real pro."

"You guys are my dad's friends," Milo said. "You don't have to impress me."

"You really *are* good," Joey said, ruffling Milo's hair. "I *am* impressed by your playing," he commented, sincerely.

"Okay, fellows. Lets quit effing off and get with the program," Martin said. "The problem with the lead-in is it isn't smooth. It sounds like the drums are rushing us, but that's not the issue. When Cully goes da, da, daaaaaaa, the drummer smashes the symbol at the end of the daaaaaaa-uh. Bring your group in, Pete, with your series of triplets and when the symbol is struck again, pause a measure and a half for the tremor to ease off entirely, then you, Joey, wait a half rest, then bring your trombones in, softly at first, then you know—"

"You think that'll work?" Cully asked.

"Let's give it a shot," Martin reasoned.

"Yeah, we need that extra time to make the instruments sound musical," Pete declared.

"What do you think, Joey?" Martin asked. "Are you in agreement?"

"Yeah Boss," Joey returned. "It sounds reasonable to me."

"Okay, we'll try this first thing tonight," Martin said.

Minette served the band members coffee and cake before they left and Milo went back to his practicing.

Martin and Minette's nineteen year old daughter, Elaine, brought her boyfriend home to meet her parents. "Mom, Dad", she announced anxiously. "This is my friend Raymond Powell."

"Raymond," they said together. "It's so nice to meet you."

"It's my pleasure," Raymond said. "Elaine tells me that you lead an orchestra, Mister Munroe."

"Yes. You two will have to come down and dance to it some evening. We're in a good setting. You'd enjoy yourself."

"Thank you. I would like that," Raymond said in response to the invitation. He looked over in Elaine's direction and caught her smiling and shaking her head up and down, implying *let's do it.*

"Elaine tells me that you're studying to be a doctor."

"Yes sir; a surgeon."

"Any particular field of surgery?" Martin asked.

"Yes sir," Raymond answered politely, "orthopedics."

As Elaine's parents made light conversation with their guest, the sounds of scales being played, technically perfect, on a trumpet, intruded on the discussion taking place in the living room.

"My, what technique," Raymond said. "Who's playing the trumpet?"

"That's my little brother," Elaine said. "Would you like to meet him?"

"I certainly would," Raymond said. "I have this huge record collection and I recognize good horn when I hear it."

"You wait here," Elaine said, "I'll go and get him."

She showed up shortly with this nine-year old kid wearing jeans and sneakers and holding this gold plated trumpet.

"This is your brother?" Raymond asked, surprised at her brother's youth. "You were playing the trumpet?"

"Raymond," Elaine said. "This is my little brother Milo—Milo, Raymond."

"Nice to meet you, sir." Milo said.

"The pleasure's all mine," Raymond came back.

"Can I go back now?" Milo asked Elaine.

"After you play something for Raymond."

"What would you like to hear," asked Milo.

"What can you play?" inquired Raymond.

Milo looked a little puzzled that someone would suggest there might be something he couldn't play. "You name it."

"Really?" Raymond questioned.

"Really," replied Milo.

Raymond looked toward Milo's father who nodded, meaning, *go ahead, ask him.*

"Do you know *The Carnival of Venice*?"

"That's an easy one," Milo said. Then wetting the inset of his mouthpiece with his tongue, he put the trumpet to his lips and an explosion of crisp clear notes, perfectly executed and technically correct, filled the room.

Milo played the highly technical number to perfection. Raymond stood up and clapped, showing his sincere appreciation for the youngster's talent. "Whew! I never heard The Carnival of Venice played quite like that before, unless by Harry James. What do you think of dixieland?" he asked Milo. "Do you like dixieland?"

"I like it, but my mother would rather I stick with the classics. She said if you can play classical music, you can play anything."

"I have a fine dixieland collection," Raymond said. "We'll have to get together some time and go through it."

"Swell," said Milo. "Do you have any Bix? I've heard so much about him. I would like to hear him play."

"Oh yes. He's a legend on the cornet. I also have him playing *In a mist* on the piano. I think he wrote it. It's deep and way ahead of it's time."

"I'd like to hear that too," Milo said.

"Can you play any dixieland?" Raymond asked.

"Just the songs I know. What would you like to hear," Milo asked, warming up to Raymond.

"Saint James Infirmary?" Raymond asked, somewhat doubtful his request would be in Milo's repertoire. "Can you play St. James Infirmary?"

Martin was taking this all in and was delighted that Elaine's young man showed enthusiasm for music, even the dixieland idiom.

Milo put his trumpet to his lips without saying anything further and started playing the old tune in its natural drag, consistent with a strip tempo. At appropriate passages, Milo stretched his arm, cupping his little hand over the bell. He growled a down and dirty chorus that would have Sally Rand dropping her fan to react with the bumps and grinds of his music.

When the song ended, Raymond clapped again for Milo, this time with noticeable enthusiasm, turning his head back and forth from Martin to Elaine. "Wow," he said. "Can you believe it—? Little fellow you are great—absolutely great."

Milo felt special and pretended not to know what all the fuss was about. His attitude was nonchalant as if anyone could do what he had just finished doing. He looked to Elaine. "Can I go now?" he asked?

"Sure, honey, you can go now and thanks for entertaining Raymond."

"It was nice to meet you sir," Milo said to Raymond.

"The pleasure's all mine," Raymond said, walking over and putting his arm around Milo, initiating a shoulder squeeze. It was a show of admiration for Milo's talent. "I'll see you another time," he said. "We are going to be great friends. I just know it."

Minette looked at the clock on the mantel. "It's time to put your trumpet away, dear," she said to Milo. "You don't want to be late for your karate lesson."

CHAPTER 5

▼

Evanston
Four Years Later

Fuller had gone to the library to return four books and check out four more. He had no sooner walked into the house and arranged his books in the order he planned to read them when the door bell rang. It was Tyrone with a basketball under one arm. "Want to shoot some baskets," he sought with youthful enthusiasm.

"Okay," Fuller said. "I'll give you one hour. Loser buys the drinks."

"You're on," Tyrone said.

After playing nearly an hour, their score was tied as each tried his best to outshine the other. Tyrone slowed his aggressive play to a standing position manipulating the ball to a slow dribble. "Hamburgers at three o'clock," he said, referring to two full bosomed girls approaching from the quarter direction on the compass, north aligning with twelve o'clock. He was alluding to the geometry of the female genitalia with the hamburger thing as opposed to associating hot dogs with the masculine configuration.

"Hi," Tyrone said to the girls as they passed by.

"Hello, boys," one of them said.

Tyrone and Fuller gave in to a natural response to beauty over basketball and caught up with the two girls.

"You want to talk some trash?" Tyrone asked, flashing his big tooth grin.

"We are not that kind of girls," one of them said indignantly. They elevated their noses and strolled away.

"Want to go finish the game," Fuller asked Tyrone.

"Naw. Not after that brush-off," Tyrone said. "Let's go get something to drink and go Dutch."

They went to a mom and pop store on a slow street and bought a couple of cold drinks and sat on the curb outside to drink them.

"Man, them girls should have grabbed us when they had the chance," Tyrone said, trying to understand his failure to get a favorable response. "Where did I go wrong?"

"You didn't approach them right," Fuller said.

"Oh yeah! How would you know? You never catch any girls," Tyrone barked, defending his endeavor. "How would you have approached them?"

Fuller thought for a moment, then drawing from the Shakespearean demeanor he readily identified with, contended, "I would have said something elegant like this; My how lovely you ladies look today. May we escort you to a soda fountain and offer you refreshment?"

"Why you think they'd go for that?" Tyrone sparked, scratching his head. "My line wasn't sissified like yours. The girls don't go for that shit."

"They go for it alright, because it has class," Fuller insisted.

"Class, my ass," Tyrone said. "It's getting so girls is all I ever think about. How does class fit in when all you really want to do is to grab a girl by the cheeks of the ass and pull her close to you? You ever think about girls, Fuller?"

"All the time," Fuller said. "I just wish I had a girlfriend that would let me squeeze her tit and say—Fuller, you can do anything with me you want to."

"They ain't no girl gonna say that."

"How would you know?"

"Because it's more fun making you crawl," Tyrone said. "Ask any girl that will be honest with you."

"I'm telling you, they want you as much as you want them."

"What would you do if a girl said, take me Fuller, I'm yours?" Tyrone asked, anxiously awaiting Fuller's retort.

Fuller looked upward and sighed a deep sigh. "I'd kiss her," he said.

"That's all?" Tyrone queried. "That's the first thing you'd do? What then?"

Still in a dreamy state, Fuller said, "I'd look her in the eyes and give her the best kiss she ever had."

"Get outta here, Fuller. You ain't figured it out yet. Don't you ever think about layin' next to a naked girl with your skin touchin' hers? That's when you know you are in like Flynn."

"Don't look now," Fuller said. "Hamburgers at twelve o'clock. Watch how I handle this."

The two boys stood up from the curb and dusted themselves off as the two girls approached.

"Good afternoon, ladies," Fuller said. "Might I tell you how lovely you both look?"

Without missing a step, one of the girls looked straight at Fuller with a sour facial expression and expounded sarcastically, "buzz off, creeps."

"Now that's class," Tyrone insisted.

"Don't rub it in," said Fuller. "If they were ladies, they would have responded to my complimentary greeting."

"Tyrone shook his head. "Yeah, right," he said.

They wrapped their arms around each others shoulder and sauntered down the street, laughing at their withered attempts to bag the girls.

*　　　*　　　*　　　*

As the months slid by, Fuller and Tyrone's conversation about girls intensified. While both were still virgins, they reveled in their ignorance, spreading tête-à-tête regarding how their *first time* would come about. They had heard hot street talk advancing their education of stupidity regarding feminine grandeur.

"Tell you what," said Tyrone. "Lets make a bet. I'll bet you a dollar and a chocolate malt I get some snatch before you do."

"What makes you think you can score before me?" Fuller asked, nonchalantly, feeling comfortable his intellect would overshadow Tyrone's brash locution.

"Because I'm cool man. You got that? I'm cool," Tyrone repeated. "In fact I'm so cool, I'm gonna change my name right now from Tyrone to just plain Ty. From now on you just call me Ty."

"What's that got to do with getting a piece a' ass," Fuller wanted to know."

"The women, man, the women," Tyrone said. "They all like a man that's cool."

"You can pay me now," Fuller said. "I've already won this bet."

"Now how can you know that?" Tyrone wanted to know, stretching his curiosity.

"Because I am an intellectual," Fuller said, "and all the girls walk around pretending to be intellectual."

"What chew say, white black brother. We on?"

"We're on, black honky," Fuller said, "and may the best brother honky win."

*   *   *   *

Their conversation about girls aroused Fuller's erotic sensibilities. He went home and experimented with himself. He envisioned he had a serious problem when he discovered he could go through all the motions, but not reach a climax. No one on the street had ever mentioned that happening before and all of his fancy reading didn't provide him with the answers. The way he saw it, if he couldn't reach an orgasm, he was a sexual misfire before he ever had the grand experience of getting laid. Seemingly, if he had a willing partner and was unable to perform, the embarrassment would be more than he could suffer through. The truthful insight of his predicament passed him by. If word ever got out he could go more than one thrust, the girls would line up around the block to get to him. The question remained, how was he going to win his bet with Tyrone?

Fuller read his high-minded books until early afternoon the next day. Tyrone came by again with his basketball wanting to know if Fuller would shoot some baskets.

"I'm tired," Fuller said. "I've been reading all morning. Let's go by the soda fountain, get a pick-me-up then shoot some baskets."

"Whatever," Tyrone responded.

The soda fountain was crowded. They took the last available booth and ordered sodas and talked trash. Two girls appeared from out of nowhere.

"There's no place to sit," one of the girls said to the two loners. "Do you boys mind if we sit with you?"

Fuller and Tyrone could both smell the gravy on the pot roast. They saw the pot roast thing as a metaphor of things to come, and made room for the girls to join them.

"My name is Fuller and this is my friend Ty," Fuller introduced himself and his competitor to the girls.

"I'm Judy," one of the girls said, sitting down next to Fuller. "And this is my sister Hazel," she said as Hazel seated herself next to Tyrone.

Judy was Caucasian and Hazel was clearly Hispanic.

Fuller thought it strange that all girls in groups of two claimed to be sisters when it was obvious they were just hanging out.

"I'm very pleased to meet you," Tyrone said, wondering if his greeting was intellectual enough to please Fuller. "Would you ladies care for refreshment?" he asked, continuing the pretense.

"That would be nice," Hazel said. "We're tired from walking and something to drink would really hit the spot."

The roast was smelling better with two potatoes in the mix.

I'll find your spot, Tyrone's lust dominated his thoughts.

When Tyrone spotted the soda jerk, he snapped his fingers. "Over here, my man" he said pointing to the girls in full display of his self-appointed big shot image.

"What chal gonna have?" the waiter asked.

Both girls ordered a lime coke.

"What grades are you girls in?" Tyrone asked as he dragged a big gulp of soda through his straw.

"We're sophomores in high school," Hazel said.

"What grade are you in?" Judy asked.

"We're in the eighth grade, but we decided to lay back a year," Tyrone said, reaching for some kind of parity with the girls educational alignment of one-upmanship.

"You're funny," Hazel said. "I've never heard of anyone taking a grade over on purpose."

"Yeah, I know," Tyrone said, "but look at it this way. We're going to be a year smarter when we do graduate."

Fuller looked down at his lap and shook his head. He was beginning to feel as stupid as Tyrone's comments made them out to be. In deference to Judy and Hazel having to listen to Tyrone's off the wall comments, he insisted the girls have something to go with their drink, on him.

"Since you put it that way," Hazel said. I'll have a banana split."

"I'll have one too," Judy said.

Fuller had something less expensive in mind, but figured the payoff would be worth it if they got lucky.

Tyrone was hoping Fuller had enough money to back up his generosity. There was no way he was going to pay for banana splits or he would have one.

When the refreshments were consumed, Fuller paid his share of the check, including the banana splits, and he, with Tyrone and the two girls left the soda fountain together. Fuller and Judy were lagging behind Tyrone and Hazel. Fuller watched Tyrone as he held his basketball under one arm and took Hazel's hand with his free hand.

Holding hands with Hazel was the smartest thing Tyrone has done all day, Fuller thought. He let his hand brush by Judy's and she made the first move by taking his hand in hers. He was delighted and wondered what luck had in store for him and his buddy. Their meeting with the girls was going so smooth, he and Tyrone's bet would cancel out, if their luck held steady for the rest of the afternoon.

Tyrone had chosen an out of the way neighborhood to stroll through, while holding hands with Hazel. Fuller and Judy straggled along behind them. They ambled onto a street behind an elementary school where a rusty yellow school bus was slowly falling victim to time and the elements. The tires were flat and large rust spots engulfed parts of the deteriorating body.

"I have an idea," Tyrone said. "Let's go sit in the school bus and talk."

No one objected, so he led them through the door of the old bus. They waded through dust and broken glass trying to find a usable seat. He and Hazel found one midway down the isle while Fuller and Judy continued until they reached the bench seat at the rear extreme of the bus.

Realizing that Fuller had taken the ideal seat in case he got lucky, Tyrone was scolding himself for not going to the rear of the bus when he had the chance. Fuller and Judy melted into each other's arms right away and started smooching while Tyrone strained to catch their action from the corner of his eye. Tyrone decided to go for a kiss as Hazel sat stiffly, staring toward the front of the bus and looking bored.

"I don't kiss the first time I'm with a guy," she said emphatically.

"Aw, come on. Just one for old times sake," Tyrone managed, realizing he had lost the war before the battle began. There were no old times linking them together.

"I'm sorry, Ty," she said, "I'm just not that kind of girl."

Meanwhile, Fuller and Judy were in a hot and heavy smooching session in a reclining position on the bench seat. Judy noticed a used condom on the floor close to them. "Ooh, what is that," she asked, pointing.

"Don't touch it," Fuller said, "it's nasty."

"I know it's nasty," Judy said. "It's a rubber. You didn't think I knew, did you?"

They both laughed and settled in for a long wet kiss.

Tyrone was keeping up with the levity coming from the rear of the bus. It sounded like Fuller had made it, big, and he couldn't get a kiss from Hazel. Tyrone through in the towel, giving Fuller the benefit of winning their bet.

Fuller could feel the bunching of Judy's breast mashing against his chest. He positioned his hand so he could slide it upward on her torso and cop a feel. When he reached the pinnacle of his search, he squeezed it, hoping she would say something like, *I'm yours. Take me.* He had never felt anything quite like it before. He took another liberty and squeezed again. This time she reached up grabbing his wrist, pulling his hand away. After a few more blazing kisses, he decided to go for the buried treasure.

"No baby," she whispered warmly in his face. "I can't."

"Why not?"

"Because I'm saving myself for marriage," she returned.

Somehow, he felt that one coming. He wasn't thinking marraige, but realizing he had a good thing going with his smooch make-out, decided to make the most of the situation and not ruin it by being too aggressive. From what he knew about himself, he wasn't confident he could pull it off if she did submit to his advances. Perhaps, it was better if they didn't connect sexually. Besides he had heard street talk about gonorrhea and syphilis and wasn't sure he was ready for that trip based on here-say.

By now, Fuller and Judy were completely flat on the back seat with only their shoes showing when Tyrone looked back to check on their progress. They had reached a platonic understanding which freed them up to enjoy each others scrumptious smooches without being hindered by how far they should go sexually. He would say something and she would giggle and vice versa.

Tyrone couldn't stand it. He could visualize the worst or perhaps the best coming from the rear of the bus and he couldn't even be successful landing a kiss from Hazel.

The sun had started to recede in the west when Tyrone decided it was time to move on. He was ready to get the hell back on the street and ditch Hazel.

Fuller on the other hand was enjoying limited fulfillment with Judy, but they realized it would be dark soon and brought their dallying to a necessary end. They disengaged from their awkward positions, gaining footing on the narrow isle between the seats of the old bus. He and Judy stood up and repositioned parts of their clothing that had gotten mussed up.

The girls went in one direction and the guys in another. Fuller had lipstick all around his mouth. "You asshole," Tyrone said assuming he had lost the bet. "Here's your freaking dollar and another one for your chocolate malt."

Fuller ruled that Tyrone was testing him. If he had not made out, he thought, Tyrone would expect him not to accept the money. Fuller fooled Tyrone. He said, "thank you", and pocketed the two one dollar bills.

West side

The past four years had brought Milo and Raymond closer together as friends. Raymond's record collection introduced Milo to a new world of original jazz and an introduction to the old time musicians. He also learned of contemporary music and musicians which had an appeal to a more sophisticated circle of devotees. Raymond and Elaine were now constant companions. The ingredients of Raymond's record collection and his association with Milo's sister, solidified the bond between him and Milo. Eventually Raymond proposed marriage to Elaine and she accepted. They were married on the day Raymond completed his residency. Milo had progressed habitually in his karate lessons and his trumpet playing had no boundaries. He was recognized by his father's friends as a natural; a little young perhaps for his achievements, but none the less a natural on par with the best playing music for a living.

*   *   *   *

Martin was fronting his orchestra at the hotel ballroom when he was overcome with cold sweats and a sudden weakness. His stability tottered.

Cully Tujaque noticed Martin becoming feeble. He rushed up to offer aid. "Here take this," Martin said to Cully, handing him his baton and grabbing his chest. "I have to go back stage and sit down."

Cully motioned for Joey Crabtree to escort Martin backstage to the musicians lounge. He found Martin in a cold sweat laboring to breathe and helped him to a sofa. He loosened Martin's necktie and elevated his feet by resting his legs on the armrest. He rushed back to the stage and interrupted Cully as he led the band. "I think Martin's having a heart attack," Joey said, trying to catch his breath. Cully grabbed the microphone in the middle of a dance number and ask if there was a doctor in the house. The orchestra trailed off unevenly to complete silence. Two men came forward claiming to be doctors. By then, Pete Scalibib was involved and led the doctors backstage to the sofa supporting Martin's motionless body. They performed a cursory examination and agreed with Cully that Martin had had a heart attack. "Someone call an ambulance," one of the doctors ordered as the other performed CPR on Martin.

"I already have," Pete said. "They're on the way."

When the paramedics arrived, they loaded Martin into an ambulance and sped off in the direction of the hospital. Someone called Minette, who in turn called Elaine. She and Milo rushed to the hospital where they were to meet Elaine and Raymond. They were met by Pete and Joey with a somber look on their faces. Minette started asking questions concerning Martin's condition when suddenly she felt the dour mood within the surroundings. "Nooo," she cried. "Where is Martin? Take me to him—"

Joey stepped up and seizes her by the arms. He asks Pete to "go get the doctor."

Milo was petrified. He lowered his head, covering his eyes with his hands. The doctor came into the room. "I'm sorry," he said to Mrs. Munroe. "We did all we could."

Minette broke down. Her knees buckled and she collapsed. Joey caught her, and Milo helped him get his mother to a chair. Shortly, Elaine and Raymond arrived. Minette stood up and embraced Elaine. "Your father is dead," she said mournfully.

*   *   *   *

Milo tried to radiate an aura of strength in the presence of his mother. When by himself, he didn't fare well. He found himself sinking at times, while at other times, gathering courage and confidence, because of the responsible person he had become. He had gained instant adulthood in light of his father's death.

The funeral was held on a chilly, overcast day. The prevailing gloom from the weather, coalesced with the gloom in the hearts of the Munroe family and friends. It seemed to close in, surrounding them with dreadful desolation. Following the funeral was this heavy weight, languishing like an lonely black-magic entity encapsulating a hollow body. Minette had lost her husband and best friend. Milo had lost his father and connection to the real world, and Elaine— Elaine also lost her father, but she had the companionship of a husband who loved her, softening the personal loss that was testing her strength to endure. The band members attended the wake and one by one offered their condolences. It was a necessary time for a new beginning with Milo as the head of the Monroe family.

*   *   *   *

Cully had taken Milo on as his protege, teaching him all the techniques required to play professionally as well as the demanding stride to play in a symphony orchestra. Milo was capable of playing any kind of written music while exercising his technique at improvising. He practiced his fathers charts until he knew all the popular music of the day by heart. He was zeroing in on the lifeline of the dixieland standards. He had it all for a guy, at any age, let alone a thirteen-year-old boy, still wet, but drying fast behind the ears.

Cully Tujaque was the natural *shoe-in* to take the reins of the Martin Munroe Orchestra, but because of his commitment to the Chicago Symphony, he declined in favor of Joey Crabtree. It was decided to continue with the designation, Martin Munroe's Orchestra, because of name recognition.

The orchestra was warming up for their first show of the evening when the first trumpeter's wife called in, making excuses for her husbands inebriation.

"He's just plain drunk," she allowed. "I can't get him to the car to drive him down there—What shall I do?"

"Give him another drink and put him to bed," Joey replied, coming to her rescue. "He's no good to us in his condition."

Cully had a performance with the symphony, so Joey called Pete Scalibib over to discuss the situation. It was too late to get a union replacement. "What are we going to do?" Joey pegged Pete for an answer.

"Let the alto sax play the first trumpet part?" Pete said, unsure of his suggestion. Then from out of nowhere, an idea popped into his head. "Joey boy, don't fret," he said, hitting on a solution. "I'll call Milo to fill in."

"Are you crazy!" Joey came back. "He's only a thirteen year old child, for Christ's sake."

"He can do it," Pete said emphatically. "We both know he can do it."

"I know he can, but we'll get in trouble with the union and probably the civil authorities if we so much as think it."

"Not a problem," Pete said. "I can seat him behind Tiny in the reed section. It's only for one night and no one will even know the difference. We can get a union guy tomorrow."

"Pete, you've lost your mind," Joey said, beginning a slow panic.

"You got a better idea?" Pete asked hurriedly, knowing they were running out of time.

"Make the call," Joey caved.

*   *   *   *

Pete made the call, hoping Milo would answer.

Milo was home when the telephone rang. "Shoot, it's your nickel," he answered.

"Milo. Thank God you answered the telephone." Pete said. "What's your mother doing?"

"She's watching TV," Milo reciprocated. "What's up?"

"We got a problem. The lead trumpet is out drunk and Cully's playing with the symphony tonight. Joey wants you to fill in for him."

"I can't do that. I'm on my way to Elaine and Raymonds to play monopoly."

"There's fifty in it for you—"

"Dollars?"

"The long green stuff," Pete said, rubbing the tips of his fingers together, "and wear a white shirt."

"I'll be right down," Milo said, excitedly.

"Who was on the telephone, dear?" his mother asked from the parlor.

"It was Elaine wanting to know when I was leaving," he contrived.

"Have fun, dear. Tell them I said hello."

Milo dialed Elaine's number. "It's me," he said softly when she answered the telephone. "I can't play monopoly tonight."

"Why are you talking so low? I can barely hear you."

"I don't want Mom to hear me," he said. "The lead trumpet in dad's orchestra is out drunk and they want me to fill in for him."

"You can't do that. You're only a child. It's against the law."

"I have to. Joey's going to pay me fifty dollars."

Raymond had picked up the extension and heard their conversation. "We'll meet you down there," he said. "I want to be there when they arrest Joey."

"Whatever you do," Milo said, "don't tell Mom. She'll go bananas."

"We'll see you down there," Raymond assured Milo. "I'm betting you can do it."

Milo said goodbye to his mom, fetched his horn case, and rolled his bicycle down the front porch steps. He was on his way to his first remunerative gig.

*　　　*　　　*　　　*

Milo slid to a stop at the delivery entrance to the hotel and chained his bicycle to a parking meter. After securing his wheels, he went in the supply door of the hotel where he found Joey pacing up and down, nervously.

"Here," Joey said. "Put these on." He handed Milo a black bow tie and standard jacket worn by the orchestra members. "Then go to the musician's lounge and have *Charlie the Queer* put some makeup on you. He's waiting." *Charlie the Queer* managed the musician's lounge and was fearful of running out of time when Milo walked in. "Oh, thank God you made it on time," he said sashaying around the chair he wanted Milo to sit in. "Wait a minute," he said, dusting off the seat then inviting Milo to hop onboard. He put a barber's bib around Milo's neck and commenced applying a mustache over Milo's upper lip with an eyebrow pencil. Using a lighter pencil, he sketched lines in appropriate locations to add up to ten years on Milo's young face from a distance.

Pete Scalibib was waiting for Milo when he was ready to be seated on the orchestral stage. "Let's go kid," he said, yanking Milo from *Charlie the Queer's* chair. He led their first trumpet player for the evening to a chair directly behind a 350 pound reed player named Tiny.

"You'll do okay kid, just stay behind Tiny," Pete told Milo while arranging the charts on his music stand.

Milo scanned the audience for Elaine and Raymond and caught sight of them when they entered the main entrance to the ballroom. He watched carefully as they were escorted to a table so he would know where they were sitting. That way he could observe them keeping an eye on him.

Joey raised his baton, the lights came on and the orchestra opened the evening's musical tour with a short introduction to *Over the Rainbow*. Milo fitted right in and was comfortable in his substitute role as first chair in the trumpet section. There didn't seem to be any jealousy. He wasn't taking anything away from other musicians as he was a only a temporary imposter to help the band through their obligation to the hotel. The trick was not to get caught by the authorities.

Say It Isn't So was the first dance number. Milo played note for note with the other musicians and was so close with the Orchestra environment, he didn't experience the butterflies that normally fluttered in the mid-section to hinder the performance of a newcomer. He came to a part that read ad-lib. Scribbled in long hand was an entry to *stand up*. He followed directions to Joey's chagrin. Milo stood up and started on this beautiful improvised solo that caught the attention of everyone in the ballroom, including the band members. His beautiful solo enthralled everyone within listening distance. *Charlie the Queer* was first after Joey to see Milo's faux pas. He sashayed hurriedly to the lighting director, holding his hands limply above his mid-drift in an effeminate manner. He placed his hands on his hips, obviously aggravated at Milo, and ordered the lighting technician to put a purple spot light on Milo so he would be unrecognizable and ordered him not to waste time doing it. Pete had forgotten to tell Milo not to rise during solos, no matter how the charts read. Joey was fit to be tied, but maintained his composure and exhibited a phony smile as he turned from side to side to scan the audience reaction.

An elderly widow woman in the audience checked Milo out before *Charlie the Queer's* intervention. She was a regular customer; an imposing dowager type, obstructed with gaudy jewelry and large, overly exposed, sloping breast tops, giving the impression they were straining to break free of their choking inhibitors. She always sat at the same table by herself. "Oh waiter," she said, catching one on the fly. "Go tell Joey to send that young man playing the trumpet to my table after this set."

"Yes Mam," the waiter responded.

Joey received the message and turned in her direction, still with a forged smile on his face. *Oh God,* he thought. *Milo's pushed her buttons?*

Doctor Powell went back stage at intermission to congratulate Milo on his superb performance. Elaine sent her best wishes with her husband. Joey grabbed Raymond Powell by the arm and pulled him aside. He frantically explained the problem facing him with Milo and the old dowager and asked if he would go have a talk with her without giving Milo's impression away.

Raymond approached the old woman's table. "I'm Doctor Powell," he said introducing himself. "I'm physician to the trumpet player you requested to visit your table. May I join you for a second?"

"Please do," she said, showing concern. "Is there anything wrong?"

"Well—yes and no," he said, in a deliberate attempt to be vague. "I'm here to thank you for your support. It was a wonderful gesture on your part to invite my patient to your table and I've been asked to offer you his gratitude for being so attentive to his role in the orchestra. You see, he is afflicted with *chronic chromatic-oconiosis,*" he said, yanking the phony diagnosis off the top of his head. "He's restricted from visiting anyone not directly associated within his environment."

"Oh, I see," she said, taking a back seat to the occasion, not knowing what the hell that was all about. She didn't see at all, and wondered the purpose for the doctor's visit.

"I knew you would," Doctor Powell said.

"Is it serious?"

"It can be," Doctor Powell informed the old woman. "Now, if you'll excuse me, I have to get back to my patient. Order anything you like," he said, as he stood up to leave. "The Martin Munroe Orchestra will pick up the tab."

"Why—thank you," she said, enthusiastically, as she sank deeper, but modestly in her chair. Her fingers pointed between her oversized bosom, seemingly surprised, but happily extending her gratitude to Doctor Powell for his generosity. He caught her eyeballing a bottle of champagne at the next table.

Joey bitched erratically when informed the old lady's tab was being charged to the Orchestra. He finally accepted the dowager's food and drink bill for one evening as fair trade to maintain Milo's obscurity.

The evening ended on a successful note and Joey gave Milo his fifty bucks. "Here kid," he said, "Go tip *Charlie the Queer* a five spot for your make up and saving your ass from a fate worse than death." Joey was alluding to the old dowager's attempt to get her hands on Milo. Milo accepted the money graciously, wondering what that fate thing was all about. He apologized to Joey for standing up during his first solo and promised never to do it again, that is, assuming Joey would risk using him again.

"That's okay, Kid. Forget it," Joey said.

After giving *Charlie the Queer* his five dollars, Milo packed his horn in its hard case, washed the make up off his face and went outside to his bicycle. He was satisfied with his performance and just as proud of his forty-five dollar emolument for dipping in the well of professional music. Riding home on a simple bicycle, his thoughts gave way to illusions of being transported by limousine. After all, he was the star of his first one night stand.

*   *   *   *

Saturday was just another day for Joey and Pete. They had sat down to discuss their progress after early rehearsals to have a drink and relax. Joey had finished lighting a cigarette and took a sip of his gin and tonic when the bartender handed him the extension phone.

"Who is it?" Joey asked, cupping his hand over the mouthpiece.

The bartender hunched his shoulders. Beats me," he said.

"Joey here," wishing he didn't have to talk to anyone until he and Pete finished their discussion following rehearsal.

"Hey Joey. Remember me? It's your friend Izzy. You forget I live on this planet, or something?" Isadore Rosenbloom was a squatty fat man with a thin mustache, and clearly visible clockwork on his white rolled down socks. They were bright contrasted below the cuffs of his dark colored trousers hiked up between his cheeks. Izzy ran a Jazz Club with a skimpy clad chorus line on South State Street. His place was a booze palace where social misfits gathered to drink the hard stuff, be charmed by the nearly nude dancers and forget their troubles.

"Hi there, Izzy," Joey said. "How's my favorite Hunsucker?"

"If what you mean is Jew boy," Izzy said, "I'm your man."

"What's up, Jew boy?" Joey asked.

"I got troubles, Joey. I'm up to my ass in hard knocks." Izzy complained. "My horn player flew the coop. I think his girlfriend's husband is after him. Can you lend me one of your guys for tonight?"

"Izzy, come on—I'm fresh out of spare trumpet blowers. I have the same problems myself. Have you tried the union?"

"Joey—Joey—I need a trumpet player. You're not cooperating. You know the guy they'd send me couldn't blow the thistle from his whistle. I need someone who can play the raw sound, the down and dirty stuff without a lot of practice. I'm hard pressed, Joey. I need a favor."

"Sorry, Izzy. Better luck next time," Joey said, trying to ditch Izzy and go back to his conversation with Pete.

"I guess I can blow my brains out," Izzy said in his permanent state of desperation, "then you can eulogize at my funeral."

"Can't do it? I don't have anything nice to say," Joey teased.

"Don't kid around with me, Joey; my bad heart and everything. We're like brothers, you and me, and don't you forget it."

"Right, Izzy. Come to think of it, this might be your lucky day."

"Why? What do you mean?" Izzy asked, half suspicious but gullible.

"Remember Martin Munroe?"

"Everybody remembers Marty Munroe," Izzy said. "What's the deal?"

"His son blows some mean horn, if he's available."

"What do you mean if he's available?" Izzie insisted. "Why wouldn't he be available?"

"You know, Izzy, hazards of the trade."

"See if you can get him for me," Izzy said. "I'll owe you one."

"If I get him, you'll owe me another one," Joey reminded him.

"Whatever," said Izzy, somewhat relieved. "We rehearse at four. See if you can get him down here before then."

"I'll see what I can do," Joey countered, "but I can't promise anything."

After hanging up from Izzy, Joey dialed Milo's number. His mother answered the phone. "Minette? Joey here."

"Oh, Mister Crabtree. How nice of you to call."

"Thank you," Joey said. "Is Milo home?"

"He just came in from a karate lesson. He said he was going to a movie with his sister and her husband. Hold the line, please. I'll see if I can catch him." She found Milo in the kitchen washing down a plate of oreo cookies with a glass of milk.

"Milo, the telephone is for you."

"Who is it, Mom?"

"It's Mister Crabtree," she said. "I wonder what he wants?"

"Probably something about music. I'll find out and let you know," Milo said, suspecting another job with Joey's orchestra. "Thanks Mom."

Milo passed his mother in a hurry on his way to the parlor. He picked up the receiver and in a muffled tone, said, "Hey Joey. What's up?"

"Milo," Joey said. "You want a gig tonight?"

"Sure," he said, keeping his voice low so as not to arouse his mother's curiosity. "Will I make another fifty dollars?"

"Maybe, maybe more," Joey said, courting Milo for his friend Izzie.

"I'll do it," he whispered.

"Good boy," Joey said. "Meet me at the Club Orleans on South State Street not far from the loop. It's a dixieland joint with dancers. Think you can find it?"

"I'll find it," Milo assured Joey.

"Good. Don't forget to wear a white shirt. Rehearsals start at four. Try to be early."

Milo got off the phone with Joey and called Raymond. "Hi, Bro," he greeted his brother-in-law. "I've got a gig at a dixieland joint on South State Street close to the loop. I don't guess I'll be going to the movie after all."

"A dixieland joint—South State Street—Are you crazy, Milo? That's a seedy part of town."

"Yeah, I know," Milo said. "I was hoping you and Elaine would meet me at Hopkins Drug Store. I can park my bicycle and ride the rest of the way with you. That way you can keep an eye on me."

"I have enough to worry about without taking you to raise, little brother," Raymond joked with Milo. "We'll go listen to the music and if you're any good, we'll stay till closing time and drive you back to the drugstore. If not—well—"

"Why thank you, Doctor Powell and my thanks to your lovely wife." Milo said, mimicking Raymond's witty play on words. I have to be there a little before four. If you leave now, you'll beat me to the drug store.

"Fine," Raymond said. "We'll be waiting for you." When Milo showed up, he chained his bicycle to a parking meter, hopped in Raymond's car and they headed toward State Street and the Club Orleans.

Raymond parked on the curb a few doors down from the entrance to Izzy's club. Joey was sitting in his car waiting for Milo to arrive. They connected and entered the club together. They had to abandon their sense of well being and adjust to the dusky dampness, the stench of stale cigar smoke and beer. The place was dank, and gave the impression it had never been aired out or opened to let the daylight in.

Joey grabbed Izzy by the sleeve and pulled him over to meet his substitute horn player.

"You must be my trumpet player," Izzie said to Raymond.

"Izzie Rosenbloom, meet Milo Munroe," Joey said, initiating an introduction to the kid.

Before Milo could shake Izzy's hand, Izzy flattened his left hand across his chest when he saw his substitute trumpet player was borderline pubescent. "I've got to sit down," he said, breathing somewhat heavily and searching his shirt pockets for his stash of nitro pills. "Goddamn you, Joey. You're going to be the death of me yet. How the hell do I use this kid in my show?" Izzy said trying to recover. "If he sees my naked girls, I could get the death penalty for contributing to his delinquency."

"Not a problem," Joey said, trying to relieve Izzy's tension. The kid's savvy. "I'll go across the street to the Wig Barn and pick out a fake mustache. All you have to furnish is a straw hat and striped jacket."

"I'm going crazy, Joey. You know that," Izzy said to Joey with a discouraging look on his face. "They're going to throw me in the caboose and take everything I own—all because of you, Joey."

"Just get him backstage at intermission and don't let anyone meet him. It'll work, Izzy. You'll see," Joey said.

"I don't want just anybody playing in my band," Izzy complained.

"He's not just anybody, Joey. He's Marty Munroe's son. Cully Tujaque taught him to play. Need more?"

"How do I know the kid can play?" Izzy asked.

"You'll find out in a few minutes when they rehearse. If you don't like him," Joey threatened, "I'll take him off your hands."

Milo kept looking first at Joey then to Izzy. Izzy finally agreed to listen to Milo play. Joey introduced Elaine and Raymond to Izzy, then went across the street for Milo's fake mustache.

Izzy went behind the stage and returned with a red and white striped jacket and flat top straw hat. "Here kid," he said to Milo. "Try these on."

They fit like they were tailored for him. When Joey returned, he fitted Milo's mustache.

Izzy clapped his hands. "All right, let's clear the stage. Everybody off stage. Let's bring the band out. Here kid," he said to Milo. "Put these shades on. They'll make you look cool."

Joey suggested that Milo be covered with a dark colored rotating light. This would be distracting for all practical purposes and keep Milo incognito. Besides, the band will be far enough behind the chorus line that no one will have an opportunity to see him up close.

"Okay, Guys. I want you all to respect our substitute trumpet player. Start off with *Monin' Low*. I want to hear some growl so Sadie will have something to shake her booty to when she removes her skirt. Joe!" he shouted to the lighting director. "You keep a red light on her G-string so the crowd will focus on the glitter. Okay, Mousy," Izzy said to the piano player. "Make it happen."

The first two bars after the piano intro, Izzy knew Milo could play the trumpet. After four bars, his Saturday night jitters began to dissipate. By the time Milo's guttural sounds in *Monin' Low* had passed, he was thinking about putting Milo on regular. "Hey Kid," he said to Milo after rehearsal were over. "Come to my office where we can talk in private."

Milo followed Izzy into a messy little hole in the wall Izzy called his office. The walls were laden with faded autographed pictures of burlesque stars nested together. "Have a seat, Kid," Izzy said. "You looking' for a job?"

"I'm not looking for anything," Milo came back. "I'm still in school, for crying out loud.

"What-a you want-a-do?" Izzy asked outright, flipping the ashes off his cigar stub. "You name it, kid. We can work something out. I take care of my people. Ask anybody who works for me."

"I can work Saturday and Sunday except when Joey needs me."

"What? You working for Joey, now?"

"Yes sir. Only when he needs me."

"Whatever he's paying you? I'll double it," Izzy said, pulling a roll of bills from his pocket that would plug the dikes. He tempted Milo nonchalantly like a fox keeping an eye on the hen house. It was working. Whatever else they said to one another, Izzy made sure Milo kept his eye on the *long green* he was manipulating as they talked.

Milo was innocent and not street wise, nor was he a negotiator. He was leaning on fairness and truthfulness when he opened his mouth to tell Izzy he had worked for Joey for fifty bucks one night and would work for him for the same amount. He stopped short of saying fifty as the word started to leave his mouth. He immediately metamorphosed from an inherent honest lad, to that of a smart-ass, speaking in a hoodlum vernacular. "A big one," Milo said, arching an eyebrow, not certain how much *A Big One* represented. It seemed to be in the context Joey and Izzy were talking to each other and had a cool ring to it. It was up to Izzy now to come up with the amount he was willing to pay.

"What? A hundred a night? Are you crazy? That's more than I make, for Christ sake," Izzy bitched defensively. He knew the kid was worth every penny of it after hearing him play, but what surprised him beyond his understanding, was a youngster his age asking for so much money.

"Yes sir," Milo returned innocently, while hoping Joey didn't pop in and spoil his negotiations.

"Okay," Izzy conceded, "but if you can't cut the mustard, you're out of here. Right? The officials might try to close me down if word gets out I've got a kid on my payroll. If you see anyone suspicious, pack up your horn and high tail it out the kitchen door."

Milo's juvenile instincts prompted a silent "WOW" in disbelief of Izzy's generosity, but he managed to contain his jubilation, maintaining a balanced decorum to keep from queering the deal. Izzy had mentioned his willingness to double what Joey paid him, but Milo's common sense warned him not to push it. A hundred dollars a night was more than ample.

Milo went to be with Elaine and Raymond while waiting for the nightly show to begin. Meanwhile, Joey needed to return to Pete and his orchestra. Izzy walked Joey to the exit, thanking him profusely for coming to his rescue in such an emergency situation. "That'll be the best fifty bucks you will ever spend," Joey said to Izzy as he walked out the door.

Fifty bucks, Izzy echoed. "Why that little fucker." He grabbed his chest and sat at one of the tables, fishing for his nitroglycerine tablets. He realized he had been had by a thirteen-year-old.

Milo's sister, Elaine, and brother-in-law, Doctor Powell, were stage side at each of Milo's gigs. Raymond especially liked the jazzy tunes. Milo, knowing he would be old enough to drive in a couple of years, wanted to save his money for a new car. Doctor Powell kept Milo's money in a separate account and was careful not to let Milo's mother know he was accumulating so much money. It was best she didn't know where it was coming from.

*   *   *   *

Doctor Powell received an offer to be the head of the orthopedic department from the Methodist hospital in Waynesford, Indiana. The proposal raised his salary to commensurate with the title. After talking it over with Elaine, he accepted. Milo was depressed that they were moving south as he was close to his sister and was thinking of the doctor as the brother he never had. He was devastated to know they were leaving. Elaine assured him that Waynesford was not so far he couldn't come south for a visit from time to time and that they would be coming back to visit her mother as well as Raymond's family. Raymond made arrangements to continue depositing Milo's money in a separate account and assured him they would keep mum on the subject to his mother. Another shortcoming about them leaving was, he was going to miss their presence in the audience during his gigs.

Joey and Izzy continued risking the use of Milo on an escalating basis and soon his presence on either stage was taken for granted. Milo was enjoying his side hustle as his bank account increased by multiples of squares. His highschool progress suffered accordingly.

CHAPTER 6

▼

Evanston
Three And A Half Years Later

Fuller was lounging on the sofa reading and his mother was in the kitchen preparing the evening meal when his father arrived from work.

"Hi, son," Bernard greeted Fuller. "Where is your mother?"

"Cooking supper," Fuller responded.

"Come in the kitchen with me. I have something to share with you and your mother."

After greeting his wife with a kiss, Bernard said, "come sit at the table, dear. I have some good news."

"What's up, Dad?" Fuller inquired.

"Well," Bernard started off, "I'm considering tenure at City College in Waynesford, Indiana. They asked me to be Dean of their engineering school. They offered me a huge bump in salary, should we decide to go. We can be there in time for Fuller to start his senior year in high school." After a short discussion, Maggie agreed to support her husband in whatever decision he made. Fuller thought it would be neat to separate from his antagonists who has sent him a continuous deluge of degrading name insults since his early days in elementary school. If it wasn't *dumb as* maligning Nostradamus, it was *full-o-crap,* impugning his middle and last name, Fuller Kreppe. Tyrone was his best friend and the only person from Evanston he would miss. He gave his father thumbs up if he wanted to make the move.

The girls in Fuller's life were left with more to desire after dating him a time or two. The ones that expressed a willingness to go all the way with him, were left holding the bag after he confessed he was saving himself for marriage. He wasn't really saving himself for matrimonial obligation. If anything, he was saving himself the embarrassment of failing to perform. In his naivete, he longed for a faithful relationship where he and his partner could just be in love without the burden of flexing one's sexual muscle to hold the relationship together. He wished for splendor on the spiritual side of togetherness, knowing there would be time to face his dysfunction at some point in the future. His lofty ambition was to be like other couples, walking the halls at school while holding hands with his special someone. To him, that represented peer status. He still measured the quality of a girl by the strength of his desire to take them home to meet his parents. He would fair well without the girls already in his life.

His father made the decision to move south. After they were fully packed and ready to leave, the only thing left were saying their goodbyes.

The Kreppe family were bidding farewell to Tyrone's family while Tyrone and Fuller were on the verge of lamenting as they faced each other.

"Well, white black brother—I'm gonna' miss ya'," Tyrone said.

"I'm going to miss you too, black honky," Fuller reciprocated.

They snapped together in a masculine embrace, patting each other on the back.

"You take care now, you hear?" Tyrone said.

Fuller reached in his wallet and pulled out two one-dollar bills. "Here," he yielded, "this is one I owe you and this one is for the chocolate malt."

"I don't understand," Tyrone questioned innocently.

"That day on the rusty school bus?" Fuller confessed, "I didn't score."

"You dog," Tyrone accused Fuller.

Fuller entered his father's automobile and waved goodbye to Tyrone and his parents as they drove off, departing Chicago.

West side

Minette had made the decision to sell her house. It was too much to take care of for just herself and Milo. She found a suitable apartment near the loop and made the move. A problem soon developed with the neighbors over Milo practicing his horn. While conversing with Elaine on the telephone, she mentioned the neighbor's complaints about Milo's practicing. Elaine suggested she let Milo come stay with her and Raymond for a while and added, "we'd love to have him. Besides it would give you a break."

"Oh, I couldn't do that," Minette said. "What about his schooling?"

"Mom, look. You deserve a break. If he comes now, he will be in time to start his senior year here. They have a wonderful high school in Waynesford and besides, he can practice all he wants at our house and no one will bother him."

"You think this would work?" Minette asked. "How would Raymond feel about Milo coming to stay with you?"

"Mom, they're the best of friends. They're like brothers. You know that."

"Well," Minette said, "let me talk it over with Milo and see what he has to say."

"Swell, Mom. You do that and let us know."

"Say hi to Raymond for me, dear and I love you," Minette said, winding down their conversation.

"I love you too, Mom—bye."

*   *   *   *

Both Milo and Raymond were equally receptive to the idea. Milo had saved enough money to buy his new car and Raymond couldn't wait to have his source of live dixieland jazz back in his life.

Milo, as a growing teenager, had become an Adonis to the girls at his Chicago High School, enough so that he could afford to be particular, choosing only the girls that suited his fancy. Leaving his girlfriends behind was the only thing he would miss besides Cully, Joey, Pete, Izzy, Charlie the Queer and of course, his mom.

Elaine and Raymond had left a vacuum in his life when they moved south and he was excited about regaining their relationship and camaraderie. For some reason, he never found the opportunity to visit them in Indiana. He was either too busy with schoolwork or his gigs with Joey or Izzy held him back.

Joey was disappointed Milo was leaving, but happy for the kid and his future. He knew Phil Davenport, the leader of a popular orchestra in Waynesford, and made arrangements for Milo to have an audition.

"Wait til' you hear him play," Joey told Phil, "and dixieland—man he eats that stuff like gorging on grapes."

"I'm happy to hear that," Phil mentioned to Joey. "I've been thinking about taking a few of my boys to play an occasional dixieland number as a novelty act. But you know Joey, I can't promise anything."

"Just listen to him play," Joey certified. "You'll want to throw rocks at your other trumpet players."

Izzy, on the other hand, was sickened at the thought of losing Milo. "Let me sit down," he said upon hearing Milo was moving south. "Where are my pills? You can't ever the find the damn things when you need them. Milo—Son," he pleaded. "You're a headliner here. Down there, you're just a another pair of lips behind a mouthpiece. Think about it, Milo. For my sake, huh? Tell me you're not going to leave me, baby. We've become close, you and me. I love you like a son."

Milo assured Izzy he would give it some serious thought without telling him his mind was already made up. He was moving south to Waynesford, Indiana.

*   *   *   *

Before boarding the Indiana bound bus, Milo kissed his mom goodbye and promised to write regularly and call at least once a week. It was a sad moment leaving his mother, but his destination held the promise of a whole new beginning for a young man spreading his wings ahead of his time. Chicago wasn't so far away that they couldn't visit back and forth at impromptu intervals. Milo assured his mother everything was going to be okay, as she would see, but for now he was anxious to see Elaine and Raymond and renew their kinship.

"Now you stay in school and study hard," his mother admonished fearing his life would run amok detached from her control.

"Don't you worry, Mom," Milo said with assurance, "nothing is going to change, you'll see."

Elaine and Raymond were at the station when Milo's bus rolled in. Milo was sitting by the window with his trumpet case in his lap. He had checked his luggage in the bus' underbelly, but the trumpet stayed with him. Elaine spotted Milo first and jumped up and down, waving excitedly trying to attract his attention. When Milo saw Elaine he knocked on the window, blowing her a series of kisses. When the bus eased to a stop, the air brakes sighed, signaling journeys end. The driver opened the door and the passengers filed out. Milo stepped off the bus into Elaine's arms for an emotional reunion. Raymond stepped up and embraced Milo, exchanging salutations. Through all the emotional, outbreaks, Milo retained possession of his trumpet case. Raymond retrieved his luggage and loaded it in his car. They stopped to have dinner at a restaurant before completing the drive home.

The first thing they did after walking into the house was to call Minette and inform her that Milo had arrived safely. Milo's first task was to go car shopping the next morning and Raymond offered to make the rounds with him to the various dealers.

"What kind of car you want, little brother?" Raymond asked at the breakfast table the next morning.

"I know what I want," Milo said, "but I have to balance that with being pretentious."

"What do you want?" Raymond asked again.

"I want a black Buick Super four door with white sidewall tires," Milo responded. "What do you think?"

"I think you have enough money for an airplane if you want one," Raymond said. "Let me check with the hospital. We'll go car shopping as soon as I can shake lose. By the way—in who's presence are you afraid of being pretentious?"

"It's just a kink I have," Milo said, "me being so young and all."

"Whatever you want little brother, you buy for yourself. You know what it took for you to make the money. I can attest to anybody that you earned it."

*   *   *   *

Milo drove his new car to his audition with Phil Davenport.

"How's Joey doing with your dad's orchestra?" Davenport asked after meeting Milo?

"Joey's doing great," Milo said.

"I guess Pete and Cully are still hanging in there."

"Oh, yes sir," Milo said. "They're doing swell also."

"Well, Milo, lets get to the business at hand. Joey tells me you're right up there with Bunny Berrigan and Harry James. Those are some mighty large shoes to fill. You think you're ready?"

"Joey was a friend of my dad's. I guess he's just trying to help me get started,"Milo said, modestly.

"Understood," Phil said. "You know I can't promise you anything until I hear you play and maybe not even then, but I did promise Joey I'd give you an audition."

"Yes sir," Milo came back modestly.

"Okay, son. Let's go out on the set with a couple of the boys and see what you can do."

Milo followed Davenport out to the orchestra platform clutching his trumpet case.

The platform was shielded from the dance floor by heavy draperies which afforded the orchestra the privacy they needed to practice during the day. They had it all to themselves until the crowd arrived in the evening.

Phil Davenport introduced Milo to the band members at hand and selected him a chair. "Okay," he said to Milo, "pick a chart on your music stand and lets see what you can do."

Milo selected a beautiful slow tune, *Blue and Broken Hearted*, because of its sensitive quality and beautiful chords. It would allow him to expand and show Davenport he had more to offer than just putting a horn to his lips and making a sound.

Joey was right on target. Milo was up there with the greats of the day. It was only when he improvised his solo that his true talent emerged and astonished Phil Davenport, making him aware of young Munroe's potential. He tapped his baton on his music stand. "That's enough," he said. "Let's go into my office and talk." He offered Milo a whopping salary he couldn't refuse as long as he could make practice every afternoon after school. Milo assured him he could not only be there, but be on time. He picked up the telephone and made arrangements to have Milo measured for a standard uniform consisting of slacks and blazer. "Come down in the morning," Phil said. "We'll need to get you in the union."

PART II

CHAPTER 7

▼

The First Day Of The Senior Year

The fall season emblazoned by the morning sun settled over the serene landscape. It was the first day of the last school year for the seniors' at Anthony Wayne High in Waynesford, Indiana. The consuming ambience was interrupted by a recurring chill as the schoolyard blossomed from early arrivals milling around the grounds to an overcrowded encampment of aspiring hopefuls.

The near, to affluent students were stylish in their attire. For the girls, sweaters, plaid skirts and saddle shoes were the fads of the day. Some of the girls wore penny loafers. The mainstream boys wore argyle sweaters over white shirts with suspenders and necktie.

The dregs showed up smoking cigarettes, breeding their contempt for school with a moody anxiety. It was as if they were depending on luck to get them through their final year. Separating anxiety from the "I don't give a shit" attitudes was a no-brainer; they just didn't give a shit. Most showed little desire to finish with a satisfactory average as graduation to them seemed like a lost cause. If the burden became more than one could bear, "what the hell," one could always find a plausible excuse to drop out.

The minorities bent on finishing high school under the watchful eye of demanding parents were tenacious to a fault as learning to them was more important, though excruciating, than for those preparing for college.

This was a time for renewing old friendships and checking out the new kids who were noticeably timid and kept pretty much to themselves while waiting for the bell to ring.

An old Chevy convertible clattered curbside with a ragged sounding horn and the guttural rumblings of straight exhaust pipes. The combined sounds announced the arrival of the school's hoodlum hierarchy. The old car belched

and backfired as the ignition wires were disconnected. Two Latin dandies air-
lifted themselves simultaneously over opposite sides of the car and started worm-
ing their way towards a group of nicely dressed girls who projected an aura of
refinement and showed signs of wanting to remain aloof. As the guys approached,
the girls closed ranks, rather snobbishly, and moseyed toward the building. The
fellows showed no imprint of having been scorned by the clan of feminine beauty
and looked around for another cluster of girls to harass.

The owner of the convertible, Ricardo "Rico" Castro, projected an image of
self confidence that often betrayed him. He led himself to believe all girls were
flirts and that their attention was personally directed towards him. The painful
truth was, he and his buddy, Jesus "Snake" Morales, were only attracted to their
female counterparts and even they were more responsive to the clean cut young
men. Rico exhibited himself as the guy the boys on campus should desire to emu-
late. They too, like the girls, mustered personality constraints to tolerate his stupid arrogance and avoid confrontation. He allowed his superego to support his
self-image of "Big Man on Campus" status as he rallied in his reputation as the
lead, school bully. He knew his limitations as a menace and kept his distance
from the jocks.

Jesus, known as Snake affectionately or without affection, depending on who
was addressing him, was seriously behind the least student in his class scholastically. He was constantly working his way out of cracks he couldn't protect himself from falling through. The gap in the intellectual prowess between him and
his peers, provoked him to turn inward and claim pride in his bully power over
brain power. It satisfied his perception of machismo and confirmed to himself
that he was a bad ass to be reckoned with. In reality, he was just another hoodlum
with a limp posture and crew cut. His side profile was slouchy and closely resembled that of a capital "S." His vocabulary was more visual than audible and
expressed mainly in finger gestures signifying "I've got mine, how are you doing?"
or just plain, "screw you." He sported a colossal onyx crucifix with silver
enhancements at the intersection of the cross and on the four extremities. It hung
on a heavy silver chain around his neck leaving one to reconcile what he stood
for, a finger marksman or a religious zealot.

There were no escaping Rico and Snake as two misfits linking themselves
together as sidekicks. They tolerated each other for the sake of having someone to
bond with socially otherwise they would be loners in the sea of humanity surrounding them.

✶   ✶   ✶   ✶

In the office were two new boys waiting to see the registrar with needed information to complete their application for admittance. One of the boys introduced himself to the other. "I'm Fuller Kreppe," he said, befriending the stranger with extended hand.

"Milo Munroe," returned the stranger, completing the hand shake. That handshake was the beginning of the school's most bonded friendship of the year.

✶   ✶   ✶   ✶

Fuller was average looking compared to Milo. Then he had this name thing. It was just a question of time when his kaleidoscope identity would ignite the indignities he would have to endure his last year of public school.

He knew his self-assurance would be tested in this new environment if the name calling ever started. It was beyond him to take it in his stride and let it roll off his back, but having no choice other than nasty fist fights, he'd have to relent. This brought about a shy side in his disposition and sometimes revealed an irreconcilable complex of inferiority. Inadequate feelings robbed him of the security necessary to be content. This weighed heavily on him and manifested a life of its own. He found himself in constant self analysis that would eventually detract from his confidence in social activities on campus. Off campus, it didn't matter. His activities consisted mostly of youthful fantasies and heavy reading. He was blessed with one natural unstated asset; his I.Q. was off the charts ranking him with the academic geniuses of all time and complimenting the name, Nostradamus.

Putting all of his intellectual resources aside, all Fuller really wanted was to find a girl that took him at face value rather than being embarrassed by his peculiar name or impressed by his academic performance. With a loyal girlfriend by his side, he could find the strength to fight off attempts by others to humiliate him.

Milo, on the other hand, had developed into a handsome, mature lad with dark wavy hair. Every strand laid neatly in place. His deep blue eyes were set in masculine sockets telegraphing his congeniality, but maturity overlaid his disdain for adolescent pranks and schoolyard punks who readily yielded to him because of their natural feeling of inferiority by contrast. His lower jaw was squarely chiseled leading to a small clef in his chin. He was dressed like his next stop was to be the country club or other formal gathering. He was adorned in his band uniform. It consisted of a navy blazer with a gold bullion crest over the lefthand breast pocket, a starched white shirt and red necktie. His neatly pressed gray flannel trousers over black, spit shined shoes complemented his ensemble.

The girls that passed by Milo in the hall did a double take unmasking their momentary infatuation of the guy. He never knew the threat of rejection by the girls he knew, as the *cream of the crop* competed for his attention.

*   *   *   *

The bell rang and the halls cleared rapidly. Eventually, Fuller and Milo were called separately into the registrar's office, then asked to sit outside. "Someone will come after you shortly." Soon, a young student assistant arrived and led both of them to the same homeroom. Milo's entrance aroused an impassioned swoon by the majority of the female assembly. Most were unable to refocus on the blackboard as quickly as they took to him. The boys weren't so detached. They made facial contortions and outward signs toward each other implying the dressed up dude was probably queer and Fuller a wimp.

The teacher tapped her desk with a ruler and regained everyone's attention, then said, "Students, I have an announcement. We have two new pupils joining our class today. Please introduce yourselves," she said, extending the lead to Fuller while holding steady her attempts to keep her furtive glances directed away from Milo. She too noticed he was exceptionally handsome and tugged at her natural instincts to be neutral as protocol required between teacher and pupil.

"I'm Fuller Kreppe" he said, accepting the teacher's invitation to introduce himself. He swept past his last name with a slurred murmur.

"Milo Munroe," Milo followed with assurance. After making an inconspicuous once over of the girls in his class, Milo focused on the only female in the room that pushed his buttons on sight—the homeroom teacher.

"Thank you," the teacher succeeded Milo, still having trouble with a focal adjustment in his direction. He had unknowingly become the guiding edge of her peripheral vision.

"We are very fortunate to have these gentlemen join our class. I'm Miss Hatcher," she said, pointing to her name on the blackboard.

"Class," she continued, demanding attention, "let's give Misters' Kreppe and Munroe a real Anthony Wayne High School welcome."

A parade of unintelligible welcomes resembling a "nice to meet you" rambled through the classroom mingled with halfhearted applause, then attenuated to complete silence.

Unfortunately, Rico and Snake were assigned to the same homeroom. Fuller looked around and his eyes braked when he saw Snake shooting him the finger. He tried to ignore it but was put on notice that sooner or later they would probably clash.

Snake read Milo correctly. He knew he was outclassed and was intimidated by Milo. He refrained from the expressive assassination he so rudely telegraphed to Fuller.

Miss Hatcher was in her early twenties. She was a pretty lady, petite and tastefully dressed. The classroom males had trouble keeping their chins off the floor when they were fortunate enough to cop a clear rear end view. Her three inch heels changed her pretty status to that of a fleeting beauty. The heels caused her calves to tense as she walked, infusing a captivating mystery and preoccupation of the boys as they tried to separate their secret thoughts from her teacher's persona.

The rest of the day was spent going from class to class with lunch somewhere between. Fuller and Milo shared most of the same subjects and joined each other for lunch. Fuller recognized Milo as a friend from the beginning. He discerned that Milo was a man of character and integrity—the kind of person he was reared to be, and he knew from the beginning they were destined to be good friends. He needed someone to bond with and become close to.

The disappointment of the day was when it became apparent that Rico and Snake were on the same schedule as he and Milo. *It's going to be a shitty year*, Fuller surmised upon receiving this news.

He spent the class changes keeping up with Milo. When the final bell rang, they paired up and evacuated the school together.

"Can I give you a lift?" Milo asked, angling off toward the parking lot.

"Sure," said Fuller. "What direction are you headed?"

"I'll take you wherever you want to go," Milo said. "I just have to be downtown in forty-five minutes."

Milo stopped beside a new black Buick Super with white sidewall tires, stuck the key in the lock and opened the door.

"Jeeze," Fuller said, "who does this baby belong to?"

"It's mine," said Milo, "all mine."

What's this guy do, when he's not going to school? Fuller wondered silently, *Rob banks or deal drugs?* "The kind of money it takes to buy one of these babies, doesn't grow on trees."

"You bet your ass it doesn't," Milo said in agreement. "I worked for it," he flashed Fuller a winking smile.

"I've got to hand it to you," said Fuller, pairing up the car with the clothes Milo was wearing, "you've got good taste in automobiles and threads."

"As much taste as the money you have to spend will buy," Milo said. "She's a beauty, isn't she?"

"She's a beauty, all right," Fuller agreed. "You'll have to fight the girls off when they find out this little treasure belongs to you."

"Not really. I have a career and don't have much time for girls."

A career. Fuller thought. *What kind of career can a high school senior have that yields classy automobiles and designer clothing. That's the career I want.*

"I saw the way the women came onto you today," Fuller said, "including the teacher."

"Don't let it fool you," Milo said. "For some reason, girls are intimidated by me."

"Yea, right," said Fuller. "If I was a girl, I would be all over you. Huh,huh."

"You're not pretty enough," Milo said. "Now if you were Miss Hatcher, I'd buy you a see through nighty and we could play bed tag till you caught me."

As Milo drove out of the school parking lot, he decided to relieve Fuller of the mystery surrounding his new car. He paused, wondering if it was safe opening up to a stranger he had just met earlier that day. *A guy needs a friend,* he resolved, *and Fuller had the demeanor of someone he would like as a friend.* "I'll tell you a secret, if you'll keep it to yourself." He was happy showing off his new car and wanted someone he could share his joy with.

"You can trust me," Fuller assured Milo, warming up to hear something underhanded.

"I made a deal with my mom," Milo informed Fuller. "She would let me move here with my sister if I agreed to stay in school and practice every day. Hell, I had to wait till I got to Waynesford to buy this car. I couldn't have bought it when I was living at home. My mom would have accused me of dealing drugs or something. My sis and her husband think it's neat and they back everything I do. They won't squeal on me to my mother."

"What's that have to do with practice?" Fuller asked.

"Oh, I didn't tell you? I'm a professional musician."

"Get out!" Fuller said, showing keen delight. "What do you play?"

"I play trumpet with the Phil Davenport orchestra. We play nightly at the Anthony Wayne Hotel Ballroom. Remember, this can't get out," Milo cautioned, "or they would kick my butt out of school."

"They wouldn't do that," Fuller said with a puzzled look on his face. "What's the difference in playing a trumpet for money or delivering a paper route?"

"If you have to ask, you wouldn't understand." Milo said. "I'd quit school today if it wasn't for my mom. It's important to her for me to graduate."

"Well, you could've knocked me over with a feather," Fuller said, recovering from the shock of surprise.

"Remember now, you can't let this out," Milo insisted.

"Hey man. You can count on me," assured Fuller. "I won't tell a soul. Are you in the school band?"

"Oh, hell no," blurted Milo. "I'm not school music material after playing the real stuff."

"Playing in that Phil—what's his names orchestra must account for the nice threads and wheels," Fuller implied, curiously.

"Yep, I'm wearing my work clothes. We have an early practice every day and I have to be on time for rehearsal. There's not enough time to go home and change."

Passing a drug store that had a soda fountain, Fuller said, "I'll get off here," and then backtracked and offered to buy Milo a Coke.

Milo checked his watch then said, "Just what I need. Thanks man," and searched for a parking place. "I can't stay long or I'll be late for rehearsal."

They took a corner booth in the reaar of the fountain and both ordered cherry cokes.

"Where did you move from?" asked Fuller.

"Chicago—"

"Fantastic. That's where I'm from," Fuller showed delight. "We lived on the north side near Evanston. What part of Chi are you from?"

"I grew up on the west side, but we moved to an apartment near the Loop after my dad passed away."

"Oh, I'm sorry to hear that," Fuller said, expressing his sympathy.

'Thank you," Milo said, accepting Fuller's condolence. "It was kind of sudden so he didn't suffer. My mom sold our house. I couldn't practice in the apartment so I moved here to live with my sister. She owns her own home and the noise doesn't bother her."

"Your sister—what does she do?" Fuller quizzed.

"Shops all the time. She's married to an orthopedic surgeon and he's got more money than Jesus Christ."

"That's what I'd do if I had lots of money, read and shop," Fuller squandered his ambition to Milo. "You get along with your brother-in-law?"

"Oh yea. He's a man after my own heart and we're great friends." Milo answered. "He's a dixieland jazz freak and I keep his appetite for the music well satisfied. So you're from Chicago?"

"Yeah, I knew we had something in common," Fuller said. "You look like you're from Chicago. I knew it the first time I laid eyes on you."

"What kind of work does your dad do?" Milo asked.

"He was an engineering professor at Northwestern. He accepted a tenure at City College here in Waynesford and here I am."

They finished their cokes and went outside together. Fuller agreed to meet Milo at school the next morning.

Fuller remembered how Milo, in his finery, had diverted the girl's focus on school business. He wondered how he would affect the ladies if he came to school every day, looking swift like Milo. He quickly accepted Milo's glitter over his own insipid appearance and dropped the subject. He lived nearby and strolled home.

After supper, Fuller borrowed his dad's car and drove into the downtown area of the city. He found the Anthony Wayne Hotel and drove around the block several times before deciding to park and go in. He ventured into the lobby and cased the place until he found the ballroom. The band was in full swing. For no particular reason, he thought it best Milo not see him shadowing the band. He loitered outside the main entrance listening to the music. The sounds were like all the big bands of the day rolled into one and Fuller was sponging it up. He would peek in now and then, and on one occasion witnessed Milo stand up and take an inspiring trumpet solo. He could tell it was well executed even though he knew nothing about musical technique. *Man, he is soooo good,* Fuller kept repeating to himself. He was thrilled, he had a friend the same age as he, who had made it as a professional. It set him to wondering what profession he could apply his high level reading to besides teaching. He went *Ugh* at the thought of becoming an educator. He reconciled that his reading experiences were supplemental to his formal education and his professional aspirations were still before him.

While Fuller was standing outside the ballroom in a euphoric stance, a man in a suit came up and wanted to know if he could be of any help. Fuller didn't know he was the house detective. He just knew he spoke with authority and was going to be a kill joy.

"I was just listening to the music," Fuller told him, having a feeling what was coming next.

"I'm sorry, son," he said. "If you don't have official business in the hotel, I'm afraid I'll have to ask you to leave."

Fuller felt discriminated against, being kicked out of a public place, but didn't argue with the man. It was still early, so he decided to drop by the popular drive-in burger joint for a snack on his way home and check out the carhops.

Sitting in his dad's car, Fuller ordered a burger and shake from a scanty clad carhop on roller skates. He made a personal evaluation of each of the girls as they glided past his car in their cheer leader style costumes. Their short fluted skirts flexed in the breeze relative to the speed they were skating. Fuller set a numerical priority on the girls he was viewing. He measured them by how strong they influenced his desire to take them home and introduce to his mother and father. None really passed the test as the standard he set for himself was higher than he had a right to expect. He had been there on occasions when some of the girls would leave with boyfriends on motorcycles or in hot rods after their shift ended. The girls' cute appearance passed his visual inspection, but their male counterparts left risky impressions of suitable traits to be desired. It followed, if the girls character attributes were parallel to those of their boyfriends, then their charm and beauty endowments were superficial. The sweetness part of their aesthetics, Fuller could buy into, but their overall culture left a hollow hole in his psyche that was disenchanting and contrary to the standards he set for himself.

He paid no attention to the occupants of the car that pulled in the parking space behind him. He caught a quick glance in the rear view mirror revealing a smooching session in progress, but Fuller went back to his car hop appraisals which were more fulfilling to his fantasies. His analysis of the girls was becoming more fascinating on the one hand, but their physical presence grew farther from his reach on the other. It was highly unlikely he would get lucky enough to drive one of the girls home.

After relaxing his inspections of the carhops, he glanced again in his rear view mirror. He saw overtones of seduction evidenced by the kissing and lumping together of bodies in the car behind him. It made him jealous of their conspicuous intimacy.

Subsequent to paying his tab, Fuller stepped out of his car and headed to the restroom. He didn't notice the occupants of the car behind him. It was the two Mexicans from school; Rico and Snake with their girlfriends.

Snake thought he recognized a familiar figure get out of the car in front of them. He did! "Hey RRRico," he whooped, rolling his R's. "Esee who dat is? It's dat freaky new kid in our class. I'd know him anywhere. He kinda hanged around dat queer looken' dude with the coat and red necktie. Know who I'm talking about?"

Rico showed his annoyance. Snake had interrupted his locked up position with his female companion. He disengaged from the torrid smooch with the girl he was enmeshed with, making a sucking slap sound. "Es-shut-up," Rico commanded, "can't you es-see I'm in conference."

Snake was momentarily taken aback. "I was just gonna say—"

"Can it, but thole. I ain't got time for youse right now."

There was a four minute lapse of time as Snake nursed his hurt feelings.

"Hold it," Rico interrupted, tacitly apologizing for bruising Snake's self-esteem. "He's coming back."

They watched as Fuller re-entered his car. Snake stretched out of Rico's convertible and sauntered in a cocky gate over to Fuller's open window. He rested his elbows on the window ledge with the middle finger of one hand locked in a vertical *in-your-face* pose.

Startled, Fuller turned his head toward the window, almost nosing into Snake's fiendish green tooth grin. He was close enough to feel the warmth of Snake's body and smell the stench of his fumy breath. Then his eyes converged on the finger.

"Ain't dat a purdy es-sight?" said Snake, stroking his finger. "This one's es-stiff enough for you to es-spin on, new boy, and big enough to es-stuff. Know what I'm es-saying?

Fuller remained silent, hoping the Mexican would go away.

Snake raised himself, still grinning and blew on the tip of his projected finger as though clearing smoke from the barrel of a freshly fired hand gun. Just as he turned to go back, the girl he was with shoved past him and pushed her head through the open window of Fuller's car, planting a long, wet kiss on his mouth. Pay no attention to him," she whispered, referring to Snake. "I think you are cute even if he thinks you are just another finger object."

Snake, grabbed his girlfriend by the hair and jerked her back from the window of Fuller's car. "You my bitch," he snarled. "Whud I tell ju bout flirting wid udder guys. If you know what's good for you, you better not let me catch you flirting again." He pushed her hard on her sternum sending her stumbling back toward Rico's convertible. He looked back at Fuller. "Keep yo hands off my es-stuff," he threatened, "or I'll be kickin' your ass every time I see you. You got that, gringo" Snake turned and headed back in the direction from whence he came, Rico's car.

Fuller was uncomfortable at Snake's confrontation and was glad it was over. He paid his tab, drove home and went straight to bed with his worrisome experience to inhibit his peace of mind.

CHAPTER 8

▼

Fuller was walking to school when Milo pulled up in his shiny, black beauty. "Hop in, I'll give you a lift," he said.

After entering Milo's car, Fuller sat by quietly enjoying the prestige as a passenger in an upscale automobile, but was still sulking over his experience with the Mexican the previous evening.

"You're mighty quiet, stranger. Something bothering you?" Milo asked trying to get Fuller to open up.

"I had a run in last night with that Mexican that uses his finger like a stiff dick. You know the one," Fuller said. "He's the one with the big cross around his neck."

"I know the one. What happened?" Milo asked.

"You know the drive-in near the theater on Indiana Avenue?"

"Yeah, I know the place."

"I stopped on my way home to get a burger and shake and these jerks pulled in behind me. I don't even know their names and they've got it in for me already."

Fuller coughed up the story in its entirety. "My dad lent me his car last night and I went by the hotel hoping to hear you play and some guy ran me off. On my way home, I stopped by the drive-in. The Mexican's girlfriend gave me a big wet kiss, right on the mouth, in front of him."

"That doesn't sound good," Milo stated. "Why did she do that?"

"That's the problem. I don't know, but he's plenty pissed about it."

"Who ran you off at the hotel?"

"Some man in a business suit."

"That was the house dick," Milo said. "I know the guy. Next time you want to come hear the music, wear a dress jacket and tie. If he gives you any shit, tell him you know me. During the week, I can get you a table near the bandstand and at intermission, I'll take you backstage to meet the guys. They are a great bunch of fellows."

"You're a good friend," Fuller complemented Milo. "I'll do that next time." He slumped in his seat and released the tension brought on from talking about his run-in with the Mexican.

Milo assured Fuller it was a new day and not to worry. "The Mexican will come around—You'll see."

The halls were like super highways with students rushing in all directions to be on time to their designated classes. Fuller looked up and saw Snake and his girlfriend coming toward him. He nudged Milo to change directions at the next hall intersection. Before Milo could implement Fuller's instruction, Snake cut them off. He was in a sullen mood and in a hurry to get something off his chest. "Hey man," he greeted Fuller with a half grin on his face, "I got to tell you es-sump'um, I'm es-sorry bout' las night, you hear?"

Snake looked at his girlfriend and she pushed his shoulder with the palm of her hand. "Go on, dammit," she prodded. "Do it." His head drooped slightly and his eyes aimed at the floor. "Let's shake hands and you and me be friends," he sought timidly.

Fuller and Milo glanced toward each other, surprised, but suspicious of Snake's sudden change in attitude?

Snake's girlfriend nudged him again. "Go on, Goddamn it," she said forcibly.

In a low monotone, he asked, short of begging Fuller, "Please?"

Fuller hesitatingly took his hand like a gentleman and said, "Okay, bygones are bygones."

Snake had no idea what that meant.

As Snake's girlfriend started to leave, she took hold of his right hand and gave a jerk temporarily dislodging his balance. As he recovered, he sent a quick finger maneuver, ensconced beneath his scroungy grin, toward Fuller. He and his girlfriend were soon blended in the stream of hallway traffic. Fuller was dumbfounded, but he got the message. Snake could not be trusted.

Fuller and Milo couldn't figure it out. There had to be something stranger in Snake and Lupe's relationship other than their eccentric treatment of one another.

Later, during the day, Fuller and Milo were changing classes when Fuller remembered he needed to stop by his locker. "You go on ahead, I'll catch up," he said to Milo. "I need something from my locker." After rounding several corridors, he approached his locker and opened it. Upon concluding his locker visit, he reached for the door handle to close it when he heard a girl address him with a "Hi there." She stuffed herself between him and the open locker door. It was Snake's girlfriend.

"I want to apologize for Snake's behavior last night," she said. "Sometimes he can be such a dork, but we grew up together. You know, like he's my brother or something?"

"An apology's not necessary," Fuller assured her.

She flirted with Fuller, with fluttering eyes, then asked, "You have a name?"

"Fuller," he said, flatly, resenting the fact she had forced herself on him in the privacy of his open locker.

"I'm Lupe Alonzo," she returned.

"Well Lupe—tell me, what powers do you hold over your boyfriend after the way he treated you last night?"

"You mean the apology thing, this morning?"

"Something like that."

"You really don't know, do you?"

"I could guess."

"That's won't be necessary," she said. "I'll tell you. I wouldn't put out last night. On top of that, I threatened to cut him off for good if he ever treated me that way again. He knew I meant business when I said that included shaking hands with you."

Fuller thought, *for a tough guy, Lupe's boyfriend was helplessly pussy-whipped.* Last night, he threatened to cut her off and now it was her doing the threatening. Fuller was oblivious to their wrenching of each other, but he wanted no part of their lover's grip.

Lupe startled Fuller by letting a hand fall thigh high and sliding it palmside across his crotch. She ad-libbed a finger tap as her hand brushed over his private area. Her other hand supported books upon which rested her oversized bosom. "If you want to go out sometime, I'm available and some say I'm a pretty good lay," she said, popping her chewing gum and winking. She tilted her head back slightly, grinning salaciously and slowly turned it in his direction as she leisurely strolled away.

He was momentarily aroused as he stood there surprised and dumbfounded. *Thank God she's gone,* he thought. "There is no way I would involve myself with that bitch."

Fuller spent the rest of the day trying to erase Lupe from his memory, but he was preoccupied with Lupe's finger dance across his crotch and her spicy lingo, offering him a good lay. *Why was he torturing himself,* he wondered, *when he couldn't stand the sight of the girl?* He didn't tell Milo of this incident, partly because it gave him something secret to fantasize about. As far as he was concerned, she had made him a bonafide offer to get laid. If he never took advantage, it was like having a deposit in the *pussy* bank. For now, he would not consent to testing her generous proposition, but the tangibility of her proposal was a source of arousal he could use to electrify himself in his spare time or when alone. He savored the fantasy of teasing himself with the idea. Next, he recalled the cheeks of her buttocks grinding together as she walked away. That was another matter and could not be visually avoided unless he closed his eyes. They resembled two twenty-pound canines loose in a toe sack. If he could discern mentally as to whether or not she *would* be a good lay, he could relieve his imagination of this heavy burden by checking it out or letting it go.

It was a long day for Fuller. He spent it in an uncomfortable, compromising position trying to dump Lupe from his head without success. He was glad when the final bell rang.

He caught up with Milo and was offered a lift. Long before they reached Milo's car they saw Rico and Snake sitting on the fender, feigning a jovial conversation.

"It's me they are after," Fuller assumed bravely. "I'll go lead them away." He was being protective of Milo and his new car. He could only assume they were there to hassle him as he started walking in their direction.

"It's my car," Milo said, grabbing Fuller by the arm. "I can deal with these assholes myself."

"No!" Fuller said. "It's me they have a *hard on* for."

It wasn't like Fuller to go headlong into trouble, but he was loyal to his new friend. "I'll try to talk our way out of this. If I can't, you call the cops."

"You're a good friend Fuller, but like I said, I can handle these assholes by myself."

Fuller felt obligated to address the situation alone, but was pleased Milo was willing to spare him the trouble he volunteered to face on his on. He figured together they could play the hand dealt them and maybe save face with some semblance of parity if the Mexicans started anything.

When they reached their adversaries, Milo said, politely, "That's my car you're sitting on. May I help you with something?"

"Well, maybe," Rico answered. "Me and my friend here wuz jist wunderin' about es-sump'um and figgerd you could answer our question."

"I'm your man," replied Milo, "what can I do for you."

Fuller was amazed at Milo's self assurance.

"Me and my boy here was jist wunderin' if you was a queer or jist a plain ol' pussy," Rico taunted.

Snake jumped in, "yeah, that's what we was a-wunderin'."

"You are about to find out," Milo said, standing tall, "then you can tell me."

"Come on you guys. Leave us alone," Fuller pleaded. "We don't want any trouble,"

Milo removed his blazer. "Here, hold this," he said to Fuller, dusting it off as he carefully placed the coat across Fuller's arms. "You stand back," he ordered. "I can do this alone."

With that, Rico and Snake detached themselves from Milo's car and eased shoulder to shoulder in Milo's direction with a mean spirited determination showing on their faces.

Fuller had a feeling this wasn't going good and was prone not to look. To his surprise, Milo initiated a spinning karate move that caught both Rico and Snake off guard. He blazed past their chins with the edge of his shoe, sending them reeling back and forth against each other until they fell limply to the ground.

Milo slapped the dust from his hands, then reached for his coat.

"Allow me," Fuller said, as he held the coat open for Milo.

What is it this guy can't do? Fuller thought privately. "Congratulations, Milo," He spoke with pride. "You really fucked them over. Maybe they'll jerk straight from now on and leave us alone."

Rico and Snake raised up to a sitting position, shaking their heads. They were both stunned by Milo's karate maneuver. Milo reached out with both hands and helped Rico and Snake to their feet.

As Rico reached an upright position, he started to laugh, softly at first, then moderately loud, then roared as he faced Milo and grabbed him by the shoulders. "Whud you go an do that for?" he said to Milo, forgivingly. "We was just testin you, that's all. We yo Frans—*Ah-MI*-goes," his voice increased in volume as he continued to laugh.

Milo stepped back, distrusting anything Rico said. With his hands, Milo reached up and grabbed Rico by the forearms prying Rico's grip from his shoulders. Snake started to shoot Milo the finger, then reminded himself of what had just happened. Milo saw Snake nearly unfold the finger movement and said squarely to his face, "You screwball. You are nothing but a cheap prick."

Rico started laughing again and said to Snake, "He's right, you are nothing' but a prick; a cheap prick" and started laughing louder.

Snake, realizing he was on a limb by himself, decided to join the laughter aimed at him and said, "yeah, RRRico; right! he knows a prick when he see one," he laughed louder. "I'm a jolly ol' prick, ha-ha, ha-ha. That's exactly what I am, a prick all right, but I'm a big prick." Rico and Snake entwined their arms across each other's shoulder and had a prolonged, self-debasing laugh, patronizing Milo and Fuller.

"We gonna' call you prick from now on," Rico said to Snake. "You are now Mister Prick," he said accelerating his laughter.

Milo, was disgusted. "C'mon," he said to Fuller, "let's get the hell out of here." They got in the car and backed out leaving Rico and Snake pleading. "Don't be that way, we your friends. Aw come onnnnn—"

As Milo drove off, Rico berated Snake for letting that "gringo" get the drop on him.

CHAPTER 9

▼

After supper, Fuller turned in early. "Don't you feel well, dear?" his mother showed concerned for his moodiness.

"I feel fine, Mom. Just have some studying to do." That went smooth. Fuller went to his room and engaged in his new favorite past time, daydreaming of Lupe's finger dance across his crotch and promiscuous proposition that she was a good lay. He remembered the smell of her cheap perfume and the supple grind of her buttocks which sent his hormones banging into each other, clamoring for gratification. He was willfully torturing himself and found it difficult to let go. Finally he wore himself down, mentally and physically, and succumbed to a restless night's sleep with short snippets of erogenous replays of the day, during the night.

*   *   *   *

Fuller was a virgin and for a very good reason. He envisioned he had a serious problem when he discovered that it took him up to thirty minutes to reach an orgasm, if it happened at all. He avoided sexual encounters because of the impending embarrassment if he failed to complete a satisfactory performance. This was a source of deep concern and mental controversy to him. He had heard that women sometimes faked orgasm, and wondered if sometimes men didn't fake it also—and if so—were that the thing for him to do. Faking could get him past his orgasmic rebellion. If both persons in a sexual duo *faked it* to give the impression they were not faking it, the rhetorical phrase, *was it as good for you as it was for me,* would take on a new meaning. It would be meaningless and not good for either party. Neither partner would achieve the sought after conclusion. Combining all of his intelligence with his instant wisdom on demand, he was helpless to unravel the mysterious nuances of contact with the opposite sex. If he couldn't reach a climax, then in his mind, something was malfunctioning with his equipment. He was determined to seek medical help before getting seriously involved with anyone. He decided to reserve the *fake deception* as a last resort.

Fuller was lacking experience in dealing with medical providers other than his pediatrician as he was growing up. His instincts directed him to a pharmacist at a drug store distanced from where his parents traded so there would be no family connection to discuss. He asked the clerk behind the counter if he could speak with the pharmacist. The accommodating clerk went behind a curtain and returned momentarily with a female druggist. Fuller, too embarrassed to deal with a woman, asked where he might find the chewing gum. She motioned to the display on the counter between the two of them. His predicament manifested a noticeable nervousness, causing him to turn red while trying to control his trembling extremities. He selected a package of chewing gum, paid for it and left the store in total frustration. He set the gum on an outside window ledge as he set about to find a pharmacy with a male druggist.

He rounded the neighborhood on foot looking for a place he could comfortably discuss his problem. He ultimately found one. Behind an elevated counter stood a tall gentleman with a bland facial expression, compounding medicines.

He spotted Fuller loitering on the main level, presumably mustering the courage to ask for prophylactics. This was common since most *very* young men were too reserved to come straight to the point and outright ask for rubbers. Prophylactics were generally stored in a drawer behind the counter.

When Fuller's fortitude stabilized, he approached the druggist's window and asked to speak with him privately for a moment. The pharmacist came from behind the counter and down two steps to hear what Fuller had to say. If he was there to buy prophylactics, the pharmacist was determined to make him go through the agony of asking for them. Fuller stumbled through several false starts before gaining a foothold on his purpose for being there. He finally made his case. The pharmacist realized Fuller was not there to purchase gratification accessories and began listening intently as Fuller labored through the details. When he was through, the druggist urged him, compassionately, to see a urologist and went so far as to recommend one.

Fuller followed through and made an appointment with the recommended doctor and subsequently visited his office as scheduled. He was handed a clipboard with a questionnaire attached, and was blind sided by all the questions.

The first question asked for the identity of the responsible party. Naturally that would be him. Why did they need details? All he wanted was to see the doctor, then make arrangements to pay for the visit. He listed himself as the payor.

The next question asked for his insurance company. When it reached the purpose of his visit, he had just about had it. How do you explain his sensitive problem in the space allowed? He could picture the women in the office passing his questionnaire around, finger pointing and laughing at him. After much thought, he decided to appeal to their professional acumen and wrote, "personal matter." He finished answering the remaining questions as best he could and returned the clipboard to the receptionist. He took a seat in the anteroom and waited for what seemed like forever. An elderly lady sat down beside him and struck up a conversation. "I'm here for my incontinence," she said. "My urine is dark yellow and has a strong odor to it. What are you here for, sonny?"

"Christ," Fuller winced silently."I'm here for the same reason," he answered off the top of his head. He abhorred the old lady's geriatric problems and didn't wish to become involved; he was carrying enough weight with his own. Getting up from his chair, he went to the magazine rack and selected an old issue of the Readers Digest, then found a chair distanced from the talkative oldie. After glancing through his selected material, he fell asleep.

As he dozed off, a nurse opened a door and called for "Fuller Kreppe." When he didn't answer, she called the next in line to fill his opening.

When he awoke, he discovered a half hour had passed. He went to the window and asked the receptionist "how much longer?"

She called the nurse and asked his status. The nurse scanned her clipboard which revealed she had called him earlier. She said, "We can take you now, Mister Kreppe", without mentioning her earlier canvass of the waiting room.

Bleary eyed from his nap, Fuller followed the nurse to a treatment room. After another *forever time lapse*, the doctor entered and introduced himself as Doctor Mason. He was a portly gentleman with a shiny bald head, reflecting the light from overhead.

"Well, young fellow, what do I owe the pleasure of your visit?" the doctor asked, assuming from Fuller's youth, he had a discharge which usually leads to lab work and a gonorrhea diagnosis. He anticipated his patient leading off with "I have a friend—"

Fuller, somewhat nervous, said, "Doctor Mason—I have this friend—"

Just what I thought, Doctor Mason concluded, silently.

Fuller managed to repeat the story he had disclosed to the pharmacist. His complaint stretched the doctor's imagination. As Fuller spilled his guts, Doctor

Mason became interested and tuned in carefully to understand what was really troubling young Kreppe's friend. When he had nothing else to say, Doctor Mason scratched his head and thought about it for a moment. He had been practicing medicine long enough to recognize when someone starts off with, *I have a friend*, they are generally speaking for themselves. It makes no sense to send a friend to your doctor's appointment.

"You say your friend has this problem?" the doctor asked.

"Yes sir," Fuller answered.

"I see," Doctor Mason continued. "Can you tell me why your friend sent you instead of coming himself?"

"He had to work," Fuller pulled this answer out of the air, realizing it was thin. He became more nervous in the process and suspected the doctor had been this route before and was going to trap him.

"You are aware, of course, that I can't discuss a patient's medical history without written consent. First he has to be examined and diagnosed. Now what is it I can do for you?"

This time, the doctor had Fuller against the wall. He scrambled for his next contrivance. "Well, Doctor Mason, it seems I also have this problem and was going to discuss it with you."

"Fine," Doctor Mason said. "You will need to be examined. We need to draw some blood and get a urine sample. The nurse will bring you a gown and a cup. I will return shortly."

God, Fuller thought. *What have I let myself in for?* Nothing seemed to be working for him.

The nurse brought him a gown to squeeze into and a plastic cup for a urine sample. "A lab technician will be along shortly to draw some blood," he was told.

The gown was two sizes too small and half the ties were missing. After the blood withdrawal and another long wait, the doctor returned with the nurse. She took his temperature and the doctor monitored his blood pressure.

"You have no fever and your blood pressure is normal," the doctor said. "Now, bend over the examining table and lift your gown up over your rear end."

Fuller thought, *this has gone far enough.* He was too modest to moon the nurse while the doctor watched, but there he was, bending over a table, half naked, in full view of the doctor and his nurse, not knowing what was coming next. He decided he had had enough for one day, partly because of the way things were going for him and partly because of his modesty for having to stand there *bare assed,* with a short sleeved strip of cloth hanging from around his neck. Just when he was about to call an end to his visit, Doctor Mason rammed a rubber gloved finger, hard up his rectum and rolled the tip around what Fuller imagined to be his tonsils. Several times, the doctor partly withdrew his finger and reinserted it to the hilt causing stars in Fuller's crown and a pain in his ass. The one thing Fuller learned from this examination, was when the doctor finally withdrew his finger, it felt so good, it set him free. He kidded himself—*It was almost worth a trip to the doctor to feel this good.*

"We will have to wait for the lab report, but until we hear from them, I would have to say you are the picture of health."

"But Doctor—"

"Son," Doctor Mason interrupted. "If I had your problem, I'd get on my hands and knees and give thanks to the Virgin Mary. If you indeed, have a problem, it's a good one. Do you know how many men on this planet would trade places with you right now? You have a gift, my boy. My advice to you is to stand proud and not worry yourself unnecessarily."

"I hear you doctor—," Fuller hesitated, then asked if they could speak privately for a moment. Doctor Mason nodded an okay to the nurse and she left the room. "Doctor, you say I don't have anything to worry about. I think I've been cursed. Do you know how much I dread being with a girl? I'm not sure if I can deal with the embarrassment of not being able to—you know—there *must* be some treatment you can recommend."

"I can tell you this," said Doctor Mason, "there is nothing physically wrong with you. Your condition is known throughout the medical profession as an infantile arrestment. In lay terms, that means an undeveloped penile organ. It doesn't imply a malady in your case, it simply means you have an extended misfire. The entire syndrome cannot be measured by an occasional failure to have an orgasm. This condition has been thoroughly researched in Scotland and covered in the English Medical Journal. No evidence was ever suggested that the physiology of this disease causes any permanent detriment to the human body or masculine performance. A lack of confidence perhaps in your case, but what I'm saying to you is this: the odds are, in time, your condition will correct itself. Take my word, young fellow. Go about your business realizing that you've been blessed and don't let your imagination undermine your libido."

"Okay," Fuller surrendered. "I'll try to make an adjustment in my thinking to accommodate your advice. Er—Doctor? I need to ask you—may I please pay your bill a little at a time?"

"There is no charge, son," Doctor Mason said. "You go and live a happy life and don't forget what I told you."

"I don't understand," Fuller inquired of the doctor.

"I didn't do anything," Doctor Mason said. "It's always a pleasure to speak with the young folks. Thank you for your visit." He had every right to levy his usual fee on Fuller, but to charge a scared kid for a little free advice would have been taking advantage. He was happy to negotiate with the lab for the blood test and hoped he had been instrumental in educating a young person to the cost in discomfort and money for investigating *frivolous* symptoms.

*   *   *   *

Fuller was confused. How could a gift of this nature be so damaging to his sense of well being. Sooner or later his so called gift was going to jump out and bite him on the ass. How could he utilize such a gift without revealing his abnormality. From his perspective, if he couldn't climax, there was something wrong with him and he wanted it fixed.

Here he was, an "A" plus student on the verge of getting an "F" in his view of a four letter action word—if he ever got that far. The degradation could have a lasting effect on the rest of his life and ruin his chances with the girls forever. He could visualize himself remaining a virgin for life as he pulled away from society to become a recluse. He couldn't get it through his head that if word of his sustaining libido ever got out, he would be the number one studmaster amongst the sexually active girls in school or anyplace else for that matter. There was only one way to tell for sure where he stood on a scale of one to ten as a satisfactory lover, and that was *not* to weasel out of his next opportunity to have sex. He thought about it until he was satisfied all elements were in place. His final decision was to take the high road if no one of the opposite sex threw themselves at him. He would lay back and wait for his dream girl. If he ever found a true love, they could work through anything lovingly together, or he could fake it lovingly with her, or they could fake it lovingly between themselves. He reconciled that things of this nature would take its rightful place in the pecking order of life and he couldn't do a damn thing about it, but play the hand the Almighty dealt him.

CHAPTER 10

▼

Miss Hatcher was very professional in the performance of her duties. She kept an eye on all of her pupils and two eyes on Milo. She was careful not to jeopardize her objective of peeking from time to time. Milo couldn't help noticing her interest beneath her cover of professional scruples. He could feel her fleeting glances ricocheting off him at the most peculiar times in class. He perceived her copping a random glance to be a personal thing between the two of them and hopefully would not become conspicuous to the assembly. To him, this was up close and personal and he wanted it to remain that way. *What a shame,* he thought, *their teacher/pupil relationship had to be under such strict authority.* She was more in his league than all the teeny-boppers he was forced to smile at and mince words with everyday. He was satisfied, by osmotic perception, that she was attracted to him also.

Snake continued his inept finger distractions toward Fuller, and Rico flaunted his mock Lordship over the fearful male students foolish enough to put up with it. Lupe continued to put the make on Fuller without success and Fuller continued to fantasize intimate get-togethers with Lupe.

Just when things were about to level out and become boring, the latest test scores were pinned to the bulletin board. Rico and Snake could have just as well stole a smoke outside the building as nothing in their learned status had improved.

Snake noticed it first and pointed it out to Rico. There for all to see was the name Nostradamus F. Kreppe.. The first name was enough for hazing mileage to last the rest of the school year, but Fuller Kreppe? That was choice. In all their illiteracy, they deducted the "F" correctly as standing for Fuller. They clipped each other on the shoulder and broke out in a low mentality laugh, repeating, "Nostra-doe-mas, Nostra-doe-mas.Doe-mas". Nearly the Spanish equivalent of *two more*. Snake was fascinated by the sounds resembling words in Spanish. He repeated it quizzically until it finally caught on and migrated to repeated chants of "dum-ass" by both he and Rico. Another round of low mentality laughter erupted, this time with a higher pitch and louder volume.

"NOooo, NOooo," Rico slobbered. "That would be dum-ass, fool-o-crap."

"Hyh, hyh, hyh,hyh," one more outburst of rowdy laughter.

A crowd was starting to gather. Fuller walked up unnoticed to get his grades, but when he heard Rico and Snakes loud voices working him over, he moved on.

Later when he met up with Milo, he was congratulated for his grades.

"What did I make?" Fuller asked.

"The highest in the class," answered Milo, "a double A-plus," as if there were such a value.

"Hey that's pretty damn good," Fuller reacted, not taking his curiosity beyond Milo's jesting. "How did you do?"

"Not bad, considering I don't ever study." Adding truthfulness to his answer, he confessed, "I'm flunking."

$$*\qquad*\qquad*\qquad*$$

Fuller had taken Milo up on his invitation to come by the ballroom wearing a dress jacket and necktie to listen to the music. He made it over there as often as he could. True to his word, Milo found him a table near the bandstand and summoned him backstage during the band's intermission. Ultimately, over time, Fuller had been introduced to all the musicians and knew them on a first name basis. During intermission, the band had hard drinks backstage, but Milo drank beer without being questioned by his colleagues and Fuller had a coke. The house picked up the tab. Fuller was actually becoming part of the in-crowd and he loved it. Even the house detective was beginning to recognize Fuller's presence as Milo's friend and sometimes joined the intermission breaks.

The next day in school, Fuller ran into Rico and Snake in the hallway.

"Well, lookee here," Snake babbled, highlighting one of his middle fingers."Is it Mister dum-ass or is it full-a-es-shit?"

"You dingbat," Rico scolded Snake.

"It's full-o-crap."

Fuller ignored Rico. He looked directly into Snake's face and mustering the necessary courage, said sternly, "Out of my way, prick."

"Hey, watch who you callin' prick. I'll whup yo' ass," Snake retaliated.

By then Fuller was lost in the hallway crowd.

"Come on, prick. Let's keep it movin'." Rico said to Snake.

"Right, RRRico," Snake retorted, "but go easy on that prick thang, huh?

*   *   *   *

As the bell rang the students started filing out of the room. Miss Hatcher snagged Milo with the wave of her pencil and asked him to stay a moment after school. After the classroom was clear of her charge, she asked Milo to have a seat. She wanted to discuss his grades with him. This was the first time they had been alone, one on one. Miss Hatcher was careful not to let her guard down. Milo was fantasizing how the two of them could make music together in a cozy sack somewhere.

"Why is it a young man, who seems to have it all, is letting his grades slip?" she questioned Milo. "It's as if you don't care to culminate your last year in high-school with a diploma."

"I'm sorry," he said. "I have an afternoon job that is probably holding me back. I'll try to do better, Miss Hatcher," Milo smiled while imagining her in a compromising position.

She too was exercising her imagination. She saw Milo as the best looking hunk since Clark Gable. "It is my job to see that you succeed," she said curtailing her fancy. "If you need help, I will stay after school a couple of days each week and see that you get it."

That would be great, Milo thought, *but it can't be on the same time schedule as my job.* "If I can't improve on my own," he pledged to Miss Hatcher, "I will stay after school and let you help me—I promise."

His music came first, but he obligated himself to try and improve his grades so he could stay in school and appease his mother. To stay in school just to further his education didn't register with Milo. He already had a well-paying profession and didn't need the toil of waking up every morning and wasting his days in some funky ol' school house.

"Consider this carefully, Milo; I know you can do better. Remember, I am your teacher and your safety net. Call on me anytime, if you need help."

You can count on it, Milo thought. "Thank you, Miss Hatcher, I will."

Fuller was waiting in the hall. "Well—what was that all about?" he pumped.

"I'm falling behind in my grades," Milo said. "She wants to tutor me after school."

"Yea, right." Fuller commented. "She has the hots for your body."

"I honestly think she was trying to be helpful."

"Oh hell, if you need tutoring, I can do that," Fuller promised. I'm better at it than she will ever be."

"I love you Fuller, but I'm not interested in taking you to bed," he elbowed Fuller with a wink and a grin.

"Oh I see—I don't wear my skirt high enough. Is that it?" Fuller kidded. He was aware that any extracurricular activities after school would interfere with Milo's job. He restated his offer, this time seriously, to which Milo answered, "If I can't work things out, I'll give you a shot at it."

*   *   *   *

On the way out of school, they stopped by the bulletin board. Fuller caught a glimpse of Rico's and Snake's grades. They were in worse shape than Milo's. He noticed they were barely balancing on the negative side of the failing mark. Fuller's first reaction was, "Good, the son-of-a-bitches need to fail." His following reaction was characteristic of his upbringing: "Shit, I didn't mean that," he said to Milo. "They have a right to an education, just like the rest of us."

"I'd say they are well educated in flipping people off."Milo replied.

*   *   *   *

During school hours, Fuller had started evaluating the crop of female seniors by the same standards he ventured with the carhops at the drive-in. He vacillated through the herd to see if he could find one worthy enough to take home to meet his parents, or lucky enough to strip him of his virginity. He was fearful of being the only virgin in his senior class, but was also fearful some young *split tail* would unmasked his alleged sexual dysfunction and expose him to the entire school population. He was caught in his own crossfire of staying a virgin or being exposed by some loose lipped rib of the male species; a quirk of fate mother nature had tagged him with.

CHAPTER 11

▼

Friday was going to be an off night for Milo. A traveling orchestra with name recognition would occupy the hotel ballroom for a one night stand. He was glad to have a night off and accepted an invitation to a party by one of the stylish girls in his class. She said they were going to listen to records and to bring a friend, adding "the more the merrier."

Milo concluded they were short of boys. He invited Fuller who readily accepted. Milo parked across the street from the target residence. The girl that invited him was Calley O'Malley from their homeroom. She was on the porch with several other girls when she saw Milo drive up in his expensive automobile. She rushed over to greet him with a kiss on the cheek and was anxious to be seen with him. His shinny new Buick gave impetus to their togetherness. "You must have a super dad, for him to lend you his new car," she said as they walked across the street.

"I do," Milo lied, taking advantage of the opening she gave him. The car needn't be her excuse to want to be seen with him. "He trusts me and knows I'll be careful with it," he said. After a little idle chit-chat he excused himself to inform Fuller about the car belonging to his dad and reminded him not to let it slip. They chuckled and winked at each other sealing Fuller's promise. Milo returned with Fuller and introduced him to Calley O'Malley. *There is the only girl out of the whole damn school including the Drive-in herd,* Fuller thought, *that he would take home to meet his mother and father.*

Milo's girl of the evening sat on the rug near the speakers and patted the floor next to her for him to have a seat. He arranged himself into a comfortable position and settled back next to her to listen to, and enjoy the music. She grabbed his hand and used it to pull his arm around her neck. His hand was hanging limp against her upper arm and she reached up and ever so gently eased it closer so it molded to her shoulder's contour. She rolled her head back and smiled directly in his face with a sparkle in her eyes. He returned her smile sensing a possessiveness he had become familiar with. He was used to girls putting their claim on him rather quickly, but he, like the jocks, had his pick of the crop and didn't take any of them seriously.

Calley was lovely and fresh as a bouquet of daisies. Milo's movie star looks against the backdrop of Calley's innocence, gave the appearance of a platonic friendship sparked by fond admiration for each other. His mind, however, was preoccupied with lingering thoughts of Miss Hatcher.

Fuller was giving the once over to the girls present, but his gaze kept snapping back to Calley. He had trouble believing he was actually coveting his best friend's lady of the evening. He definitely decided she was the only girl he had met since coming to Indiana that he would take home to meet his parents, but there was no way he would compete with his friend for her affections. He couldn't anyway. He didn't have Milo's savoir-faire. The other girls were busy pawing their boyfriends or huddled in a gossip session, so Fuller retreated to a cushioned arm chair in the far corner of the room.

Why hadn't he noticed Calley before? She was in his homeroom at school. He later discovered a partial explanation. She had the fourth desk directly behind him so it wasn't easy for him to catch sight of her. Meanwhile, he continued to be touched by her simple beauty.

Artie Shaw's *Back Bay Shuffle* was on the turn table when the door flew open and in popped Lupe Alonzo, confident as ever and ready to take over as life of the party. Seems she knew everyone there and they proceeded to greet each other, some with phony hugs and kisses that stopped short of their mark.

She spotted Fuller and wove her way through the frivolous humanity and bulky furniture to get to him. "Poor baby," she cooed, "no one noticed him over here all by himself but me. Isn't that right, honey?" She smoothed out the material atop his thighs making room for her abundant carcass in the middle of his lap. "I think I'll sit here so you won't be so lonesome—Okay, Sweetie?"

Not waiting for an answer, she climbed aboard. Her inexpensive perfume flared his nostrils with an intoxicating blend of overly sweet, but sensual fragrance. It was strong enough to kindle a smoldering, uncontrollable, arousal within him which he was trying to ignore. Lupe wasn't surprised at the growing enlargement she had sat on and began to take advantage of the situation by squirming on his lap.

"Mmmmm, I like that," she whispered blowing a soft stream of warm breath on his ear.

He liked it too, but his intuition prompted a thought about her boyfriend. "What's Snake doing tonight?" he asked before letting her titillating go further.

"Oh, don't worry about him." Lupe answered. "He smokes pot on Friday nights with his buddies. That leaves an opening for you, get it?"

Fuller got it all right. She scrunched her bottom against his lap again and he completely slackened his attempts to control the involuntary surges raging through his loins.

He had the presumption something profound or precarious was pecking at the edge of his sanity. He made up his mind once he would have nothing to do with this woman. His only use for her was her being the object of his fantasies in the secret games he played at home or when he let them infiltrated his school period. His life was rearranging itself to match his imagination. *How unusual,* he thought. *What's it going to be?* The choices were getting tougher to make, the more thought he put into them. *Either get it on or forget* it, he told himself. He knew he couldn't have it both ways. He also knew he was slipping in the direction of her undisciplined behavior and wouldn't be able to hold out if she kept molding her butt against the vertex of his lap. *Everyone knows a stiff dick has no conscience,* he reminded himself, *but forget the mind games?* If he was going to surrender his morals to Lupe, it would only happen under the duress of temptation, otherwise he couldn't stand the bitch.

The rest of the evening was spent listening to big band records and Fuller warming up to Lupe's invasion of his eroding tease-resistence. She had him confronted with a dichotomy of sensuous overlaps. One resonating in step with debauchery because his hormones were spiraling out of control, while the other hindered his eagerness to succumb by clashing with her obnoxious momentum he determined to avoid. He was also wary that at least one of the guests would inform Snake of the heated action going on between himself and Lupe.

As usual, Milo came to Fuller's rescue saying he had volunteered to take Calley home and offered him and Lupe a ride. Lupe was first to jump at the idea. Getting Fuller in the backseat of Milo's car seemed the perfect place to put the make on him.

Throughout the evening, Calley had been lightly affectionate towards Milo, but remained mannerly and ladylike. Fuller, on the other hand couldn't say Lupe had been ladylike because she had him pinned to his chair all evening with the overwhelming force of her body weight.

Once in the car, Calley snuggled up to Milo and he wrapped his arm around her shoulder as he started to drive. It was expected and he complied.

Lupe positioned herself toward the rear of the car with her torso mashed against Fuller—her face within inches of his. She began breathing in heaves against his chest and shrouding his face with an intermittent stream of her moist hot breath. Her demeanor sent the message that she was ready and willing to fulfill any of his fantasies or desires that needed gratifying and that included proving she was the good lay she professed to be. Fuller's resistence wilted rapidly into a sensual preoccupation as the temptation she was thrusting upon him intensified. He glanced down at the top of her blouse, ingesting the bulbous constriction of her cleavage. This was the first time in his life he had been so closely connected to such a complete mixture of feminine potpourri. Her blouse top had been pushed up by the pressure of her heaving bosom against his chest. It was open just the right amount for a hand to slip *an in and under maneuver* to the full roundness of an awesome breast. He looked up to catch her eyes focused disarmingly at his. Their anticipations linked as one as their expressions dissolved into a mutually weakened frown. They both looked down at the open top of her blouse then slowly back to each other with bland expressions. She was offering the next move to him. He accepted her tacit invitation to explore and slowly eased his hand downward through the opening. When his fingers reached the nipple, she gave a deep sigh followed by a faint moan as it erected to a rigid, sizable nubbin. Lupe leaned backward and tapped Milo on the shoulder. "We'll get out at the next block and walk the rest of the way," she said.

What the hell, Fuller thought. He was game for anything after her willingness to allow his exploration between her skin and under garment. He saw himself as being liberated from the bondage of innocent adolescence once he performed with *live ammunition on a genuine female target,* all in one experiment. It wasn't like he had planned it this way and certainly not with the girl of his choice, but he was confident now that he could perform like a champion. His anticipation of exploring the unfamiliar, but often dreamed of feminine attributes, overwhelmed him. A fleeting thought about Snake temporarily deflated his ego. His next thought: *Piss on Snake.*

Once on the sidewalk, they wrapped their arms around each other and staggered like a couple of drunks, mostly because of the difference in their heights. Every now and then Fuller would squeeze one of her breasts as a symbol of his new found authority. She would reach up and kiss him on the cheek in response. He would squeeze again and think of Snake at random intervals. He actually held in his hand, an *off-limits* bundle that he thought, until now, belonged exclusively to Snake. He reveled in the fact that he was about to make out with Snake's girlfriend and Snake couldn't do a damn thing about it.

They stopped at an abandoned old filling station. She raised up on her toes and whispered in his ear, "I have to pee, you come hold my hand." She took him by the hand and led him to the rear of the old building which was overgrown with weeds laden with rubbish. She clung to his arm while she squatted, then used a handful of green leaves to wipe. She offered to hold his object if he had to go, but he was repulsed and rejected the idea. She then led him behind a lattice board fully covered with overgrown vines hiding a door hanging loosely from the bottom hinge. The top hinge was totally detached from the door frame. It was the entrance to an unused dilapidated store room attached to the filling station. Inside was an old musty cot with a mattress caked with dust and a bunch of worn out tires strewn about on a clammy dirt floor. The ensuing petroleum smell was discomforting to Fuller. He felt grimy and greasy, but managed to suppressed any second thoughts he might be having.

There was a couple humping on the cot when they entered. The lovers sprung up, surprised and unnerved, as if caught by the sex police. They scurried to get dressed. "We were just leaving,"the guy said shuffling on one foot while trying to slip into a shoe with the other. His female counterpart was busy fumbling with buttons and snaps while rushing to follow her lover through the exit trying to hide her identity. She covered her face and twisted to one side, as she passed the intruders.

She's been here before, Fuller surmised of Lupe. He wondered how many people knew of such a remote place in the middle of the city and how many fellows had she lured to this out of the way love lounge? He deducted that the chances of her taking him someplace she had shared with Snake was far remote. She knew Snake was a loose cannon and catching them together might spin him off into a rage he wouldn't easily recover from.

They moved toward the cot where she sat down and motioned for Fuller to sit beside her. He honked a breast with a free hand while they immersed in one long, insatiable kiss. Just as smooth as the machinery in a juke box, she slid out of her skirt and wiggled clear of her constraining girdle. With her next move she popped open her bra exposing two huge, beautiful titty teardrops with erect nipples.

Fuller was aghast. If this were a dream, *don't let it end now,* he thought, fighting to keep his wits about him. He was in the process of descending on one of her booby peripherals when she jumped up sliding her hand under her butt and bitching in Spanish. He was beside himself with fear of being caught as they had intruded on the couple before them. "What in the hell's going on?" he demanded.

"That son-of-a-bitch left some of his sticky shit on the mattress," was all she could say.

Fuller sighed, somewhat relieved. Here he was, about to get laid for the first time in his young life and he was disoriented by Lupe's impulsiveness to side track their passion. He was alarmed by the thought of being caught with his pants down, literally, and being led to his mom and dad's house half naked, embarrassed and handcuffed to a female policeman. Any sound or irregularity on Lupe's part scared the bejesus out of him. Was this the time and place for his first sexual experience? It didn't look like it was going down well. He might have to throw in the towel if there were more surprise interruptions.

She looked around and found a dirty oil rag with a clean side in the window sill and shoved it under her butt covering the sticky mess. "Come on, baby," she cooed, with outstretched arms. He quickly surveyed the dirty little room. He was anxious to continue, but was skeptical whether the room would remain safe. He determined it necessary for his masculinity to give it at least one more try and pray that Murphy's Law had run its course. He was warming up to her by tweaking her nipple with his tongue when he noticed she was fast becoming restless, then irritable. He could tell the heated passion was rapidly slipping away and rationalized that she wanted his mouth on her other nipple to solve the problem. He had barely reached it when she pushed him up by her palms against his shoulders.

"What are you waiting for, slugger?" she sought, becoming more irritated.

He hadn't initiated any foreplay other than the selfish pleasure he derived from callously nibbling her nipple.

"What do you want me to do?" He appealed for help.

"Take your pants off and lets cuka-monga," she said in a "pepper hot" Latin accent while skillfully shaking her shoulders, causing her heavy tits to rotate in opposite directions.

That could only mean one thing, he judged. Wary of being caught with his pants down, Fuller dropped his trousers and shorts from the waist to around his ankles, making sure they could be retrieved on a moments notice. He clumsily eased on top of her trying to steer without the use of his feet, which were uselessly bound together by his trousers and underpants choking off his ankles. He proceeded to push his artillery against the crest of her mound in repeated attempts to make it disappear in what he perceived to be her bull's eye. His efforts to be cool betrayed his innocence. He kept poking at her pelvic bone in a futile attempt to find his target. If he continued to miss the feminine mystery he was prospecting for, he would go down as the dumbest son-of-a-bitch in school and never live it down or have opportunities with the other girls. Lupe was sure to blab word of his bungled pursuit.

"You don't know anything, do you?" Lupe bitched, sensing she was being used by a cub explorer. "You're a fuckin' virgin," she complained. "Get the hell off me." Her pride was in being a good lay and he was depriving her of a chance to make good on her promise. He was experimenting with the birds and bee thing at her expense. "You used me, you asshole! That's it, Gringo-boy. Cover your dickie, we're outta' here." She was taking charge of the situation while putting herself back together. It took a little longer for her to desecrate the elastic stretch of her girdle as she remolded her fleshy abdomen and butt within its confinement.

Neither had anything to say the rest of the walk to her house. When they reached the steps to her front door, Fuller wanted to say something friendly as a means of disengagement, but she beat him to it.

"You've got a lot to learn white boy. Maybe somebody will teach it to you, but it sure as hell ain't gonna' be me." She was in the house before he could say, "I had a nice time."

Unbeknownst to her, she had missed the opportunity of a lifetime. Had she offered him a little more help and less temperamental criticism, she may have had the distinction of literally being the only female in history to have her brains fucked out. Being aware of his potential, Fuller felt a little less beat up on and reconciled that they were both losers.

*   *   *   *

Milo picked Fuller up on his way to school Monday morning. Fuller dumped on him his Friday night's experience with "that jumping bean bitch".

"How did *you* make out?" Fuller asked.

"Me and Calley?" Milo, questioned.

"Yeah."

"I didn't," Milo said. "She is one of the nicer girls. I didn't want to get anything started."

Fuller was glad to hear that. At least Milo had given her high marks inferring she was not soiled merchandise.

"We parked in front of her mom's house after we let you and Lupe off and had a nice long talk. I came forward about the car. Other people at school know it's mine, so I figured why lie to her? She just laughed, thinking I was funny—well, anyway, I explained that while I had a wonderful time, I was not available. She seemed a little disappointed, but seemed to understand. I did tell her you were my best friend and she expressed an interest, saying you were cute. She knew you weren't tied to that Mexican girl. She's known Lupe since their first day in grade school and that's just the way she is with all the guys."

"What did she say when you told her about me?"

"Nothing really, except if you wanted to call her sometime, it was okay."

"Did you get her number?"

"Oh yeah."

"Well?"

"Well what?"

"Aren't you going to give it to me?"

"Of course, silly," Milo said, reaching in his shirt pocket, retrieving a piece of paper and handing it to Fuller.

"OH KAayy," Fuller beamed with enthusiasm. His being with Lupe was beginning to pay off in different ways. He reconciled that he couldn't be unlucky all the time.

"Not so fast," Milo suggested to his friend. "You will want to treat her different from the rest. She's sort of the private type—like you—and me. I think the two of you would hit it off nicely," Milo said, drawing up one corner of his mouth and making a two note clicking sound.

*   *   *   *

Fuller retuned his attitude for his inevitable face to face meeting with Lupe at school. He had to be prepared for her, otherwise she would bury him in shame with her big mouth. It would even be worse if he ran into Snake and he had found out about Friday night. Fuller's enthusiasm for Calley dulled for the moment and took a back seat to his apprehension regarding contact with Lupe or Snake. After two days, Fuller was satisfied that Lupe hadn't mentioned anything to Snake about the disastrous night at the filling station. Snake was his same ol' self, shooting Fuller the finger and calling him dumb-ass. Fuller was fine with that and felt he had a reprieve from Snake, since he hadn't been confronted by now. That was one he owed Lupe, but he was not willing to hunt her down and thank her for it. The one thing Fuller and Lupe had in common was the secret they shared about each other and both were better off if Snake never found out.

He was hoping he would not have to face Lupe, but sooner or later it was destined to happen. He didn't see how he could ever overcome the humiliation she staked through his heart as opposed to being the good lay she advertised herself to be. The only way he could neutralize his feelings and get on with his life was to compromise within himself that time was on his side and little by little his pain would taper down and go away completely. This thing about time being on his side, was repeated over and over in one form or another from the books he had read. It was these teachings that gave him the stamina and confidence to sustain himself during these periods of trial.

Rico was now calling Fuller "Mister full-o-crap". In addition to Rico and Snake, his nick names were catching on with the delinquent crowd as he knew it eventually would. Fuller's only line of defense was to either ignore or endure the obscenities as they came at him. Sometimes they rolled off his back. Sometimes he had to forge on without showing his animosity. Sometimes he felt like beating the shit out of the next guy that opened his mouth, but he knew he would never do that. Either way, it was coming down as he had imagined. Then he thought about Calley. How would she react to the insults raining on his parade? Would she not respect him?

Fuller was starting to fantasize about he and Calley as a team even though they were nearly strangers. While he was sloughing off insults, an unexpected development was taking place at his school. He was being recognized by the faculty as the most intelligent student in their enrollment.

*   *   *   *

It took Fuller three days to work up the courage to call Calley. He was relieved and overjoyed to find her at home and receptive. Her telephone voice complemented her appearance as he remembered it. It was delicate and matched her fragile beauty. Their conversation ended on an agreement to meet for sodas after school. He was fixated with the prospect that he had hit pay dirt; a proper girl he could respect and be proud to introduce to his parents.

CHAPTER 12

▼

Milo had the pleasure again of being summoned by Miss Hatcher for an after school conference regarding his studies. He was impatient and looked forward to another session alone with her even if it was to hear her gripe about his teetering grades. This time, while being very tactful, she came down on him—hard. "Now I can help you or your mother can employ a tutor to come to your house, but whatever you choose, it is very important for you to improve your grades if want to graduate with the capable students," she said. "I know you are better than your grades reflect." This time she showed more compassion than a desire to scope him out. "Now, my offer still stands to help you a couple of afternoons after school each week."

"Thank you again, Miss Hatcher," Milo said, wishing he could take her up on her offer. "I promise to get some help," he lied. She was backing him into a corner. Sooner or later his grades would collide with his job, then what? He wasn't about to give up his chair in Davenport's orchestra for a mere high school diploma.

Fuller was waiting for Milo outside Miss Hatcher's room when he came out. "What was going on in there?" he asked.

"I wish," Milo returned. "I'm slipping in English, math and history."

"Is that all?"

"Yeah."

"Hell, that's everything," Fuller said.

"I know. I'm going to stop goofing off on Saturday and Sunday and work on catching up. I owe it to my mom and my sister. If I flunk, my mom will blame my sister," he said, referring to his sister's generosity for letting him stay with her and her husband.

"I promised once I would help you," Fuller said. "I meant it then and I mean it now. Let me chew on the best way to make it work and I'll get back to you."

"We are friends, Fuller. You don't owe me anything."

"More than you'll ever know," said Fuller. "I'm going to figure a way to help you catch up. Just leave it to me." He knew if Milo quit school, he would lose his friend.

Milo thought his situation was impossible, but was beginning to feel better because of Fuller's positive interest in rescuing him from the clutches of educational doom.

*   *   *   *

That evening at the ballroom, Milo had a steak dinner sent to Fuller's table with his compliments. Fuller acknowledged Milo with a nod of his head and a facial gesture which signified a fond "Thank you".

Milo grinned at him from ear to ear and winked back in response. The music was super as always, but Milo's solos seemed more inspired this night. Fuller had temporarily taken the heat off him, if only with lip service, but Milo had his doubts that he could be helped without injecting some extra time into his already congested schedule. He respected Fuller and was confident that if help was to be had, Fuller would be the one to make it happen.

Fuller was also inspired, because to offer his support to a special friend was a sincere inclination for him to help. Milo's need to show his appreciation with a steak dinner was superfluous and not necessary. But my how Fuller enjoyed it. The steak was his first fine cut of meat in memory. It was so professionally prepared, he was not likely to forget it. He was in a position to help his best buddy and knew he could find a way to do it. He would just have to settle on a plan. The rest would be easy.

*   *   *   *

Fuller saw Calley in the halls once or twice everyday. She was pretty much a loner, but was always cheerful when they stopped to speak. They accidently ran into each other outside Miss Hatcher's room as both were headed to the next class on the other side of the building.

"Here, let me carry your books," he offered.

She looked up at him with her sparkling eyes and said in the most cordial tone, "You are sooo sweet."

Fuller's knees nearly buckled. He handled her books as though they were a bag of breakable feathers. "Calley", he said, stopping momentarily to face her, "May I walk you home today after school? We can have that soda."

"Why thank you, Fuller, I'd like that," she said, then remarked that she lived at least ten blocks away if he wanted to change his mind.

"Oh, that's okay. The walk will do me good." He knew Milo would give them a ride if he wanted one, but today he was anxious to enjoy Calley's company all by himself. He was so upbeat, his mood was to dance Calley home.

When they reached class, she said, "Thank you for carrying my books."

Fuller answered, "My pleasure. That'll be my job from now on."

She didn't say anything and Fuller felt he was being stupid for making that assumption up front, leaving himself open for rejection.

*　　　*　　　*　　　*

Sometime during the day he told Milo he was walking Calley home after school.

"Good," said Milo, "I'll pick you up in the morning and you can fill me in on the details."

"Your happy ass," Fuller said. "I'm coming to the ballroom tonight. If there is anything worth telling, you'll be the first to hear it."

*　　　*　　　*　　　*

The final bell rang and Fuller pushed his way through the outrush of students into the hall outside Miss Hatcher's room. Milo gigged him in the ribs with his elbow and grinned his approval as he passed by. Lupe came out, masking a stern facial expression. She purposely brushed past him as though he didn't exist.

Slut, Fuller thought to himself.

Calley followed close behind her. Fuller had to quickly reconfigure his role from hatred of Lupe to Mister Personality for Calley. He was so into his first real meeting with Calley that Lupe evaporated completely from his mind.

"Oh, hi," he said to Calley. "Here, let me take those," he said, reaching for her books.

After they were out of the school yard and by themselves on the sidewalk, he showed his pleasure of her company by taking her hand to hold while they walked. She was a quiet girl and very much content with herself. He was obsessed with her neatness and simple beauty and the fact that she held his hand. Her legs were shapely with burnished, dark brown loafers covering her feet. The penny in the cutout of the bridge of her loafer added a measure of fascination to his delight and complemented her dainty white anklets. She wore a plaid skirt, just the right length below her knee which enhanced her youthful appeal to his pleasure. The soft, pink sweater covering her lacy white blouse, tastefully completed her ensemble. Fuller was even smitten by her little gold charm bracelet and the way the sleeves of her sweater were bunched at the elbow. A small gold cross hung from a delicate gold chain around her neck. It added to her angelic aura. *Why was she not popular with the guys?* Fuller pondered. She took to Milo and was now taking to him. He finally concluded she was not extroverted enough for the run of the mill peer group. He and Milo were a group within themselves and never associated heavily with the other students. The three of them must be cut from the same cloth, he concluded. The in-crowd's loss was his gain.

They reached the drug store soda fountain and went to the farthest booth from the crowd. They each ordered a soda and were clumsy in their attempts to get a fruitful conversation started. He finally grabbed both of her hands. With sweaty palms and mustering his courage to the maximum, he bravely looked her straight in the eye. "I think you are the most beautiful girl in the whole world," he stumbled through the words and was glad to get them out. Her eyelids drooped. Again he felt stupid for laying himself open for rejection. They were still holding hands when she lifted her pretty eyes square with his. They reflected a flickering gleam, most definitely announcing her approval of Fuller's compliment.

"That is the nicest thing anyone has ever said to me," she said, absorbing his compliment. "You are pretty neat yourself."

The afternoon ended with him walking her the rest of the way home. They shared pleasant goodbyes at her door step. "I'll see you at school tomorrow," he whispered.

"Until tomorrow," she said winding down their conversation. She was standing on the first step of her porch and bent down to kiss him on the cheek before retiring inside.

He glided euphorically through the streets to get home and change for his trip to the ballroom, vowing to never wash his cheek again. He was trying to decide whether or not to inform Milo of his kiss from Calley when he came across one of the boys from his class.

"Be on the lookout," Fuller was warned. "Snake's after your ass."

Fuller remembered a line from Cyrano de Bergerac. "Mere mortals—bring me giants." He was riding high with a fresh kiss on his cheek from Calley and nothing was coming between him and his excitement of the moment.

He called Calley after supper and they talked at length on the telephone. His call became a nightly ritual they both looked forward to.

CHAPTER 13

▼

Fuller had been to the ballroom often enough that he knew all the regulars by sight and all the musicians knew he was Milo's friend. From his usual table, he began to notice this well dressed middle-aged woman sitting at the end of the bar nearly every time he was there. Shortly some guy would go sit beside her and buy a round of drinks. After a brief encounter, they would leave together. Fuller watched her leave with different men three times during the evening. Milo pointed out to Fuller that she was the resident hooker. She also recognized the regulars, including Fuller. They began nodding greetings to each other the first time their eyes would meet each evening.

One night in the middle of the week, it was slower than usual, with only a few couples on the dance floor. There was nothing going on with the hooker either. She grabbed her hand bag and lazily made her way to Fuller's table. She picked one of three empty chairs. "Are you saving this for anyone?" she asked. Fuller displayed his hand, palm-side up, in a polite gesture suggesting she have a seat.

She explained, up front, assuming he knew about her, that she wasn't hustling him. The evening was stalled and she just wanted someone to talk to. Her candor put Fuller at ease.

"My name is Alma," she said, offering a hand.

"Fuller," he replied, shaking it.

"I see you here quite often. What business are you in?"

"I go to school," he answered. "I have a friend in the orchestra and come just to hear him play."

"Who is your friend?"

"Milo Munroe."

"Oh, he's good," she said.

Fuller grasped the dual meaning of her statement, applying both versions of how she meant it, to his imagination. She could mean he was good as a person or as a customer or both.

Their conversation was idle, but friendly. "He is good," Fuller said.

"I know all the fellows in the band," she said. "They invited me to Mister Davenport's birthday party last year. They treat me as one of the gang and are really a great bunch of fellows."

The small talk lasted until closing time. Fullers' assessment of Alma was that she was a nice lady despite her occupation.

"It was fun," Alma said upon getting up to leave. "Maybe we can do it again sometime."

"I look forward to it," Fuller reciprocated truthfully. He was sympathetic towards her for having to prostitute herself to make a living.

*   *   *   *

Once in the car, Milo said, "I see you've met Alma."

"Yeah, she came by my table just wanting to talk. Said it was a slow evening."

"Did she put the make on you?"

"She was bored and just wanted someone to talk to," he reaffirmed, then added capriciously—

"From the handwriting on the wall, she knows you too. She said you were good."

"Huh huh, don't believe everything you hear," Milo said. "She knows everyone in the band. They are all good."

"You've been with her then?" Fuller seemed surprised.

"Oh God no and neither has anyone else I know. She's a fixture in the hotel. You're completely safe around her." Fuller had been put at ease twice this evening concerning Alma. He relaxed while Milo drove him home wanting to know everything about his encounter with Calley OMalley. Fuller told him what there was to tell; the soda and the kiss on the cheek. He felt like he was in love, but how could he tell Milo he had fallen in love after walking a girl home one time? That would be stupid and he had done several stupid things that day. Besides, he had nothing to show that she had any feelings for him in return. He asked Milo to come by his house Saturday morning. He had a plan for reconstructing his grades.

*   *   *   *

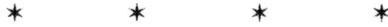

Saturday morning, Milo showed up at the Kreppe household ready for his miracle catch up by way of Fuller's ingenuity. After the niceties of meeting Fuller's parents for the first time, Milo was escorted by Fuller to the enclosed porch on the side of the house. His mother brought refreshments then left. "Okay, here's the deal," Fuller said. "In six weeks you will be the second smartest son-of-a-bitch in school, me being the smartest naturally."

"Naturally," Milo agreed.

"I write ten questions every day. Read one every chance you have during the day until you know it by heart, then go to the next one. By the end of the day you should know the ten questions. I'll quiz you with the answers during the band's intermission in the evening. What you don't get during intermission, we will tackle on the way home. If it requires a few extra minutes after we reach my house, so be it. We'll start again the next morning. On Saturday and Sunday, we will mix up the questions you've learned during the week and I'll quiz you until you've got them all down, week by week. Got it? Only ten a day. Sixty a week This is important. This process will catch you up in a reasonable time and you won't have to kiss Miss Hatcher's ass anymore."

Don't mess with Miss Hatcher's ass," Milo instructed Fuller facetiously.

Ignoring Milo, Fuller continued, "In six weeks you'll be three hundred and sixty questions smarter. That should catch you up and then some. How does that sound Gabriel?" Fuller asked, sounding like a smart ass.

It sounded reasonable and made good sense to Milo. He was excited. He looked around confirming Fuller's parents were out of ear shot, then said, "God-damn, you're one smart son-of-a-bitch. I'll be the only asshole in class that don't stink. When do we start?"

"Right now."

"Man, if we pull this off, I'm gonna personally buy you a piece of Alma's ass." They laughed and punched each others shoulder, then began to build their trophy of Milo's success by neutralizing the educational system. Fuller would infuse his brainchild into Milo's idle daytime moments, designed to catch him up, exponentially and faster than he was falling behind.

Monday morning after giving Milo his ten questions, Fuller met Snake head on in the hall. Snake grabbed him by the arm and shoved him against the wall. "You weren't listening when I told you to leave my woman alone," he said, sputtering droplets of his nasty breath in Fuller's face.

Recovering from Snake's respiratory defects, Fuller thought fast to disarm his antagonist and avoid a fistfight. "Snake," Fuller said earnestly, "Lupe's your woman and I respect that. You know I would never violate a trust between me and an amigo. We are amigos, amigo—remember?"

Snake was caught by surprise. He had never been treated as an equal before, by anyone, not even by his compadre, Rico. While Snake was figuring it out, Fuller breathed a sigh of relief. He knew he had completely confounded Snake and if he ever found out the truth, he wouldn't recognize it.

"Yeah, right," Snake said, trying on his equality. "If you find out who's been messin' with Lupe, you let me know and I'll break him in half."

"Right on, Amigo," Fuller said assuredly, breaking away in the direction of Miss Hatcher's homeroom.

CHAPTER 14

▼

Fuller waited for Calley outside his homeroom between classes. "Hello, Miss Good Looking," he expounded with confidence as she exited the classroom. He realized what he had been missing and gave thanks to all above for allowing him a special someone to express himself to.

"I bet you tell that to all the girls," she said affably.

"All the girls rolled into the one I'm looking at," he said, trying to be cool.

"You sold me," she said pleasantly, manifesting her share of the ongoing congeniality.

He took her books and she grabbed his hand as they started down the hall toward their next class. He was beside himself. His dream was coming true and he didn't have to do anything to make it happen, except carry her books. He remembered the old cliche' of *heaven being here on earth* and surrendered himself through earth's pearly gates to Calley's ineffable tenderness. His aspiration to walk hand in hand through the school halls with the girl he considered his soul mate was a powerful and wonderful feeling. He was excited he was actually having this experience.

Before entering the next class, he asked Calley, "Walk you home from school today?"

"If that's what you want, then I want it too," she answered.

Fuller was in hog heaven looking forward to being alone with Cally once again when school let out.

*   *   *   *

Between another class, Fuller saw Milo further down the hall and ran to catch up. "How you coming with your questions?" he asked.

"Hell, you won't believe it, but I've learned em' already."

"All of them?" Fuller showed surprise.

"All ten of them," Milo answered. "I can see where this is going. I believe your Martian antics are really going to pay off. I said you were one smart son-of-a-bitch and I meant it. This idea of yours is really great, Fuller, and would make you rich if you could bottle it."

"Hang in there, boyfriend—you'll surprise the entire faculty by how quick you catch up," Fuller shoved off in the opposite direction.

*   *   *   *

Fuller and Calley met in the hall after the final bell and left the school grounds together. They stopped at a park on the way to her house and sat at a picnic table to visit. They told each other about themselves and as expected, had plenty in common. She was making all A's like Fuller. He told her about his name and assured her she would be embarrassed if she continued hanging around with him. He also told her about Rico and Snake and how they rocked his boat with their brand of vulgarity every time they met in the hall. He mentioned about Milo playing in the hotel orchestra, swearing her to secrecy, and explained how he was helping his friend improve his grades.

She related Rico and Snake to two hungry wolves and urged him not to be intimidated by anything they said or did. She knew them as hoodlums as she grew up through the school system with both of them. She assured him that nothing they could say or do, where he was concerned, would embarrass her. They were talking frankly now with no fluff in the threads of their conversation. She related how sweet it was of him to help Milo with his school work and how much she enjoyed him walking her home.

It was becoming apparent that they had the ingredients for a meaningful relationship. Their beginning was based on an optimistic promise of friendship and respect for each other. They were bonding rapidly and both had an innate sense of well being when together.

It was getting dark when they reached her house. Her mother drove up with a load of groceries while they were standing outside and Calley introduced Fuller to her mother.

"So this is the Fuller I've heard so much of, lately?" her mother said, sweetly. "You're all she ever talks about. It's Fuller this and Fuller that. I'm finally glad to meet you."

"Oh Mom," Calley teased, feigning embarrassment, "you are giving my secrets away."

Fuller made a hit with Calley's mother by carrying her groceries into the house.

When they were alone again, Calley bent down from the steps as before, this time kissing him on the forehead.

He headed home satisfied he was on the fringe of something wonderful and discovered it didn't come in one package as he had envisioned. It was spread out in layers he would have to wheedle through, one layer at a time to fully understand the true meaning of friendship with a girl.

*   *   *   *

Calley's mother was sweet like her daughter. Her husband had left her for another woman when Calley was a little girl. Calley's grandfather owned a haberdashery where he employed his daughter until he died, leaving the business to her. She sold the business and has lived in a sound financial environment ever since without remarrying.

*   *   *   *

That night as Fuller entered the hotel, he was startled by a larger than life poster. It was in a glass frame, positioned on a brass easel at the hotel entrance. In the frame was a full-sized portrait of Milo playing his trumpet. The wording on the poster read in large letters, "Phil Davenport's Orchestra Featuring 'MILO STAR' and his Golden Trumpet." Fuller was excited and amazed. "Talk about big time." He bought a single rose from a lady vendor on the sidewalk. At the desk, he wrote a note, saying "From your partner and lover, congratulations," and without signing it, waited until intermission. He had a bellman deliver the note with the flower backstage to Milo. He followed the bellman as far as he could without being detected and peeked in to see if there were any reactions to his shenanigans from the band members. It soon became news and the entire band commenced teasing Milo about turning queer and went overboard with gibes relating to *Mister Star*. Phil Davenport gave Milo the name Star and he wore it proudly as it seemed to fit his personal esteem despite the ongoing harassment from his contemporaries.

Milo instinctively knew who was behind the charade. Combining the event of the note with the rose, he waited for the opportunity to have his own fun. When Fuller appeared on the scene, Milo said, "Don't everybody look at once, but here comes Nostradamus." That was a new one on the band members and when they found out it related to Fuller, they had a ball at his expense with the legendary name. It wasn't meant to offend, but to show that weird kind of fellowship usually prominent during moments like these. It was these times that Fuller felt closest to the gang. Milo knew he could get away with it and not offend his friend. Fuller congratulated Milo on his promotion with a hug and pat on the back and the ribbing for turning queer started over again.

When the intermission was over, Fuller went to his usual table. He looked up and caught Alma at the bar. She gave him a little smile and waved hello which he returned. It turned out to be a hectic evening. They were going to run late attaching answers to Milo's questions, but it had to be done and Fuller was dedicated to the cause. When the dance ended, Milo drove Fuller home. They sat in the car in front of Fuller's house while he drilled Milo over protest that he was tired and needed sleep. As Fuller had predicted, Milo ingested the answers he was behind on in ten to fifteen minutes.

Again Milo was amazed at his success in such a short time and was glad Fuller hadn't caved. He pushed Fuller out of the car with their brand of camaraderie, saying, "Get the hell out of my car, task master," followed with "and good night."

Fuller went in the house, hit the sack and drifted off to sleep wistfully thinking of Calley.

*   *   *   *

Time had pried the days off the calender one at a time until a month had passed. It went by quickly. Milo Munroe was up to speed with Fuller's tutoring and *Milo Star* headlined Phil Davenport's Orchestra nightly. Miss Hatcher was amazed at Milo's learned advancement on her advice to engage a tutor and Milo vowed to himself again that they would become lovers one day. Fuller and Calley went to the homecoming dance but left because they had more going than the dance could offer. Neither was a party animal and both enjoyed each other's company more than being with their so-called peers. Alma and Fuller were becoming best friends as she tethered herself to him, fostering motherly advice while Rico and Snake remained the same old assholes.

Fuller had fallen in love with Calley and told her so, as Milo continued to insist it was only puppy love. Calley returned Fuller's affections, but in typical female fashion, insisted she had to be sure before she could return his commitment to love. How could she be certain of her love for him if he didn't show his love for her? All he ever did was say "I love you." True, he once said that she was beautiful, but never has he indicated she was desirable or showed it in someway other than a short kiss on meeting and departure? Sure they smooched when alone, but according to her, they had known each other long enough to test the waters of temptation.

Walking Calley home from school, they stopped at the park and took to their favorite picnic table.

They sat close together and Fuller put his arm around her. "Calley," Fuller said, searching for a response that she loved him, declared, "I'm falling deeper in love with you."

"I like you too, Fuller," she returned, looking up at him and brushing the windblown hair away from his eyes.

The difference in their ritual was injurious to Fuller's self esteem. It was so obviously dissenting, it was like a loud bang from a nearby cannon. It would have added so much to the tenderness he felt for her had she responded with an "I love you, too."

"Calley, didn't you hear me?" he lunged for a more acceptable comeback. "I just said I'm falling deeper in love with you."

"I heard you," Calley said. She moved in closer, laying her head against his shoulder, hoping that would deflect his need for an immediate answer. "You are the swellest boy I know, Fuller."

Fuller's mood changed from that of confidence in love to disappointment and anxiety.

Calley picked up on his changing quality of spirit. "What makes you think you love me?" she asked sweetly, trying to warm up to him.

"I just do," Fuller came back. "You are everything I want in a girl."

"How can you be sure you love somebody if you've never—you know, done it with them?" "If you are in love, you know it and don't have to prove anything," Fuller said, somewhat annoyed. "If you have to prove you're in love, it didn't happen."

"Have you ever *done it* before?" she asked nuzzling closer and picking at the top button on his shirt.

Fuller was caught by surprise. *Uh Oh,* he thought. He hadn't expected this level of candor. "No," he answered truthfully, then added, "not actually," recalling how close he came that night with Lupe.

"Then you're a virgin?" she contended with assurance.

He felt awkward by her questions. "Yes," he replied sharply.

"I'm glad." She said, as she clung tighter to his arm. I can tell. "I am too. Don't you see, sweetheart, that makes us the perfect match for each other? We each have within us the gift of love. Wouldn't it be right to share our love with each other?"

"Calley—" Fuller began, but Calley wasn't through.

"We are fortunate, to have each other at this special time in our lives. We could give and take this wonderful token of our love, unselfishly and without guilt. That's what makes it so right."

"I guess," Fuller grumbled, uncomfortably.

"Have you ever wanted to do it?" she persisted.

He paused, then said modestly, "I suppose at one time or another. What about you?"

"It depends," she said softly, burying her head tighter against his shoulder. "I intended on waiting until I got married, but you became part of my life."

Fuller wasn't ready to engage in sexual activity of any kind until he had settled, or at least compromised the one thing that was holding him back, his ability to be an equal partner in a sexual union. He was at a loss as how to respond, so he remained silent. He pressed his hand against the side of her face and swept her windblown hair behind her ear.

She leaned her head back and blew a soft stream of warm breath on his ear. He quivered. "I believe it's up to us, Sweetheart," she whispered, "to claim our right to know if we are right for each other. We owe each other that much. Besides, how can we be sure of our true feelings, if we don't do it. I would feel special, darling" she continued, "if you told me you needed me." Her breath smoked from the chill in the air.

"Yea, I guess so," he said, wishing the direction she was dragging him would take a turn toward more modesty and less aggression. He failed miserably with Lupe and needed a morale boost to even discuss the subject intelligently.

She reached up and stroked his face and said, gingerly, "Sweetheart—I'm willing if you are."

If *doing it* was expected of him, why was his value system so far behind the mores of his peer group? Why wasn't he jumping at the opportunity? He was delighted to hear her say she was a virgin and admit her willingness to go all the way with him, but he wanted to wait until he was ready.

"Where could we go?" he asked, thinking he had found a temporary safety zone because there was no place except the back seat of his father's car.

"There's this old filling station with a run down store room in the back—"

Her answer to his question got Fuller's immediate and complete attention. "How do you know about that?" he snapped, surprised and suspicious at the same time.

"Everybody knows about it," she said. "That's where everyone goes to do it."

"Calley, I'd die if I thought you've been there with another boy. Tell me it's not so."

"Oh, Sweetheart," she rose up to kiss him on the cheek. "I could never lie to you. A boy wanted to take me there once and I wouldn't go. I just told you I was a virgin. Don't you believe me? You'll know I'm telling the truth when we *do it.*"

"I'm feeling sick," Fuller feigned. "I think I'd better go home."

"Is it something I said?" Calley asked, with concern.

"No baby," he said. "I'm just not feeling well at the moment."

Fuller finished walking Calley home. They were silent and reflective. When they reached her mother's house, he kissed her goodnight, then went straight home and to bed.

✳   ✳   ✳   ✳

Calley's mother had accepted Fuller as Calley's "nice young man." Fuller and Calley's minds took independent forks in the road regarding their feelings for one another. Her tine led her down a curious path as to why he wasn't more physical when they were alone. His led him to abstaining from making passes superfluous to a platonic relationship because of his abiding respect for her for one thing and his imaginary sexual dysfunction for another. She made it clear she didn't want to be his trophy on a pedestal, she just wanted him and their feelings for one another mutually dispersed between them. Neither knew how the other interpreted their budding romance as it slipped into a lingering habit. How was he going to handle his dysfunction with Calley when the time came for him to put up or shut up? He wanted her to say she loved him, which she artfully side-stepped. Life was returning to normal, all screwed up.

CHAPTER 15

▼

Alma had come to visit with Fuller at his table. They discussed current events and were easing into personal matters. He would tell her how wonderful Calley was and she would revisit her youth by commenting on young love, how sweet and beautiful it used to be.

"Nothing has changed," Fuller reminded her, "your experience has just given you a different perspective. Don't sell yourself short, Alma."

"You're right. I'm living in the past," she said, reflecting back in time. Her brow began to furrow. She began discussing how she became a prostitute and Fuller let her ramble out of respect. She was abandoned as a mother with a young daughter to raise and no skills to generate income. A friend of hers who had given no indication that she worked the night trade, took pity on her and tendered an introduction into the world's oldest profession. Her toleration of the job eroded into remorse as she tried to explain her downfall to Fuller.

"What's a mother to do when she has a daughter to raise and has no way to pay the bills?" Her reflection was touching Fuller as she poured her soul out to him.

"What about your daughter?" Fuller asked. "Does she know what you do?"

She blotted her nose with a handkerchief, sobbing a sorrowful, "Yes."

"How does she handle it?" he asked.

"She knows I've made many sacrifices for her. She loves her mother," she said, still sniffling.

"How would you feel if she followed in your footsteps?" he pumped, suddenly realizing he was psychoanalyzing her without the know-how or her permission.

At least it was free. They couldn't pin him for practicing psychology without a license.

"We talk," she answered. "She knows it's a damnable life and I discourage it, but I can tell you this, if it comes down to outright survival—"

"I know," Fuller said, signifying his understanding and letting her know she didn't have to continue.

"It's an honest living no matter what other people think," she continued. "I don't rob, cheat or steal," she sniffled. "All of my bills are paid on time and I live in a nice house—and drive a nice automobile. You ought to see the married ladies turn their heads when they see me coming, like they're so much better than I am. One lady told me to get a job or get married. It's easy for her to say, she doesn't have to hustle to put food on the table." He mouth arched downward at the corners as she held back tears. "I'm talking too much," she said to Fuller upon regaining her composure. "I'm sorry, honey. I didn't mean to burden you with my problems."

Fuller didn't like to see her this way. If nothing else, she had gained his complete respect. One hand rested on the other as she sat there trying not to feel sorry for herself. Fuller reached over and gently placed his hand over hers and squeezed lightly. He didn't smile but his frown signaled his approval. Nothing was said, but she got the message that he fully understood and supported her.

She felt pangs of guilt for dumping her life's decline on a young school boy. She apologized again to Fuller, begging his forgiveness.

"There is nothing to forgive," Fuller said. "It could happen to anybody."

It was almost intermission time and she knew he would have to go backstage and help Milo with his quiz.

"I will never forget your kindness. Thanks for listening, dear," she said as she straightened up and returned to her end of the bar.

✳   ✳   ✳   ✳

Milo's scholarly attributes were improving daily by applying Fuller's streamlined learning method. He continued to be amazed by the improvement of his intellectual capacity. The answer sessions during intermissions were becoming so routine that it was more fun than work. Members of the band became a hindrance to their efforts by insisting on helping by making the questions and answers a guessing game. Two more weeks and they would wind up the original target date of six weeks. Milo contended he could take it from there and keep up with the best of them.

On the way home, Milo prodded Fuller for what was going on between him and Alma. He readily told Milo the whole story and both agreed it was sad, but that she was one of the "good ol' gals."

*   *   *   *

Thanksgiving was on the horizon. Fuller's Mom invited Milo for Thanksgiving dinner and extended the invitation to his sister and brother-in-law whom she had never met, but knew inviting them would please Fuller.

"She's a good cook," Fuller boasted to Milo. "You'd better take her up on it."

Milo accepted on the condition he could buy the turkey. Fuller's mom was in agreement and suggested Fuller invite Calley and her mother. She had never met them either. Fuller was elated by the anticipation of all of his friends being together on this special holiday and took the necessary initiative to finalize the invitations.

CHAPTER 16

▼

It was Saturday afternoon and the snow was falling in large flakes, melting when they hit the sidewalk. Miss Hatcher was downtown having her hair fixed. When the stylist was through with the finishing touches, she stepped out of the salon onto the sidewalk and inhaled a deep breath of the chilled, fresh air, thankful it did not contain the acrid smell of the beauty parlor chemicals. It was breezy and clean as the wind brushed lightly across her face.

Walking to her car, she passed the Anthony Wayne Hotel and did a double take upon seeing the orchestra poster featuring Milo Star. *His name wasn't Star,* she thought, unraveling the duality of name differences. *It was Munroe.* She was in awe of her handsome pupil being featured in the Phil Davenport Orchestra. For the first time, she was able to put some perspective to his mature manners, movie star looks and finery he wore to school each day. Then it dawned on her how a young man with so much going for him could fall so far behind scholastically. One thing left to unravel; how was he catching up so quickly?

She knew instinctively that Milo had his eye on her, but so far hadn't put it into language form or asked for her tutorage. She wasn't pure of thought either—eyeballing him discreetly when she felt safe to do so. She couldn't quench his success and striking appearance from her mind as she drove through the busy Chicago streets going back to her apartment.

The first thing she did, when she walked threw her front door, was to wrap a protective scarf over her freshly arranged coiffure, then sat in a comfortable chair and began taking inventory of her social life. She imagined herself with Milo as a couple. Just as quick, she un-imagined it. Her thoughts were infringing on dangerous boundaries and she damn well knew it.

Surely there was nothing wrong if she decided to have dinner at the hotel with a girlfriend and listen to the music, she thought. *She didn't have to be aware he was part of the show. If he noticed her, so what? She could just feign surprise at seeing him.*

She had a previous engagement with the P.E. coach, Charles Cagle or C.C. as he was known. They were to have dinner out and spend a quiet evening together. She threw caution to the wind and was compelled to pick up the telephone and dial his number. When he answered, she said, "C.C., I want to back out of our date this evening."

"Why, for Christ's sake?"

"I've been running around town all afternoon and lost a heel," was her excuse. "I wore myself out getting back to my car. I know you will forgive me."

"Hell, I suppose," he answered, disappointedly. "What are you going to do?"

"I have this splitting headache and I'm worn out. I just want to go to bed and sleep it off," she lied. "I feel like, if I can just lie down, I'll be all right in the morning."

"Well—okay, dawlin," he said. "I'll either be here or at the tavern if you need me." That was C.C., totally devoid of enthusiasm which in turn robbed his personality. His lifestyle was midway between red neck and trailer trash. He was a complete mismatch for Miss Hatcher. There wasn't any wonder, she digressed from C.C. when she collided head-on with Milo's refinement?

"That's sweet of you, C.C.," she said. "I'll talk to you tomorrow."

Her next call was to a girlfriend, whom she invited to accompany her for dinner at the Anthony Wayne Ballroom that evening. Her friend accepted if she could bring her date and offered to see if he knew someone for her. She respectfully declined her girlfriend's offer, but was satisfied the situation would be even better with a man at their table. Miss Hatcher called for reservations and the evening was set. She was anxious to hear Milo Star perform.

This being Saturday night, Fuller was on a drug store date with Calley. Milo was backstage warming up with the orchestra. After Miss Hatcher and her friends arrived, she quickly surveyed the ballroom and told the Maitre d', "I want that table over there." She pointed to one at the rear in a dimly lit section. It was perpendicular to the center of the band stand. They could have dinner, watch the band and probably not be noticed by Milo.

At eight sharp the music started with the orchestra's theme song. A circular stage revolved slowly, stopping when the band was square with the dance floor. Phil Davenport faced the orchestra waving his baton and directly behind him, facing the guest stood Milo Star at a microphone engrossing the crowd with the beautiful, crystal clear music emanating from his trumpet. Delores noted he also cut a fine figure in his wardrobe,.

His new position as front man, required him to wear a deep red blazer with a Gold Bullion Crest over the lefthand breast pocket. The rest of the band wore navy blazers. Phil Davenport sported a double breasted, white linen jacket. The band reeked with professionalism and could stand toe to toe in looks and performance with any of the popular big bands of the day; thanks partly to Milo.

Their first number was *You Made Me Love You*. When it came to Milo's solo, he executed it so beautifully that Miss Hatcher instinctively imagined it was being played exclusively to her. It would have been his pleasure had he known she was in the audience. The sounds were beautiful as she absorbed the sincerity of the music and perceived the passion of the musician expressing himself. Her friend and her date danced throughout the evening. She danced once with her friend's gentlemen assuming she wouldn't be noticed through the spotlight focused on Milo. From Milo' position, the spotlights underexposed the crowd on the dance floor to insignificant shadows. During the last intermission, Miss Hatcher and her company slipped out quietly.

*   *   *   *

Monday, after the final bell, the class filed out of Miss Hatcher's room. Calley's mother was picking her up her for a dental appointment and Fuller was going to ride with Milo. Miss Hatcher pointed a pencil at Milo as he was passing her desk. "Could you stay for a moment, please?" Fuller followed the other students out of the room and waited for Milo in the hall. Miss Hatcher invited Milo to "have a seat" as she pointed to the chair next to her desk.

"Tell me Mister Star, What is going on?" she asked sternly.

She knows about Milo Star, he thought, wondering how she found out. Well, what the hell. If the jig was up, he had nothing to lose but a high school diploma which he didn't need anyway. He reminded himself his only reason for staying in school was for his mother's sake. If he was forced out because of his career, he might as well go out in style. He locked his eyes in the focus of hers. She was temporarily fixated as a deer frozen in time by automobile headlights. "I think you are beautiful," he said, taking an audacious liberty that could get him expelled.

Miss Hatcher was semi-frightened by his stare, but flattered by his statement, wishing she could respond in kind. She maintained her better judgement and remained in charge of the situation. "It is inappropriate for you to talk to me like that, Mister Munroe," she warned. "It is not your place to be familiar with members of the faculty and it is not allowed."

"I'm sorry," Milo conceded. "I was just stating the facts as I saw them."

"Keep those kind of thoughts to yourself," she reprimanded. "This is a high school, not a social club."

"All I can say is I'm sorry, Miss Hatcher. I'll watch what I say from now on." *I still think you are beautiful, you sweet thing*, Milo thought to himself.

"I must say I was impressed with your playing," Miss Hatcher said, letting it be known she had been to the ballroom, "but that's not why I asked you to stay. You see your grades were scraping the bottom of the barrel when you turned them around, and quickly, I might add. As I see it, you were either cheating on your exams or you took my advice and contracted some expert help. Which is it, Mister Star, or is it Munroe?"

"Well, I have to give credit where credit is due," he said, grabbing an opportunity to put a feather in his friend's cap while evading her direct question. "Fuller Kreppe worked out a study plan and helped me implement it."

"Let's talk seriously for a moment," she said. "That may be true, but it is not plausible. I want the truth."

"That's the God's honest truth, Miss Hatcher," he said with a smile and a raspy giggle in defiance of her disbelief. "Fuller has a way about him. He can work through anything. He's the smartest person I know."

"I see," she said, as though she did not believe him for the second time. "I'm serious. If what you say is true, I may need his help. Can you help arrange it?"

I can arrange a place for an afternoon quickie, he thought *but he knew the chances were slim to none.* Before he could answer, she added, "I have some students that are in serious trouble and are not going to graduate if they don't get the help they need, and soon. Do you think Fuller would volunteer a little of his time to help them in their studies?"

"He's waiting in the hall. Shall I call him in and let you get it first hand?"

"Please do," she answered officially.

Why was everything in our conversation so damn formal? he thought, getting up from his chair. He walked over to the door and stuck his head out. There was no one in the hall but Fuller.

"Hey, Nostradamus," Milo hollered.

"What's up, handsome?" Fuller retaliated, knowing handsome was parallel to Milo's use of Nostradomus.

"In here, she wants to see you," he said, motioning with a slight bend of his neck in her direction.

Fuller came into the room and nodded a greeting to Miss Hatcher.

"Please," she said motioning for him to have a seat in the chair next to Milo. "The school needs your help and I would like to know if we can count on you for support?"

"Why yes, Miss Hatcher, I'll help in any way I can. What's the deal?"

"Mister Munroe tells me that it was you that helped him improve his grades."

"Yes, I helped him."

"The faculty is in agreement that you are the brightest student in our school. I think you are aware of that."

"I've heard rumors," he said.

"Well, the truth is—we have a couple of students who are not going to make it to the finish if they don't get the help they need. That is where you come in. Still, interested?"

"I suppose," Fuller answered. He was caught off guard and not fully aware that it was in his power to say no.

"Fine. We will get together after school tomorrow, and Fuller—thank you. Oh, by the way, Milo, would you be interested in playing in the school band?"

"I'm sorry, Miss Hatcher but that's a luxury I'm going to have to forego," he said. "Please don't tell anyone I play the trumpet."

She started shuffling papers on her desk top letting him know time for conversation was over. "No one has to know," she said without looking up.

"We'll see you tomorrow, Miss Hatcher," Fuller said upon leaving with Milo.

"Good evening, boys."

"Did you hear that?" Fuller asked after they left the room. "She called us boys. If she only knew."

"Knew what?" Milo asked.

"That you have the hots for her body."

"Hah! I guarantee she knows it," Milo said. "She also knows about my job."

"I wonder how she found out?" Fuller questioned. "I didn't tell her."

"She heard me play Saturday night at the ballroom, but said not to worry, no one has to know."

"That means, if you come to Momma, she won't tell."

"Huh huh, don't be too sure. She jumped my case for getting familiar."

"What do you mean?"

"I told her she was beautiful."

"Not really?"

"Yep, right to her face."

"Get out!"

Milo drove his car to Fuller's residence. "Will I see you at the hotel?" he asked. "Try and keep me away," Fuller said as they parted company.

*   *   *   *

It was another slow evening. Fuller was running late. The band was playing to a half full ballroom. He sat at his usual table upon arrival and nodded a "good evening" to Alma. She put out her cigarette, reached for her hand bag and did a slow walk to his table. She bent down and kissed him on the cheek followed with a "Hi, Sweetie."

"You doing better this evening?" Fuller asked.

"Thanks to you," she said, gratefully.

"I didn't do anything, but listen," he said, simply.

"Now don't you go getting modest on me," she said. "I wouldn't be over here if I didn't love you for being you." She pulled out a chair and sat down. "How are you and Calley getting along these days?"

"Okay, but we're starting to drift a little and it's not a good feeling."

"You really love her, don't you?" Alma asked, showing concern.

"Yes I do."

"Does she love you back?"

"I think so, but she won't come out and say it. Her feeling is, how can you know you love somebody if you haven't—you know."

"I know," said Alma. "What's holding you back?"

"I don't know." Fuller answered. "She hints all the time for me to get more touchy-feely. I really don't know," he said. "I'm afraid if we cross that line, our feelings for each other will change."

"And if you don't?"

"I'm afraid of that too," he countered. "You see, Alma. There's something I haven't told you about me."

"How can I ever trust you again?" she kidded.

"It's not funny—I'm serious. I have something wrong with me," Fuller said, "like some kind of dysfunction. It's not the kind of thing you discuss with your girlfriend."

"Then why are you trusting me? Aren't I your girl friend?"

"Because you are a special friend and I know I *can* trust you."

"Poor baby," she said. "Go ahead and get it off your chest."

"It's kinda personal, Alma," he said. "Maybe I need to work it out for myself."

"You know I'm here for you if you need me."

"I know, and I thank you for that."

Alma studied the situation for a moment, then said, "The only dysfunction I know is a sexual dysfunction. What the hell kind of problem can you possibly have with your girlfriend you can't discuss with me? You can look 'till doomsday, honey, and never find a better sex therapist than old Alma here. Now let's have it," she added.

"Perhaps you're right, but I don't quite know how to lay it out. It's kinda personal."

"Try me," she said. "Just start talking and see if I can follow you. Remember this is my area of expertise."

"Okay," he sighed reluctantly. "I have this thing that won't let me do it, if you know what I mean."

"What are you saying, honey? You can't get a hard on?" She questioned, forthrightly.

She was too blunt. Fuller twitched with embarrassment, but continued modestly. "No, that's not it," he said.

"You cum too quickly then?" She asked, digging for the root of his problem.

"Not that either," he said, this time more embarrassed.

"The only thing that's left is orgasm. You can't cum?"

This time her candor was shocking. It stung him like a hive of bees. "Something like that" he said, reluctant to confirm her venture into his privacy.

"That ain't gonna' get it, honey. We're talking frank here. Now let it all out."

He thought it over for a moment and said, "it's what you said."

"You can't ejaculate? Is that it?" She asked again, digging deeper.

"Alma, do we have to talk about this?"

"We do now," she asserted. "Old Alma here is going to solve your problem, one way or another. Now tell me the truth."

"I have to go a long time before it happens," he was reluctant to answer, then added—"if it happens at all. Does that make sense?"

"Maybe. How long?"

"Twenty, maybe thirty minutes."

"Goddamn!" She exclaimed. "Believe me, that's not a problem. It's a blessing. How many people know about this?"

"You and a doctor, maybe Milo. The doctor called it infantile something or other—I can't remember exactly, but he did say I had a special gift and not to worry about it. I don't think he understood what I was trying to tell him," Fuller complained.

"What if you and Calley got it on, would she understand?"

"Hell, I don't know," he answered, showing signs he was not certain of anything anymore.

She noticed him becoming more annoyed. She wanted to help him over his torment, but had already told him he was blessed. What else could she say. Just then an idea popped into her head. A trick she uses in her business on busy nights seemed to be the perfect solution to Fuller's malady. She uses it when she needs to hurry the guys along with the excuse it makes it better.

"Okay Sugar. Now you listen to me. Doctor Alma here is gonna solve your problem. Here's what you do. Go to the drug store and buy a small bottle of peppermint oil. When you're ready to get down and dirty, put a drop behind the head of your—" remembering his difficulty describing details, mimicked his tactic. "You know," she said. "I guarantee it will make you—you know, a lot faster."

He was astounded by her intensive consultation pertaining to his sex life in general and his genitalia in particular; a whore telling him how to treat a problem that even the doctors couldn't remedy. *Why not,* he thought. *Who would know more about screwing than a hooker with Alma's experience?*

"How does that help?" he asked.

"Honey, don't question the experts," she cautioned. "Just do the bidding. If you must know, it's a little warm, maybe even a little hot and stimulates your dooty. That'll make you stiffer than a fence post and the rest will follow. Believe me."

"Alma, I've got to hand it to you," he said. "You are one remarkable person and I'm glad we had this conversation. I'm going out right now and buy a bottle of peppermint oil". He was gullible and scatterbrained with anticipation and excitement. He had been discussing a private, personal matter with a member of the opposite sex as though they were stirring a cup of coffee together. Her advice was off the cuff and supposed to set him free. He was overjoyed and anxious to try it out. No one else had come up with anything positive before. At least it was tangible and not just *lip service* from a disinterested party. If she was peddling snake oil, it was worth a try.

"Good luck, sweetie. Let me know how you do," Alma said, realizing she had been away from her post too long. She angled her way back to her end of the bar and took up her position.

The place was getting ready to close when Fuller returned with his little bottle of Peppermint oil. It was stored safely in his pocket. He was jubilant at the prospects of reclaiming his life with Alma's prescription. On the way home, Milo commented how Fuller and Alma were in a pow-wow much of the evening. "What was that all about?" he inquired.

"Awe, nothing really. Alma's my buddy. I know she's just a hooker, but she's a real friend and a real nice lady to boot," Fuller commented.

The day was finally over when he stepped out of Milo's car. He darted into the house and into his room and plopped on the bed with his clothes on. Before falling asleep, he pondered if the peppermint oil was really going to help. He thought about trying it on himself. If it cut his stroking time at least in half, he would be hysterical with anticipation of what lies ahead. He acknowledged to himself that he would be resorting to trickery if he relied on his peppermint oil as crutches, but for now it was a good idea. The gift the doctor said he had, or the blessing Alma had endorsed him with, would only ring true when he was capable of performing on a stand alone basis without the aid of temporary fixes. Until then he would have to be satisfied with any application that proved trustworthy. His father had always cautioned him never take lessens in life off the streets, but here he was taking the word of a common prostitute. *Shit,* he thought, *I trust Alma because she makes sense and has seen this stuff in action.* Before he could rationalize any further, he was fast asleep.

CHAPTER 17

▼

Fuller was walking in the hall holding Calley's hand. When they approached the classroom, he squeezed her hand and she squeezed his back before letting go and entering.

Milo was especially handsome in his new red blazer. Miss Hatcher's roving eye kept snapping back to him when it was comfortable for her to do so without being conspicuous. She couldn't get the sight of him fronting Phil Davenport's orchestra from her mind.

The day was moving slow and seemed to last forever before coming to an end. Fuller had mentioned to Calley that Miss Hatcher wanted him to stay for a little while after school and asked if she would "wait for him in the hall. I shouldn't be long." He informed her it had something to do with him coaching some students that were lagging behind in their studies.

"Take your time," she allowed. "I'll read my English Lit book."

When the final bell rang, the classroom emptied and Fuller found himself alone in the room with Miss Hatcher, Rico and Snake. *So this is it*, he thought. *There is absolutely no way I'm going to spend my Calley time with these smuts.*

"Gentlemen," Miss Hatcher began by addressing Rico and Snake. "I asked you to stay today to see if there is anything we can do to keep you from falling through the cracks. Your grades are atrocious. You do want to graduate, don't you?"

"Yes Ma'am," they said in unison.

"Mister Kreppe has offered his services to help you bring your grades up. There is still time before graduation. What do you say?"

Both Rico and Snake had been *shit asses* to Fuller since the first day of their senior year. They weren't acclimated to accept his benevolence. They hem and hawed and engaged in their own brand of double speak without actually answering Miss Hatcher's question.

Fuller interrupted, "Miss Hatcher, I don't think this is a good idea. Neither one of these guys can stand my guts and I have to say the feeling is mutual."

She called Fuller aside, out of ears reach. "I see what is going on here," she told him. "Did you ever stop to think what makes them the way they are?"

Out of politeness, Fuller listened.

"Look at these two young men," she said appealing to Fuller's intellect. "People have turned their backs on them all their lives. Would you want to be the one to deny them a high school diploma if you knew it was in your power to offer the help they needed to get through school?"

"I don't care what happens to them," Fuller said, trying not to offend.

"Take another look," she persisted. "Would you want them on the street as a menace to society? At least do what you can to save them, to give them a chance to walk out of here prepared to deal with that jungle out there. It takes a minimum of a high school diploma just to get a decent job. How about it, Fuller? Don't do what you want to do in this case. You have an opportunity and an obligation to do the right thing. Take advantage of it."

Fuller's thoughts were of Calley. He wanted to do everything he could think of to keep their relationship in equilibrium. He and Calley would both have to sacrifice their time together if he decided to tutor these two ruffians. He was a reasonable person, but wouldn't accept the challenge without Calley's approval. "Can I let you know tomorrow?" he asked.

"If that is what you want," Miss Hatcher allowed.

They went back and joined Rico and Snake. Miss Hatcher told them Mr. Kreppe wanted to go home and think about it. "He will let us know tomorrow."

*   *   *   *

Calley was sitting on the stairs, reading her book and waiting faithfully for Fuller when he exited Miss Hatcher's room. He took her books as usual. When Rico and Snake were out of sight, he bent over and gave her a quick kiss on the lips. "I love you," he whispered. She snuggled tightly against him, affectionately, but wouldn't return the sentiment he was longing to hear; *I love you too*. It looked like he was going to have to take the plunge and *do it* if he was going to get her to say what he longed to hear. After all, he was prepared now. He touched his pocket to confirm his little bottle of peppermint oil was with him.

They departed the building. It was cold. He filled her in on the conference status and said the outcome of his decision, depended on how she felt about him becoming Rico and Snake's tutor. If he took the job of helping them, it would mean he and Calley wouldn't see as much of each other for a while. He was digging for her sympathy and true feelings, hoping she would admit that she was going to miss him and confess that she did, in fact, love him. He waited for her approval or comments.

"Oh, Fuller," she said disappointedly. "What are you going to do?"

"It depends on you," he said, relying on her answer. "I said I would let them know tomorrow."

"I don't know if they are worth it," she said pouting.

He responded to the guilt trip Miss Hatcher put on him by inferring it was his responsibility to carry this heavy load. He explained it to Calley in a way he hoped she would understand. They would only have to forfeit a little time in the scope of eternity, but if these two jerks flunked high school because of his omission to do everything he could to help them, it would be a red mark against him in heaven he wouldn't want on his conscience. On balance, tutoring Rico and Snake for the short haul would give them a boost that would last a lifetime and like Miss Hatcher said, "would be the responsible thing for him to do." *Besides*, he thought, extending his presumption, *their time of separation from each other might tend to draw them closer together.*

She reluctantly accepted his explanation and agreed that helping Rico and Snake was the right thing to do. She further admired him because of his sacrifice. It unveiled a conscionable side of his character that allowed him to go this distance for two guys that didn't seem to have any conscience where he was concerned. They stopped at the park on the way to her house. It was almost dark. They sat at their favorite picnic table. He put his arm around her as she laid her head against his chest. They sat there, contemplative of the forthcoming time they would spend apart. He looked down at her and she, up at him, and they gave each other an extended kiss as if to say I'm going to miss you and that everything was going to be all right. This time she whispered, "I love you, Fuller." That cleared up his doubts about her feelings for him and confirmed that working with Rico and Snake was definitely the responsible thing for him to do. He walked her the rest of the way home, their arms around each other.

On his way home, after leaving Calley, he suffered a sinking spell. The thought crossed his mind that she might get used to his absence and lose interest in him all together. The mere thought jolted him back to reality. Only moments before, she announced her love for him in an audible that he pinned emotionally to his heart. He still tasted her lips and felt the warmth of her breath, like souvenirs of their last meeting. He would reserve the memory for when he was lonely for her.

His hands were in his pockets and one was clutching his little bottle of peppermint oil as he trudged against the wind, going home to get ready for his frequent trip to the ballroom.

CHAPTER 18

▼

There was no parking near the hotel and Fuller had to park several blocks away. *He figured there was a party going on*, remembering it was the beginning of the holiday season.

He was bent forward with his hands in his coat pocket and bucking a head wind when he bumped squarely into a young lady nearly knocking her over. "Jeeze, I'm sorry," he apologized. "I wasn't watching where I was going." He straightened up, face to face with a smiling vision of loveliness; probably twenty years old.

"Are you all right?" she asked.

"I'm fine," he answered, getting a whiff of her alluring perfume. "How about you?"

"It'll take more than a bump from a handsome man like you to do me in," she answered, dusting herself off. "Are you by yourself?"

"As a matter of fact, I am," he replied, innocently. "I'm headed to the Anthony Wayne Hotel."

"Isn't that a coincidence? So am I," she said. Actually, she was going in the opposite direction. "Would you like some company?" she asked through her beautiful smile, "I'm affordable."

It was then that Fuller realized he was being hustled by a prostitute. *So this is how it happens,* he thought. His knee-jerk reaction was to decline indignantly, but his hand was still in his pocket wrapped around his little bottle of peppermint oil. On second thought, he was reminded what it was there for. Instead of thinking of her as just another pretty girl, since she has acknowledged she was a hooker, he looked upon their chance meeting as an opportunity to go nameless, and put

Alma's potion to the test. If it worked, he would legitimately claim his right of passage into manhood and could deal with Calley, one on one.

"How affordable?" he asked.

"Twenty bucks for twenty minutes. If you pay up front, I'll knock off five."

He studied the situation for a moment. How could he accept her proposition and still remain true to Calley? Acute pangs of guilt began to stack on his conscience. Could he not do this and remain true to himself? Many options and guilt formats flashed through his mind. He had something to prove and here was his first real opportunity to prove it. *It must be part of the great universal scheme of things,* he thought. Their chance encounter must be a sign from heaven. He saw no way in which their meeting was an accident. It had to be intended as an earthly source to set him free or he wouldn't have bumped into this *lay for pay* lady. *He rationalized that losing one's virginity to a whore was a meaningless ritual, otherwise he couldn't accept her offer in good conscience.* As long as he classified the decision he was about to make as sexless, sex, his outreach to justify the unjustifiable would be valid. It was now or never. At this moment in time, it made sense to have this experience. This wasn't the time to dwell; the hooker was expecting an answer.

"What do we have to do to get started?" he asked.

"Let me see the color of your money. That's all it takes."

He counted out fifteen dollars and handed it to her.

She led him to the Belmont Hotel around the corner. It was a two-story flop house. "Wait here five minutes," was her instruction to Fuller, "then come up to room 207 and tap lightly on the door. I'll be expecting you"

Fuller looked at his wrist watch and fixed the time in his mind. He wondered if he was foolish for giving his money up front. If she was on the up and up, why did she ask him to wait five minutes? If he had been scammed, he was soon to find out. He hadn't thought about this angle and was irritated for not using better sense. Had she indeed ripped him off, he would chalk his loss up to interacting with sorry people. It reminded him of his mother's often used figure of speech; if you lie down with dogs, you'll get up with fleas. When his five minutes were up, he walked casually into the lobby and looked around. The Belmont Hotel was a cheesy place with winos napping on a worn sofa and sagging chairs. The clerk had a two-day growth of beard and a sunken chest, reminiscent of a tuberculosis survivor. He was slouching on a bar stool, reading the racing forum and chewing on a short cigar stump. His feet were crossed and perched on the edge of the counter. Fuller abhorred the stale smokey environment. It made him feel furtive and unclean. When he was satisfied no one was paying attention to his appearance on the scene, he hurried up the stairs. His knees were knocking, partly from anticipation and partly from fear of the unknown. When he reached room 207, he rapped lightly on the door as instructed.

The door opened part way and his lady for a quickie stuck her head out and peeked both ways down the hall. When she was satisfied all was clear, she motioned him into the room.

"Why are you monitoring the hall," he asked, apprehensively?

"I share this room with other girls and we don't pay for it," she informed him.

"Oh," he allowed, wondering what sharing the room with other girls had to do with monitoring the hall. He stood there as she shut the door behind him and pulled the linkage closing the transom. He watched her moves curiously so he wouldn't miss anything. Walking over to the bed, his lady of the evening removed her sweater and blouse down to her bra and threw them on a chair. It crossed his mind, this was for real and he hadn't been scammed.

"There's the sink," she said, pointing to a lavatory against the wall. It was encrusted with a dirty rust ring midway up the bowl and otherwise caked with dried crud from age and usage. "Wash yourself," she instructed. "The towels are underneath."

He faced the sink, discreetly retrieving the peppermint oil from his pocket, being careful not to arouse suspicion. He washed and dried himself as instructed, then deposited one drop of the magic potion to the critical area as Alma had prescribed. He managed to hold back an "ouch." The oil shot a hot streak up his stick that brought tears to his eyes, then the heat gravitated downward to a moderate sting he could not only tolerate, but added strength to his erection as Alma had said it would. He turned around in time to catch her tossing her panties. Her bra hadn't been removed. Walking over to him, she said, "Take your clothes off and sit on the bed." He didn't know the routine and did what she asked for fear of screwing up. He was trying to absorb the vision of her nakedness as he was undressing. When he was totally nude, he sat on the bed as she had directed. He was apprehensive of being stripped naked and defenseless if the police decided to raid the joint. There were any number of things that could close in and catch him, literally with his pants down or in this case, off. For the second time, he worried about the fallout from his parents for being marched to their front door, handcuffed and naked, tethered to a policeman or more humiliating, a police woman. The first time was back at the old filling station.

"Now lay down," she ordered.

This was his last chance to back out if he didn't think he was up to what lay ahead. A wave of courage infiltrated his alter ego. He had come too far to back out now. His intellect didn't have the tools to face down the other side of his personality that was going to brand him a wimp if he didn't climb on board and prove once and for all he was a man. He leaned back on his elbows, thinking he was following her guidance.

"Flat on your back," she asserted, intimidating him.

He fell flat on his back as instructed, wondering how the first move was going to be initiated and by whom.

She grabbed hold of his mushroom and began installing a condom. "That's a nice one," she said, complimenting his manhood as she rolled the sheath down the length of his column. She figured if she massaged him as she unrolled the prophylactic, he wouldn't last long enough to get his monies worth and she would have fifteen dollars she didn't have to earn. "I smell some kind of mint," she said, wrinkling her nose.

"It's a breath mint," he improvised, deflecting her attention from his secret weapon, the peppermint oil.

She accepted his excuse, then reached for a tube of lubricating jelly and smeared a squish, between her legs. "Scoot over," she directed him. She eased in bed beside him and motioned for him to crawl on top.

He rolled over, half there, then hesitatingly asked if she would mind removing her bra, thinking that was part of the program.

"No, honey," she was adamant, "I don't want breast cancer."

He was disappointed, but he had heard of breast cancer before and her refusal made sense to him. He finished sliding on top and she guided him into her socket. He was conflicted between his success now and his failure with Lupe. The only difference he could figure was the hooker put it in for him. He always heard that nice girls put it in for you and he questioned if her initiative qualified her as a nice girl as opposed to the slut profile that shadows prostitutes. If her help was the key to success in bed, then he needed to remember it. He could have made it with Lupe if he had only known to let her take charge. He lay there in his current position enjoying the magic of the moment trying to burn every last detail into his memory.

His play for pay partner started bumping up to get him started. "Honey," she advised, "you've only got a few minutes left."

He looked at his watch and started timing himself. When he had mentally absorbed enough of the moment, he started a slow *Choo Choo* motion. He was provoked by the excitement of the moment and reached for a kiss on her lips to which she turned her head. "Mmm-mmm, she hummed," disallowing his uncontrollable passion for a kiss. Like the bra incident, he respected her right to protect herself from lip cancer if that was her reason for rejecting his bid for a kiss.

Just then someone put a key in the lock and tried to unlock the door. His heart stopped momentarily, then pounded rapidly deflating the intensity of his urge.

"Shhh," putting her finger across his lips "It's okay," she whispered. "Its one of the girls. She knows the room is occupied if the night latch is on."

"Oh!" He breathed a sigh of relief. He was having to reconstitute his punctured libido as he re-gathered his steam to continue where they left off. His remaining time was slipping away. She kept checking her watch and decided to apply an old hooker stratagem to finish him off artificially. She ran her fingernails lightly up and down each side of his spine. This action backfired. He shuddered and started to buck mercilessly out of control with long, forceful strokes.

He was so richly endowed that she involuntarily gorged on his animal like domination with each fiber of her being. She engendered a hunger for him that triggered an untamed response in kind.

She started bucking in concert with his intensifying motions, making sounds of exhilaration with each stroke. "Unh—Unh—Unh—Go faster," she said. "Can you go faster? Oh, yes."

He was already pushing top speed.

"Deeper," she cried, "please go deeper." She was huffing, puffing, and gasping for breath.

"Faster and deeper," she maoned, twisting and bumping up and down in cadence with his moves. "God—GOD—Ohhh yes—OOHH—Myyy—GHOOOD!!" she shuddered, grabbing his face with her palms and pulling it down, mashing their lips together. Using her tongue, she pried his lips open and navigated it between his teeth, forcing it deep down his throat. She was in orbit with an orgasm and forgot to notice his mouth was absent the flavor of the purported breath mint.

Having never experienced anything of this magnitude with a real girl, he wasn't sure what was happening, but he kept up the pace until he looked back at his watch. He was also huffing and puffing, out of breath, and out of time. "My time is up," he informed her as he came to a stop.

"Who's counting?" she insisted, still bumping. "Don't stop now, you idiot."

He was more than willing to continue, having the feeling he was on to something big.

She reached under his chest and ripped her bra open for her own selfish fulfillment, not necessarily giving in to his wishes to see her breast. They undulated back and forth as far as they could go, then bounced back to their original position with each of his mighty strokes. "Suck my titty," she demanded, grabbing the back of his head, pushing it down. "Suck it NOW! Oh yes, YES—Oh—OOHHhhhh., JESUS, I'm cuming again," she cried, nearing exhaustion. Upon reaching her sixth orgasm, she was totally spent. Her arms collapsed against the bed. She lay there, wasted and out of breath. Her legs remained parted, leaving him access to the kingdom as he continue his ride to glory with an audible slushing sound emanating from their crotches.

He was getting tired and perspiration was splashing, chest to chest, with each bang against her galloping breast. He glanced at his watch again, naive that time no longer mattered, and wondered if he had enough money with him to cover the overtime charge. If she would let him go a just a little longer, he was certain he could make it happen. Maybe the peppermint oil was starting to kick in. Whatever was taking place was grand. She just lay there exhausted, as he continued.

He had just witnessed a complementing display of ecstacy by a real woman, brought about by his energies. The doctor and Alma certainly knew what they were talking about with reference to his gift and his blessing. The thought of Calley crossed his mind. He imagined the whore to be the love of his life and thinking of her brought him to the line. "It's about to happen," he yelped.

She wrapped her arms tightly around his chest and gigged him in the buttocks with both heels forcing his deepest thrust. It was over and he went limp. He looked again at his wrist watch. He had lasted a full seventeen minutes, but the crux was, he brought his romp to fruition. They fell asleep with him on top for another fifteen minutes. She woke up first trying to push him off her, saying, "Wake up honey, it's time to go."

After getting dressed, he asked how much he owed her for the extra time. She was digging in her purse as he spoke. She returned his original fifteen dollars and stuffed an extra ten dollars in his shirt pocket. "This is for you, honey," she said. "Will I see you again?"

He took the money and smiled his approval of her approval and left without further commitment. He didn't notice the couple at the end of the hall as he left. They were waiting for the room and were entertained by the racket coming from within. When Lupe saw it was Fuller, she couldn't believe her eyes, remembering the blank he shot at her that night at the old filling station.

It was intermission time when Fuller reached the hotel. The band was milling around backstage getting ready to take their positions. When Milo spotted Fuller, he rushed over to him. "Goddamn, fellow, where have you been?"

Fuller leaned over and whispered in his ear. "I just got laid," he said, grinning from ear to ear.

"Calley?" Milo quizzed.

"No! I'll tell you about it on the way home."

*   *   *   *

The band filed back onto the revolving platform and began to play. The room was crowded and Fuller's usual table was taken. He looked around and caught Alma returning with a trick. She talked a few minutes with her customer, then he left. Fuller couldn't wait to tell Alma of his experience. She saw he had no place to sit and motioned for him to join her at the bar. The bartender shook his head. Fuller was underage. She motioned again, this time for him to meet her in the lobby. They occupied an out-of-the-way leather sofa.

"Okay, Doll, let it out." She could tell he was bursting a gut to tell her something.

"I just got laid," he grinned, waiting for her response.

"Calley?"

"No, a hooker," he answered with excitement.

"A hooker?, I'm offended," she said. "You could have come to me if you wanted a hooker?" She was joking, of course. She knew how to put the embarrassment on him and he was so embarrassed, his system locked up. He had to wait until he thawed before continuing. "She hooked me off the street," he said, finally, after catching his breath.

"Who is she?" Alma asked.

"I don't know her name."

"You fucked a stranger and don't know her name?"

He turned red with embarrassment. *Maybe it was a bad idea confiding in Alma.* Realizing she had come onto him too strong, she set about to tone down her rhetoric.

"I'm sorry, Love," she apologized reaching for his hand. I couldn't resist it.

"You know I love you," she said. "How much did she charge?"

"That's what I'm trying to tell you. It didn't cost me anything," he said.

"How can I stay in business if she's giving it away?"

"It's not like that," he said backtracking. "She charges twenty bucks, but if you pay up front, she'll let you have it for fifteen."

"Oh really." Alma said. "I know you're special, but if she charged you fifteen dollars, how did you get it for nothing?" Then the truth hit her. Knowing Fuller's story, she surmised that he probably screwed that poor girl's brains out. *I would pay for a trip like that,* she thought.

"I poured the coals to her for a solid seventeen minutes," he said, and she gave me my fifteen dollars back plus a ten-dollar tip.

Alma burst out laughing. "I'm safe for a while," she said, referring to the poor girl's likely inoculation from too much of Fuller. "She won't be giving any more away for at least a month. Besides, I'm in the wrong business, I need to be renting you out."

Fuller's uneasiness was neutralizing by now, but she continued to test him until his embarrassment had worn off completely, then he was flattered by her barbs.

"Wait a minute," she said. "Didn't you use your peppermint oil?"

"I sure did," he said, "you ought to package and sell it."

"Nobody needs it but you," she reminded him. "Well at least you know your limits."

He remembered through the awkwardness of the moment that it was her help that contributed to his incentive to go the distance as he had that evening. He turned a little bit more in her direction and looking straight in her eyes, solemnly said, "I'm free, Alma. I know I'm all right now and I owe it all to you—and maybe that doctor."

"What about the little lady you just humped?"

"Well, her too," Fuller admitted.

"Honey," Alma said, "without question you have to be the best lover in the world. If I were younger and know what I know about you, these baby chicks wouldn't stand a chance. I know how to treat a man."

"I bet you do," Fuller said. "You're a special friend Alma. I hope someday I can do something for you."

*　　　*　　　*　　　*

Fuller filled Milo in on his escapade with the hooker on his trip home from the ballroom. In between strips of his story, he was trying to help Milo with his quiz as Milo navigated his car. When they reached Fuller's house, he asked Milo if they could skip the rest of the quiz this evening. He had some mental challenges he needed to work through. Fuller had absentmindedly left his dad's car downtown and Milo had to take him back to get it.

Milo could tell Fuller was weighing heavy with guilt from betraying Calley. He agreed to give his friend the break he asked for. "By the way," he said. "I want you and Calley to come to the Thanksgiving dinner dance at the ballroom next Friday. I'm going to ask Hatcher."

"Hatcher? You think she'll go?"

"How can she turn me down?" Milo questioned his friend, being cute. "We love each other," he said.

"I know," Fuller said, being facetious. "She told me she loved you too, but that's bull shit. She would never sink so low," he added.

They both chuckled.

"What time Friday night?"

"I'll have to let you know."

Fuller drove his dad's car home. He unlocked the front door, re-locked it from inside and retired to his room. He was having trouble with his conscience. He was more than imbued with delight by his performance at the Belmont Hotel, but was having intermittent bouts of shame and regret when he was finally alone by himself. How could he ever forgive himself for having his first sexual encounter with someone other than Calley, and a whore at that. Making matters worse, now that he was home and didn't have the stress of temptation making decisions for him, he had to face the fact that he had actually cheated on the girl he was in love with. She had offered, by modest innuendo, to surrender her virginity to him. *Why couldn't he have waited?* He knew why. For the same reason he had the peppermint oil. After much agony and beating up on himself, he arrived at the only conclusion available to bargain with his self reproach. One of the things holding him back from being intimate with Calley had been dealt with and that's that. He had conquered the uncertainty of his sexual competence, but admitted to himself that it would have been better all the way around had he shared the experience with Calley. At the very least his conscience would be clear. His new concern was what to do next. Should he be up front and come clean with Calley? That would make him feel a lot better, but look what it would do to her. It would break her heart and the bond holding them together, plus she would never trust him again. He knew Milo would advise against it. He decided on embracing the less stressful ideal and take Milo's unspoken advice. He tried to erase his tryst with the prostitute from his mind, but he couldn't completely let go and it contaminated his ability to live normally and trust his better judgement.

*   *   *   *

The next morning, he was confronted in the hall by Rico and Snake. "Hey man," Rico greeted, speaking for both of them. "You know we your fran, right?"

"Yea, I know," Fuller returned, thinking it was all *bull shit*. He had weights hanging on him that were heavier than being patronized by these two.

"We wont you to help us, you know, like Miss Hatcher ast you to do. We whan to graduate with the rest of the class. Know whad I'm sayin'? We no treat you or your fran bad no more. You know why? Becuz we your amigo's, dat's why?"

"We'll see," Fuller said. "You can tell Miss Hatcher when we meet after school." Rico was still talking as Fuller broke away and hurried down the hall.

He no sooner got rid of them when he ran into Lupe coming down the same hall.

"Hello Fuller," she said with a gregarious smile. "I want to tell you that I'm no longer mad at you. I just wanted you to know. I hope there's no hard feelings."

You got that right, Sister, he thought to himself. *There's definitely no **hard** feelings.* "None at all," he said, expressionless and excusing himself. Why had she sided up to him? Whatever her reason, that too was *bull shit*.

Upon entering homeroom, his eyes immediately fixated on Calley. They smiled at each other and he sat at his desk. The sight of her sucked the wind out of his sails, making him feel cheap and remorseful for losing control of his better judgement the previous night. He was angry with himself. To help compensate, he decided to ask Milo to let her ride to school with them in the mornings. It would give him a little more time with Calley and perhaps help ease his conscience.

Homeroom was breaking up when Fuller asked Milo if Calley could ride to school with them in the mornings. He reminded Fuller he didn't have to ask, saying "he knew she was welcome anytime." Fuller caught up with Calley and escorted her to her next class.

Miss Hatcher had a free period and was sorting papers to grade. Milo waited for everyone to leave her room. When she looked up, he was standing in front of her desk.

"Aren't you going to be late for class?" she asked, sternly?

"I won't keep you," he said. He then leaned over slightly, bracing himself with his hands on her desk and said, "Delores," addressing her by her first name for the first time. She was astonished, but hesitant to admonish his audacity. "I want to invite you to a Thanksgiving dinner dance at the hotel ballroom. There will be a continuous buffet and afterward we are going to a recording studio to cut a record. Say you will go."

So—he found a way to break the ice, she thought. Maintaining her professional dignity, she asked, "When is it?"

"Friday evening," he answered.

"When do I have to let you know?"

At least she was showing interest, Milo reasoned, but he couldn't stand the suspense of waiting and decided to take a chance. "Now," he said.

She had reservations about giving an immediate answer on the one hand, but on the other, having been to the ballroom, she knew what she would be missing if he withdrew the invitation and took someone else. She couldn't stand the thought of his asking one of her *split-tail* pupils. "Then I'll go," she said, matter-of-factly without looking up. She fumbled with papers on her desk, suggesting to him, she didn't have time for idle conversation.

"Fine," Milo said, wanting to lean across her desk and kiss her lips. The way she accepted his invitation didn't mean anything. What really mattered was, his success was parallel to his imagination. "Give me your address and Fuller will pick you up at seven thirty sharp."

She reached in her purse, pulled out a card and handed it to him.

"Thank you. I'd better hurry or I'll be late to my next class," he said, humoring her.

She settled back in her chair and wondered why she accepted Milo's invitation without making him work a little harder. She knew why. She was smitten by the guy like all the females in her class. She was flattered that he asked her instead of one of the teenie boppers always hitting on him. Besides, it was her chance to get to know him for whom he really was instead of through fantasy or perhaps the professionalism of her faculty status insulating them from being closer friends. That's what she really wanted, but was conflicted and confused. Her final decision to accept his invitation was inspired by the beat of her heart as opposed to rejecting his offer heeding professional protocol.

*   *   *   *

After school, Fuller met with Miss Hatcher, Rico and Snake.

They sat there staring at one another. Miss Hatcher took the initiative. "Well, gentlemen," she started, "I'm glad all of you could make it. I believe this meeting rests with Mister Kreppe's decision to help you in your studies. What do you say Mister Kreppe? Would you like to share your decision with us?"

"Well—I guess so," he said stringing the words out, still unsure but willing to abide by his answer, "but if I determine that either of you are wasting my time, it's over. Is that understood?"

"You heard the man," Miss Hatcher said. "Do you want to continue on these terms?"

Snake and Rico looked at each other and Snake nodded his okay. Then Rico led off as spokesman for both of them.

"Yes Ma'am," he answered. "We gonna es-study es-so hard you whant recunize us. We don't whant to disappoint either whan o' you. We bean a leetle—you know, unfair to Fooler and whan to make it up to him."

Fuller thought for the third time the same day, *bull shit*.

She dismissed Rico and Snake, then asked Fuller to keep her informed on their progress.

Calley was waiting faithfully outside Miss Hatcher's room for Fuller. When he finally appeared, the usual routine was a quick kiss on the lips and a transfer of her books from her hands to his. They started the long walk to her mother's house.

"Guess where we're going Friday evening?" he asked, prompting her for a reply.

"I give up, Where?"

"Don't you want to guess?"

"Oh, silly, I'm no good at guessing. Where are we going?"

"We are going to the Thanksgiving dance at the Anthony Wayne Hotel Ballroom—dinner and everything."

That was something to look forward to; a real dinner date where she could dress up and feel special. She was excited.

"Oh, and one more thing, Milo and I want you to start riding to school with us in the mornings." He knew she would be as pleased to accept as he was to make the offer.

Her answer was affirmative as expected. "I'd love to," She leaned her head over to his shoulder as a momentary show of affection and squeezed his hand. "Thanks ever so much for asking, sweetheart."

*   *   *   *

That evening during intermission, Milo had a chance to talk to Fuller. "Guess what?" he enticed Fuller. "Hatcher's coming to the Thanksgiving dance and you're going to pick her up."

"Great," Fuller said. "What are you holding against her to make her go?"

"Not as much as I would like to, that's for damn sure."

"You should be so lucky," Fuller said.

"You ain't heard nothing' yet," Milo said. "Dinner is going to be a continuous buffet and when the dance is over we're going to a recording studio to cut a record."

"Gerrr-rate," Fuller said, excited that he was going on a real date with Calley and witness a live recording session all in one night.

Milo warned Fuller to advise Calley's mother not to worry if her daughter wasn't returned home until early morning.

*   *   *   *

Fuller had started his consultations with Rico and Snake. Delores Hatcher was remaining aloof from Milo in the classroom so as not to arouse unnecessary suspicion regarding the two of them fraternizing. She was also concerned that he might feel confident enough to leverage his familiarity with her in front of the other students by calling her Delores.

Lupe had stepped up her interest in being better friends with Fuller and he continued to be insensitive to her sudden transformation from a venomous bitch to a remorseful victim.

CHAPTER 19

▼

Fuller canceled his Friday afternoon session with Rico and Snake and gave them assignments. He and Calley rode to the hotel with Milo, who turned his car over to Fuller with instructions not to be late. He had to drop Calley off, go home and change, return to get Calley, then off to pick up Miss Hatcher; all this before seven-thirty.

Fuller let Calley off at her house to get ready, then proceeded home to do the same.

He did a quick change and doubled back to pick up his date. Calley was ready when he rang her door bell. He said "hello" to her mother upon entering. Calley was dressed up as never before in his presence. She was beautiful and dazzled before his eyes in a black taffeta cocktail dress with high heels. She wore her mothers mink stole and held a silver sequin hand bag.

"You have a beautiful daughter," he said to her mother.

"And she has a handsome boyfriend," her mother reciprocated. "The two of you make such an attractive couple."

"Oh, by the way," Fuller explained the time table for the evening to Calley's mother and offered to bring her home early if she didn't approve.

"Please Mom," Calley begged. "Please?"

Calley's mother was uncomfortable with the idea of her daughter returning home in the wee hours of the morning, but Fuller's willingness to bring her home early if she didn't approve, gave her the necessary confidence to put her trust in him. She bid them farewell with instructions to "have a nice time," as they walked down the outside steps, arm in arm, to Milo's car. Her mother stood in her doorway and watched as Fuller opened and closed the car door for her daughter. She was happy he was the gentlemanly type she hoped he would be, and waited for them to drive away. Her daughter was growing up and she had a discomforting qualm of emptiness.

Calley helped Fuller with directions to Miss Hatcher's apartment using a city map. Miss Hatcher was ready when Fuller rang the doorbell. Fuller took her arm and walked her to Milo's car telling her how nice she looked. He asked where she preferred to sit, in the front with he and his date or in the back where she might be more comfortable. Her choice was up the front with him and his date, not knowing at the time his date was Calley.

"Why Calley," she showed surprised. "I am so happy to see you."

"I'm happy to see you too, Miss Hatcher," Calley said.

"Please, for this evening, it's Delores," Miss Hatcher said. "You two make such a lovely couple."

A "thanks" from Fuller to Miss Hatcher and a "thank you" from Calley. The two ladies conversed as Fuller chauffeured them to the hotel parking garage where Milo instructed him to park. Walking between the ladies, he escorted them through the lobby to the ballroom.

The band was scheduled to start at eight o'clock. They were fifteen minutes early. Milo had been pacing the dance floor on the lookout for his guest. When he saw Fuller with Calley and Delores, he made a dash in their direction, sidestepping his path to grab Phil Davenport by the arm. "Someone I want you to meet," he said to Phil.

He took each of Delores's hands in his and smiling at her as a committee of one, said in a low voice, "thanks for coming," and moving his gaze to Fuller and Calley, he shook Fuller's hand saying, "and thanks to both of you for picking Delores up."

He reached for Phil and dragged him closer. "This is my boss," he said to Delores and Calley, "Phil Davenport." Then, progressively completing the introduction process, said, "Delores, Calley and you know Fuller."

When the pleasantries were over, Milo led them to the special table near the bandstand he had reserved for this occasion. Displaying his gentlemanly manners, he held the chair for Delores and Fuller did the same for Calley. Another round of "thank yous." Fuller was collecting the ladies' coats when Milo's sister and brother-in-law appeared from the main hotel lobby. Milo braided himself through another round of introductions. This is my sister Elaine and her husband, Doctor Raymond Powell. No one at the table had met them before.

Elaine said to Fuller, "It feels like I know you already. Seems like you're all Milo talks about." Fuller added her coat to the two coat stack already collected and took them to the cloak room.

Milo excused himself to go backstage and get ready for the opening theme song.

The band members let him know throughout the evening their comments regarding his date. Most thought he did quite well, but others jested about Delores in various forms. Some accused her of robbing him from the cradle, while others insisted he canvassed the nursing homes for his dates. Delores could tell through her feminine intuitions she was under curious scrutiny by the orchestra members.

The waiters were serving champagne to Milo's guest. Fuller and Calley accepted a glass and made a toast to each other. "To the loveliest girl in the world," he whispered, leaning his face close to hers.

"And to her handsome boyfriend," she whispered back to him.

Neither had experimented with alcohol before and grimaced while forcing a taste of the bubbly.

Backstage, Milo wrote little notes on a batch of little pieces of scrap paper, "Dedicated to you," and signed them with a hand drawn star. The musicians took their places. The music started and the revolving stage rotated toward the dance floor. Phil Davenport faced the orchestra with his baton, back to back with Milo fronting the band. Milo stood erect before the audience and played into the microphone with artistic fervor and explosive phrasing. The brilliance of his playing transcended the beauty of layman appreciation. His immaculate appearance upgraded the aesthetics of the glitter and polish reflected to the crowd by the klieg lights. The theme song ended on the up stroke of Davenport's baton. The audience applauded with contagious enthusiasm as the band readied for their first number.

Milo called a waiter over from his position at the edge of the stage and handed him one of the little notes he had written to Delores and pointed her out to the messenger. Milo had helped Davenport lay out the evening's program by making certain that each piece of music had an amorous nuance to its title. She read the note, and nodded a smile of approval to Milo just as the downstroke of Davenport's baton started their orchestral arrangement of *Whispering*. Delores hummed with the music. Milo carried the band with expressive emotion, crystal clear sound and natural grace.

Delores swelled with pride that it was her student anchoring a twelve-man orchestra and conducting himself with such poignancy at his age. There was no doubt about it, she was infatuated with Milo. Her infatuation began the first day he was escorted to her classroom. She was weak kneed by the threat of her emotions tricking her into an inappropriate blunder and promised herself to be on her best behavior.

Calley asked Fuller to dance. He accepted, saying he didn't know how.

"Follow me and we'll learn together," she said, leading him to the dance floor. Raymond and Elaine followed close behind.

Finishing his chorus, Milo stood his trumpet on an upright stand for that purpose and jumped off the stage heading toward Delores. The vocalist, Jan Mulvahill, took the microphone and began to sing. Taking Delores' hand, Milo led her to the dance floor.

"Thanks again for coming," he said softly.

"I'm enjoying myself. I wouldn't have missed being here for the world."

He drew her close, feeling the contour of her body next to his as they danced the slow dance. He was captivated by the fragrance of her perfume and the clean texture of her hair as it caressed the side of his face.

The last phrase of the song lyrics were, "Whis-per-ing that I—love—you." Both felt the magnetism of the endearing and lingering strain, but neither said anything. He walked her back to the table and pulled the chair out for her and thanked her for the dance. "I'll see you later," he said, as he returned to the bandstand.

Summoning the waiter again, he handed him another one of his notes to take to Delores. This time she produced an audible giggle and once again nodded her approval, smiling pensively.

Davenport's baton launched the next arrangement, Cole Porter's *'You do something to me'*.

Delores's affections for Milo contested the inner conflict tugging at her heart strings. Sooner or later she and Milo were going to have to have a talk, probably an understanding. Their preoccupation with each other was kindling into hot coals and needed downgrading to a level of responsibility. *Perhaps at another time,* Delores rethought. There were too many wonderful memories building to deal with the *right or wrong* of the moment. This was the beginning of a memorable evening and she wanted to remember the princess treatment, lavished by Milo, knowing the daily grind started over the next morning.

The buffet opened and a double file line formed, branching from each side of the food table. Fuller was behind Calley in line when he was surprised by Alma stopping by to say hello. She was on her way to the end of the line. Fuller introduced Calley to Alma, and Alma commented to Fuller how pretty his date was.

"Thank you," he said, more business like than cordial, meaning *not now, Alma.*

She took the hint and issued a "How nice it was to meet you" to Calley as she continued her trek to the end of the line.

"Who was that?" asked Calley.

"She works at the hotel," Fuller replied.

"What does she do?"

He grappled with that one for a second or two, before feigning, "She's in customer service."

"Oh," replied Calley.

Delores spoke out, saying, "She looks familiar, but I can't place her."

Phil Davenport took the microphone. "We have a real treat for you this evening. Milo Star and five members of the band are going to entertain you with a few of their favorite dixieland numbers. Ladies and gentlemen, may I present, Milo Star and his 'Original New Orleans Street Band'. Take it away, Milo, with *Bill Bailey, Won't You Please Come Home.*"

A vigorous applause filled the interior of the ballroom. The musicians had already gathered around their leader by the end of Davenport's introduction and Milo and Company kicked off *Bill Bailey* to a flying start. In jazz parlance, the joint was jumping.

Milo took the microphone to announce the next tune. "I'd like to dedicate this next number, to my brother-in-law, Doctor Raymond Powell, The *Saint James Infirmary.* It's also one of our favorites. One, two—" they were off. Brother-in-law Raymond crossed his arms and leaned back in his chair to enjoy the lagging sound of his favorite slow blues.

Calley and Delores loved the dixieland numbers. Both were overwhelmed by Milo's talent and impressed by his position in the band. After the jazz numbers, the dance orchestra reassembled and played for the rest of the evening. Milo continued to send the waiter to Delores with one of his now famous dedication notes before the beginning of each dance number. As often as he could break away after his solo, he would jump from the stage to close the number with Delores on the dance floor.

The final number of the evening was *Good Night Sweetheart.* When the lights came on, everyone connected with the band and their guests were assembling to go to the recording studio. Raymond and Elaine followed Milo's car. Milo was in the front seat with Delores at opposite ends. He patted the seat adjacent to him for her to move in closer. She eased over without hesitation. Milo started to place his arm around her shoulder, but there was something good happening to him and he didn't want to screw it up by taking the chance on making advances. Same with Delores, but she kept waffling between following her heart or conforming to faculty ethics.

Arriving at the recording studio, Milo let Fuller and Calley off at the entrance, then drove to a darker and lesser used area of the parking lot. After parking, he turned off the headlights and ignition and turned to face Delores. His musical craftsmanship and importance in his arena of expertise had enchanted her beyond the limits she had placed on herself. Easing his face in her direction, he maneuvered in for his first kiss. She was helpless. Tilting her head back so that his lips could find their target, she wrapped her arms around his neck and pulled him in close. Their lips touched for the first time. It was like fireworks on the fourth of July. They looked at each other warmly and both felt a discernible romanticism linking them together. They each savored the moment inducing a spiritual tie for one to feel the other's presence when apart. Coming back to reality, he extracted the keys from the ignition and exited his side of the car. He walked around to her side and helped her alight onto the pavement. Retrieving his trumpet case from the trunk, he took her hand and squeezed it as they began the extra long stroll to the studio. She squeezed his hand as a last minute recall of his affection before letting go to enter the building.

It was a little after midnight and Calley called her mother to check in. She was excited, telling her mother everything she remembered about the evening up until now. Her mother asked few questions as she heard the band warming up in the studio. Although it wasn't required of Calley to call her mother, they were both better off because of her thoughtfulness. Before hanging up, she told her mom, "I'll be home when you see me."

"Have fun darling," her mother said.

"I love you, Mom," Calley declared to her mother as she hung the telephone on its receiver.

Milo had helped assemble the numbers for the recording session as he had for the dance that evening. He made sure all of Davenport's songs were characterized by romantic titles. The front side of the album was "Phil Davenport's Orchestra Headlining Milo Star" and the other side was "Milo Star's Original New Orleans Street Band and his All Star Cronies." Davenports' side featured the following songs: *More Than You Know, Whispering, You Do Something To Me, I Love You So Much It Hurts Me, You'll Never Know* and *Hold Me.* Davenport had no idea Milo had such a powerful motive in selecting the arrangements. Phil titled his side of the album, "Sentimental Memories."

Milo's side featured: *Saint James Infirmary, That's A Plenty, Do You Know What It Means To Miss New Orleans, Jazz Me Blues, Struttin' With Some Barbeque* and *Someday You'll Be Sorry.*

The recording session lasted 'til five o'clock in the morning. Milo kept directing his solos on Davenport's side in Delores' direction. There was magic in the air they breathed.

When it was over, Milo's crowd stopped by the all-night diner for an after midnight snack. Their talk and laughter were artificially inspired because everyone's energy level was spent. Members of the party felt the need to cut it short and get the hell out of there and go home. Calley was the first to be dropped off. Fuller walked her to the door and gave her a goodnight peck on the lips. He wanted more, but she reminded him of the teacher in the car with Milo. Fuller was next to be dropped off.

Milo drove to Delores' apartment. He shut down the lights and cut off the engine. They sat out front and talked. Milo was willing to go in if she was to invite him, but that never happened. He no longer wanted to jump her bones for the sake of jumping her bones. His lust had levitated to a higher plane. She presented him with a beautiful, mature woman, deserving of more than he originally had planned for her. He actually found himself fostering wholesome respect for a lady. Things were going so good, he was afraid to push his luck. They discussed the contrast in their positions at school and both agreed her career came first and would be threatened if it ever got out she saw him on a social level. Their conversation softened the formality between them. He took her chin between his thumb and forefinger and turned her face square with his. They stared at each other in awe of how far they've come in just a few hours. He pulled her closer to him, both wrapping their arms around each other and locking in an unyielding embrace. He pressed his lips firmly against hers as she returned his kiss with the same energy he was imparting to her. They held each other in a persistent kiss until it became awkward, then let go. Settling into a tight snuggle, she lay her head against his shoulder. He was mesmerized by the scent of her perfume and the softness of her hair and allowed himself to lavish in the warmth of her presence. The sun was beginning to rise at the low end of the east horizon when she reminded him of the time. He could have stayed by her side forever, but knew it was time to let go. They exited the car and he walked her to her apartment. She turned to face him. "I had a lovely time," she said, "and you were magnificent," referring to his musicianship.

"Thanks," he said, closing in for one last kiss. He needed one more. This one was the jewel of the evening. It was light and short, but one he could take with him. With it, he could remember the taste of her lips. She offered to invite him in if it were not so late.

"I know," he said. "I've kept you up long enough."

She pushed herself up on her toes and kissed him on the cheek. "I had a lovely time," she said again. This time he noticed the gentleness of her beauty and the sparkle of her eyes reflected by the distant lights.

She turned to enter her apartment and he backed away to leave, both wishing the other a reluctant good night.

CHAPTER 20

▼

Fuller called Calley Saturday afternoon and divulged his endearing feelings for her and complimented her loveliness the previous night. They reminisced about the fun time they had. She was hesitant to ask, but wanted to be excused from seeing him later that day because she was *so* tired from last nights activities. The day after that being Sunday, was her day to wash her hair and get ready for school the following day. Fuller agreed to give her a rest and see her Monday morning.

Milo rejected Fuller's study routine for Saturday due to lack of interest and a wearisome body. Fuller made it known he was also fizzled and needed the rest. They went their separate ways to find relief and recovery from Friday night's abuse.

*   *   *   *

Milo wanted to call Delores, but was mindful of becoming a bore, or pushy, and wind up driving her away. His resolution to himself was to give it a rest Saturday and call her on Sunday to avoid seeming overanxious.

Delores, on the other hand, stayed home Saturday waiting for the call from Milo that never came. How could she possibly have known that a young man with the self confidence of a female lion protecting her young, would chicken out from calling her because she would think he was moving on her too fast? On the other hand, she was disconcerted for relenting to his advances, and, as his teacher, putting her reputation on the line.

She deserved at least a "next day" telephone call from him. She was slipping into a state of melancholia for letting herself get involved with one of her pupils.

Her resentment over his failure to call was starting to work on her self esteem. She was beginning to need that call to bolster her self-confidence and allow her some peace of mind. Each minute waiting for the telephone to ring seemed to drag into hours. If he did not intend to follow through, why did he trample on her affections? She became more upset when the thought crossed her mind that he would use her as his bragging rights. If he wasn't sincere, then why the Cinderella's treatment the previous evening.

She wanted to think Milo had entered her life for a reason. In one evening, he had brought excitement to her otherwise monotonous, humdrum existence as a school teacher. She was putting all her eggs in his basket. It would be worth it, if their ties grew stronger. Her past experiences with men, especially Charles Cagle, the P.E. Coach, didn't fulfill her need to feel desirable and wanted. He didn't bring anything stimulating to their relationship other than sports and numerous trips to the beer joints, which for her was a total bore. He also lacked Milo's class and refinement every girl longed for.

She was sinking deeper when she realized Milo had picked her over all his choices at school or otherwise to escort to the dance. That made her feel somewhat better, but not enough to equal the intensity of emotions she had splurged on him. She went to bed that night satisfied all young men were flippant and immature dinosaurs in their relationships with women. She was determined from now on her feminine wiles would protect her from being taken advantage of.

*   *   *   *

Missing each other Saturday was like two ships passing in the night. Sunday was a new day. Milo wanted to call Delores around mid-morning, but was afraid he would wake her. He had no way of knowing she was awake, wondering if she should call him. She closed the book on conjecture and stiffened her resolve. It was up to him to make the first move.

In mid-afternoon, he picked up the telephone and began dialing her number, then pushed down on the receiver to cancel the call. He had no idea what he was going to say.

In the meantime, she stayed close by the telephone wishing he would call. He didn't call Saturday and it didn't look like he was going to call Sunday either. She concluded his interest in her was based solely on his bent for conquest as with most young men of the day. If that were his motive, he could forget about her and get his kicks from the female teenie weenies his own age.

About four o'clock, her telephone rang. It startled her and she lurched for the handset, then backing off thinking it was about time, she allowed herself space to be natural. She let it ring three times and answered on the fourth. It was her girl-friend wanting them to meet at the cafeteria for their evening meal. Although disappointed the call wasn't from Milo, it was Sunday and she wasn't in the mood to cook. She agreed to meet her friend at the cafeteria. She put a scarf over her head, slipped into her coat and grabbed her purse. *At least her day wouldn't be a total waste,* she thought.

Milo looked at his watch. It was a few minutes after four. He resolved that the timing was right to make the call that his rationalizing had delayed until now. He picked up the telephone and dialed her number. There was no answer. The narrow margin by which they missed each other was again like two ships passing in the night.

He began doubting her interest in him. Was she purposely avoiding him? Was she on a date with some obnoxious jerk that couldn't offer the refreshing stimuli she could find in his *sphere of good times?* Everything he ever wanted found its way to him in one way or another, but for the first time in his life he was being deprived of the one thing he really went after, Delores Hatcher. He was experiencing something new for him, self doubt. His feelings for her were suddenly surging out of control. Then the truth came crashing down on him. What did he have to offer besides his *sphere of good times?* He knew there was a meaningful side of life other than fast women and dazzle and was looking for her to help him open that door. He slumped in a chair, mentally exhausted, realizing all he had was his talent, a trumpet and a new Buick Super. So he was competing in a materialistic world. Whoop-te-do. What was he supposed to do? His immediate problem was failing in matters of the heart. Milo's hurt deepened. It was worse now because he was off Sunday evening and had time to reflect and feel sorry for himself. His sister realizing his distress bought him a cup of hot chocolate. She sensed it had something to do with Delores.

"Hang in there, brother," said she. "She won't let a good thing pass her by. Believe me."

He thanked her for her concern and returned to his brooding.

*   *   *   *

Delores spoke highly of Milo when she revealed to her friend the good time she had had Friday night. After finishing dinner, they sat at the table and had coffee and a lengthy conversation. Delores acquainted her friend with superfluous images of her new boyfriend as though it were more of a reality than her imagination. Her friend agreed, based on her observations the night she was with Delores at the ballroom. Milo seemed to be everything Delores had just finished describing.

When Delores returned home, it was after seven and she jumped in the shower to wash her hair. It was at this time that Milo decided to call again. She didn't hear the telephone ring. When she didn't answer his imagination went wild. He was really hurting now. Maybe he would try once more before going to bed. He was still slumped in the chair and fell asleep. When he awoke, it was nearly eleven o'clock. He had missed his last chance to call because of time restrictions. It was now too late to call a school teacher that had to be on the job early the next morning.

Other people had trouble getting women. Not Milo Munroe. What was going wrong? Was he losing his touch? He actually showed an interest in her. What's more, she showed an interest in him. He went to bed lonely and feeling sorry for himself.

*   *   *   *

Fuller and Calley could tell Milo was preoccupied with something serious as he drove them to school the next morning. Fuller didn't dare question his buddy in Calley's presence. They could talk in detail later.

After entering the halls of the high school, Fuller broke off from Calley and Milo to go by his locker. Lupe caught up with him in the hall. "Hello handsome," she said, expecting her greeting to flatter him.

"Hello," he said, trying to ignore her without being rude beyond his normal limits. The sound of his voice telegraphed his disgust for her.

"You mad at me or somethin'?"

"How could I be mad at someone that nailed my ass to a filling station storeroom without any lights?"

"I could make it up to you," Lupe proposed

"Why?"

"Because I *like* you," she said, emphasizing the word "like".

"Snake's your boyfriend. Go be with him."

"Wouldn't you like to see what you missed?"

"Not interested."

"Have you poked Calley yet?"

"That's enough, Lupe. Beat it," he asserted.

"You'll be sorry," she said in anger. "Remember it was me that warned you."

He changed direction and left her standing alone in the crowded hall. *Why was she after him all of a sudden,* he wondered, *not that it mattered?* He wouldn't touch her with the proverbial ten-foot pole.

✳   ✳   ✳   ✳

Calley went ahead of Milo into home room and sat down at her desk. Milo was somewhat reluctant to face Delores. He needed to be careful and not make the mistake of referring to her by her first name. When he came through the door he nodded a smiling "good morning" to Miss Hatcher. She returned the greeting with a nod, half smiling. Perhaps both were checking each other for reaction. Nothing consequential was revealed except Milo noticed Miss Hatcher was all business. Meanwhile Fuller showed up and sat at his desk.

After homeroom let out, Milo hung around until the last student exited. Miss Hatcher's free period was beginning and he couldn't stay but a moment. He had no idea what to say but prodded himself into saying something, even if it was wrong.

"I just wanted to tell you I had a good time Friday night," he said, seeking her reaction.

"I'd like to talk about that," she responded, trying to be tactful.

Uh oh, he thought. *Here it comes.*

"I had a wonderful time too, but you must understand, what happened between us was a mistake. I apologize for my part and it won't happen again."

Yeah, right, he thought concerning her apology. "Thank you for being so up front," he said. "I'm sorry too, but I'm really glad you enjoyed yourself. Well, I'd better hurry or I'll be late to my next class." He didn't handle it well, but under the circumstances it was the best he could do.

What a mess. He had tried twice, in all sincerity, to reach her Sunday, but unbeknownst to him, his timing was off and his attempts failed. He had mixed emotions and was conflicted within himself regarding the warmth of their feelings expressed Friday night. He contrasted them to the formality she revealed this morning. One part of him wanted to hang onto the likelihood there was a big misunderstanding, wishing for a ray of hope. Another part of him said to let go and forget her entirely.

She on the other hand, felt she had been used for Milo's own selfish amusement and was thankful she had the presence of mind to suspend their passionate activities before it was too late. By refraining from inviting him in when he walked her to her door may have saved her reputation or it may have been because it was early in the morning and their bodies were sapped to the limits. Whatever it was, thanks to God she didn't let it go beyond a few harmless kisses.

*   *   *   *

When the school day ended, Calley took her usual position outside Miss Hatcher's classroom waiting for Fuller. His first full session with Rico and Snake was more of a routine meeting to get acquainted with the process and to check their previous assignment. It wasn't intended to last long.

Calley's mother was going to pick her up subsequent to today because of Fuller's time allocation to his new pupils. He wanted to be with her this last day.

Fuller had formulated an instruction plan similar to that used for Milo, but on a simpler scale because of Rico and Snake's ineptitude. The first session was short as planned, but they applied themselves and made it a point to absorb everything Fuller said. He was impressed but skeptical of the distant outcome.

*   *   *   *

Fuller and Calley stopped by the soda fountain on the way to her house. They sat in their usual booth in the rear and embarked on their ongoing discussion about "going all the way". This time he had something going for him. He knew he could perform and he had a ten-dollar tip in his pocket to prove it. He wanted to please Calley more than anything, but wanted his first encounter with her to be respectful and perfect; something special, since he had a new confidence in himself. With that, he saw no further need to put her off. "I love you," he said, "and I want to be with you."

She reached up and whispered in his ear that she loved him too. "I only wish we had a place where we could be alone," she cooed.

The back room of the filling station crossed Fuller's mind but he was quick to discard the thought. He wouldn't take Calley to a place like that, no matter what the incentive. There was no way they could bring their focus on each other to immediate fruition sitting at a soda fountain. They wound up in the same old argument as to where and when.

"If you truly loved me, you would find a way," she whispered softly, trying to motivate him.

"I truly do love you, honey and I am going to find a way," he said, finally capitulating, totally. "Trust me."

"Then why are we waiting?"

"Saturday, how does Saturday sound?" he asked straight out, initiating a brain storm.

"Do you really mean it?" she asked, not entirely sure where he was coming from.

"I'll get us a room in a motel Saturday?" *Just the three of us*, he thought, *you me and my peppermint oil*. "We can spend the day together. Would you like that?"

"I knew my special guy would come up with something," she said, squeezing his arm as she snuggled closer. She was cheery with expectation. She looked into the eyes of her boyfriend and said in a unique way, "I'm already looking forward to Saturday, darling."

Fuller smiled his approval of her approval. He did love her. If she wanted them to be together, then that's what he wanted, even if their reasons sometimes clashed. At the very least, the way she put it, their upcoming tryst would be a worthy expression of their love for one another. They both seemed happier now that an agreement had been reached.

$$*\qquad*\qquad*\qquad*$$

Fuller arrived at the ballroom early to discuss with his friend whatever it was that was troubling him. He sensed it had something to do with Delores. Milo opened up and began to talk. "It's all fucked up," he said. "She said it was a mistake for us to see each other again. Maybe it was a mistake, but I don't understand it. I called her twice Sunday and she wasn't home. I guess she spent the weekend with her everyday boyfriend. Anyway, I'm wasting my time with her. I knew it was too good to last."

"Don't be too hard on yourself, Milo. "If I had my pick of the women, who chase you, I wouldn't worry about some old maid school teacher."

"Thanks pal," Milo said. "I know you are trying to be helpful, but to tell the truth, I think I'm in love with her."

"Things will work out Milo," Fuller consoled. "They always do. You've got too much going for you. You'll see."

"Thanks again pal."

Milo wanted to ask a favor of Fuller. He hesitated, wondering if it was too much to ask, then decided to go through with it. If it were at all possible, he wanted Fuller to invite Miss Hatcher to Thanksgiving dinner at his house. Fuller knew his friend was out of sorts. He didn't think Miss Hatcher would accept, but if that's what Milo wanted, he would invite her anyway and let Milo discover her decision. What were friends for if you couldn't rely on them in a pinch? He left early, waving to Alma on his way out. He went home and spent the rest of the evening talking to Calley on the telepone.

*   *   *   *

Tuesday before Thanksgiving was another day of anxiety for Milo. Both he and Delores were off track in their appraisal of the other. He was confident she had turned on him because of another boyfriend and she had equal confidence his ego allowed him to pursue momentary pleasure at her expense. Because she didn't get a follow-up call either Saturday or Sunday, she reeled in her feelings for him. If his M.O. was to love em' and leave em', then he missed the boat where she was concerned. They found themselves uneasy in each other's presence at school that day.

*   *   *   *

When the final bell rang, the students were in a tizzy to leave the building. Rico and Snake were on time for their tutoring session with Fuller. They arranged some desk in the back of the room so they could face Fuller for his attention while Miss Hatcher graded papers at her desk in front of the blackboard. Fuller's teaching plan was simple and afforded his pupils the close encounter with their tutor necessary for them to progress. They were catching on and seemed to enjoy learning. Being away from the competition of the classroom and the learned students that had overtaken them scholastically had a calming effect on them. Their attention span increased rapidly as they were focused on digesting every educational concept put forth by Fuller. He was amazed at how they caught on. They realized this was their last chance and were grabbing at straws to succeed with their formal education. Fuller also realized how important it was for him to help these poor wretches catch onto what came naturally to their classmates. He felt he was using his time wisely and was very proud of himself. If they didn't make it, it wouldn't be because he didn't try. He's the one that made the difference in their life by making the sacrifice to help them. He gave up his Calley time after school to instruct them. His only compensation was their gratitude and the comfort he derived from calling Calley on the telephone every evening when he got home.

"Okay fellows, time's up," he said, on closing this session. He explained their course of home study for the evening which would lead them into tomorrow's session.

They straightened the desk in the rear of the room. Fuller followed Rico and Snake as they left, but Miss Hatcher snagged him, by the wave of her pencil. She was still grading papers without looking up. "How are they doing?" she asked.

"Believe it or not, if they don't stumble, I believe they will make it."

"It's only been two days. How can you say that?"

"Because it's two on one and I don't laugh at their stupid questions. I try to answer them."

"Good job, Fuller. I knew you had it in you. Keep up the good work and we'll see you in the morning."

"Uh, Miss Hatcher—my mom wants me to invite you to Thanksgiving dinner at our house if you don't have other plans."

"Well isn't that sweet of her. Thank your mother for me, but I'm spending Thanksgiving day with my family."

"If you want to, you can come later for desert and coffee."

She smelled Milo in the mix and wasn't interested. "If timing permits, I'll make it a point to be there," she lied, knowing it was not going to happen.

"Okay," he said. "See you later."

*   *   *   *

Fuller called the hotel and left word for Milo that he wasn't coming in tonight and would see him in the morning. He was missing Calley and wanted to visit with her. It was too cold to sit on the front porch or to go sit at their favorite picnic table in the park. They decided to take a walk and wound up at the drug store soda fountain. She was anxious to hear the arrangements he had made for Saturday. When he didn't volunteer any information, she asked him straight out.

"Today's just Tuesday," he answered. "I have lots of time, honey. I won't forget."

"You'd better not," she said sweetly, hunching her shoulders up to her ears, mimicking Shirley Temple. She placed her hand on his knee and seized it tightly as a reminder.

He kissed her on her head, smelling the essence of her femininity through the wavy softness of her clean hair. He was stimulated throughout his entire body as if covered by a mist of pheromones. "I won't let us down, I promise."

CHAPTER 21

▼

Milo asked Phil Davenport if they could play around him while he made an important telephone call. Phil nodded his approval and Milo headed for the hotel lobby seeking a phone booth. He couldn't wait any longer. He had to call Delores, now. He put his coin in the money receptacle and began dialing, then pressed the receiver back on the hook, hanging up before her telephone rang. Not having the foggiest notion what to say, he gave himself some time for thought. It was a delicate situation and needed to be approached with the utmost sensitivity. He was fearful of groveling. The best way to face his dilemma was head on with a casual demeanor and normal conversation. Putting his coin back into the receptacle, he took a deep breath to relax and keep his voice from quivering, then dialed her number. She answered on the fourth ring just before he was going to hang up.

"Hello—"

"Hi, its Milo. How have you been?"

"Fine," she said, "just keeping busy doing what teachers do. Huh huh. How have you been?"

"Fine," he said, "just keeping busy doing what musicians do when they are not in school. Huh huh."

"I wanted to call and be sure there were no hard feelings after our conversation this morning. I still want your friendship." *That was the right approach,* he thought. *How else could I sow seeds of goodwill hoping they would germinate?*

"Oh, of course not and yes we are still friends. I am your teacher, remember?" That was friendlier than she intended, but how else could she respond to a line like his without sounding like she had a broken wing.

"I'm glad," he said. "I tried calling you Sunday—twice, but I missed you."

If that were true it would change the whole character of her feelings towards him. She decided to check it out. "What time did you call?" she asked.

"Well, I called once around four and then again around seven. I was going to call Saturday, but decided to let you get some rest after keeping you up all night Friday."

She breathed a sigh of relief. He *was* telling the truth. She was having her evening meal with her girlfriend around four and was probably washing her hair when he called at seven.

"I'm sorry I missed your calls," she said. "I was having diner at the cafeteria with my girlfriend around four and was probably washing my hair at seven when you called."

He was relieved. He believed her, partly because he wanted to and partly because the times he called matched the times he was unable to reach her. "Tell you what," he said, "let me make it up to you. Have dinner with me Sunday evening."

"Oh, I don't know," she said, "I have tentative plans." She needed more time to work through this change of events and satisfy herself she was on the right course.

"Break em." He measured with some authority, confirming to himself that his clout had returned.

"I couldn't do that," she said. Her brain was spinning for a casual way to accept his invitation. She wanted to accept and not blow this second chance, but her method needed to be impassive or at least relaxed. *I could go to Fuller's house for dessert and coffee*, she thought. *No! That wouldn't work. It wouldn't be prudent to be seen with Milo in the presence of another student's parents.* "Tell you what," she said, meting out measured hope to Milo. Stop by my desk after school tomorrow. I should be in a better position to let you know."

"Till tomorrow then," he said and hung up the telephone. He was back in business and he felt better about his lingering situation. He couldn't wait to tell Fuller. He dialed Fuller's number and Fuller's mother answered the telephone. "May I please speak to Fuller," Milo asked?

"He's not here at the moment, Milo," she answered recognizing his voice. "Can I take a message?"

"Yes ma'am, tell him everything is okay with Delores."

"Who is Delores?"

"Just a girl I know," he said before hanging up.

*   *   *   *

Wednesday, the day before Thanksgiving, was Milo's Thanksgiving day. Things in his life were brighter than they had been for the past two days. He picked Fuller up and filled him in on his conversation with Delores as he drove to get Calley before heading to school.

"Well that's good because Miss Hatcher won't be coming to our house for Thanksgiving dinner."

"You asked her?"

"You asked me to?"

If she wasn't coming, it didn't matter. He had at least a fifty-fifty chance of her accepting his dinner invitation for Sunday evening. Milo thanked Fuller for his effort and continued with his high expectations.

They picked Calley up on their way to school. The day started out more relaxed for Milo. Miss Hatcher who had been serious with her students the past couple of days seemed more congenial and relaxed. Fuller and Calley were effervescent toward each other that day. Saturday was approaching with all of its promise and they were giddy with excitement.

*   *   *   *

When school let out, Fuller stayed to be with Rico and Snake for their tutoring session. Milo stopped by Miss Hatcher's desk long enough to hear her to say she was available Sunday evening. "Good," he said. "I'll pick you up at six, if that's all right". She nodded okay and he left so as not to arouse suspicion with Rico and Snake in the rear of the room.

Lupe ran into Calley in the hall and asked if they could talk.

"Sure," Calley said as they moved against the lockers, out of the way of onrushing students.

"Have you been keeping an eye on Fuller lately?"

"Why? What do you mean?" Calley asked, sensing something hateful about to vent from Lupe's mouth.

"I don't want to be the one to tell you this," Lupe began, "but your boyfriend has been with a whore. As your friend, I thought you should know."

"We are not friends, Lupe. Why are you telling me this?"

"Calley, we've been together since first grade. Of course we are friends."

"Sounds to me like you are trying to start something between Fuller and me."

"Ask him about the Belmont Hotel if you don't believe me. Anyway, gotta run. See ya'." Lupe was gone in a flash, blending with the crowd in the hallway.

Calley didn't want to believe Lupe. But suppose it was true? "NOOoooo," she cried out loud, trying to hold back tears and attracting attention. She ran out of the building and jumped in her mother's car.

"What's the matter, dear?" her mother asked, knowing only a quarrel with a boyfriend could wound this deeply. "Did you have a quarrel with Fuller?"

"Please Mom, I don't want to talk about it."

Because she was mum on the subject, her mother concluded her daughters distress had something to do with Fuller and gave her the space she needed to work it through. "In due time, baby," her mother said, patting Calley on the knee. "We can talk when you are ready."

Fuller called Calley before leaving for the ballroom. Their conversation lasted their normal range of time, give or take a few minutes. She didn't let on about her conversation with Lupe or the Belmont Hotel. She wanted to get his reaction first hand by confronting him in person. The perfect time would be while taking a walk after Thanksgiving dinner the next day. He didn't detect a hint in her voice that anything was actually awry, but her minute negativism gave him pause as to why she didn't exhibit her usual excitement when he mentioned the upcoming Saturday. And when he said that he loved her she didn't bounce it back on him. Her lack of affection was reminiscent of the past, but he reasoned it was probably his imagination. He judged she was playing it low in the event her mother was in listening distance.

*   *   *   *

It was a slow night at the ballroom. Fuller was running late. He sat at his usual table and gave Milo a thumbs up announcing his arrival. Alma saw Fuller and came over to visit.

"Hi, sweet thing," she said. "I just want to tell you how lovely your Calley is. You're a lucky young man."

"Hi, Alma. I didn't mean to be rude to you the other night." He was referring to the incident in the buffet line.

"You weren't rude, baby. Believe me I understand. Your Calley is beautiful"

"Thanks," Fuller said. "You getting ready for a big Thanksgiving tomorrow?"

"It's just me and my daughter. I think I'll take her out for Thanksgiving dinner and not cook."

"Good idea," he said. As far as he was concerned, they could come celebrate Thanksgiving with his family and friends, but he also knew it would never work, so he dropped the notion before he felt obligated to make the invitation.

The band broke for intermission and Milo came over to Fuller's table. Grabbing a chair, he slapped Fuller on the back and looking over at Alma, said, "How's it going pro-girl?"

She had to laugh. "Hello, darling," she said. "You sounded good tonight."

"That's because I am good," he joked.

"You're the best," she said. "Don't joke about it."

"What's your favorite song? We'll play it for you."

"When Your Lover Has Gone," she said.

"You got it," Milo said. "We like doing that one. Well, I'd better get going or Phil will can my ass."

Alma and Fuller watched as the rotating stage moved slowly towards the dance floor. The band's theme song ended and Milo took the microphone. "Our first number is dedicated to our friend Alma, the beautiful torch song, *When Your Lover Has Gone* with the lovely Jan Mulvahill on the vocal." The technician turned the stage lights down to a velvety purple and the music began to roll in a subdued undertone across the dance floor like an emerging fog. The dance participants embraced each other closely as they rocked slowly back and forth to the engrossingly melancholy strains of the melody. The lyrics were lonesome and heartfelt.

Jan's rendition was empathetic, word by lonesome word:
When you're alone,
Who cares for starlit skies,
When you're alone,
The magic moonlight dies,
At break of dawn,
There is no sunrise,
When your lover has gone.
What lonely hours,
The evening shadows bring,
What lonely hours,
With mem-ries lingering,
Like faded flow'rs,
Life can't mean an-y-thing,
When your lover has gone.

Fuller caught Alma at the edge of his peripheral vision while trying to keep his eyes on the band. Her attention was fixed on the vocalist. As Jan sang the powerful lyrics, Alma's friendly smile began breaking into an escalating facial pain with watering eyes. She was being touched by a memory from her past. Fuller wished he could evaporate and leave her alone with this private moment.

When the song ended, she took a tissue from her purse and blotted the tears from her lower eyelashes to catch any run of mascara.

"I'm sorry, baby" Alma apologized to Fuller. "I guess I'm a sentimental old hag."

A gentleman wondered over from the bar. "Excuse me," he said to Alma. "The bartender said if I came over, you would make time for me."

"Of course," she said. She excused herself from the man long enough for her to lean over and whisper in Fuller's ear, "Happy Thanksgiving, darling."

Fuller spoke softly in the man's presence, "Same to you, hon." She left with her trick. Fuller waited for Milo and his ride home.

CHAPTER 22

▼

Thursday was a typical Thanksgiving Day, cold and dreary with a heavy overcast. Fuller's mother was already in the kitchen when he arose around nine. The aromas from his mother's work station, led him by the nose to the breakfast table where his father was having coffee and reading the morning paper. His mother served him coffee. He was excited knowing the best part of the day was still ahead. Calley, her mother, Milo, his sister and brother-in-law were all going to be together on this festive occasion. He helped his mom around the house and did a few chores for his dad.

He called Calley and talked to her. She kept her wits about her and was successful in keeping her emotions undetected by Fuller.

"I'm glad I'm going to see you today," he said with a *lovey* tone in his voice, hoping for a compatible response.

"Me too," she said, sweetly.

He was left with high expectation as they completed their conversation.

Calley went over the entire spectrum of Lupe's conversation with her about the whore and the Belmont Hotel, trying to determine how to present it to Fuller. She wanted to arouse his best unprepared defense. At one point she decided to drop it all together. If it were true, it could be the end of their relationship. She didn't want that to happen, but still she had her self-respect and dignity to protect, and they had to be maintained. She was wounded and profaned by his philandering and he either had to come up with a respectful excuse for his activities or their romance was going to falter.

*   *   *   *

Milo and his family arrived first. After introducing his sister and brother-in-law to Fuller's parents, the men went into the parlor to watch the football game. Elaine volunteered her services in the kitchen.

Calley and her mother arrived shortly thereafter. Calley was doing a near perfect job of balancing her true feelings for Fuller as contrasted to the suspect lies told by Lupe. Fuller surmised all was not completely right by her tepid kiss on his cheek upon entering through the front door. She never let on, but there was a distant formality evident in the atmosphere surrounding her. Fuller couldn't figure it out. Maybe she was on the rag or something. Maybe her scanty greeting was for her mother's benefit. Whatever seemed to be troubling Calley was disconcerting to Fuller.

Mrs. Kreppe had prepared a lovely Thanksgiving Dinner. Everyone there complimented her on doing such a fine job and expressed their gratitude for being invited. She was in the process of making coffee to serve with dessert when Calley motioned Fuller to the porch. Calley's original intention was to take a walk, but it was too cold and the wind was brisk. They took a position on the wraparound porch to the windward side of the house.

"What's up, baby?" Fuller asked.

"Maybe you'd better tell me," Calley replied.

"I don't understand," he said.

"Maybe I can jar your memory. Tell me about the Belmont Hotel."

An unexpected freeze petrified Fuller in the head. His thinking processes were temporarily neutralized. "What the hell is that all about?" Is all he could think of to say. His response was weak and he knew it. He also knew he had been caught red handed. Only two people in this world knew about his trip to the Belmont Hotel; the hooker and himself.

"You can do better than that," she said. "Tell me about the hooker you had an encounter with. Is it true?"

He looked down at the floor, buying a little time, to clarify his thinking. He knew where she was coming from, but how she got there was a mystery. Somebody squealed on him and he had to be very careful what he said. Not knowing what she knew of the situation could either work in his favor or against him. If she knew the whole story, he was in deep trouble. If she was acting on innuendo and hunches, he could diffuse the clenches, if he could spot them. He could not bring himself to lie to her because he was confident that she knew something, and if he did lie he would just dig a deeper hole for himself. Maybe he could reason his way out of this predicament by telling her the truth. He had considered coming clean earlier.

Before he could look up and explain, she said "It *is* true, isn't it?"

He hesitated looking for an out, then admitted his shortcoming with one word, "Yes."

"How could you?" she cried?

He reached out to her and she looked him straight in the eye and snapped, "Don't you touch me." With that, she started crying. "How could you do this to me?" she blurted as she turned and ran off the porch and down the sidewalk.

He was confident that once she thought about her actions, she would come back and he could explain the truth in a way she could understand. He waited outside in the cold for half an hour, but she never returned. He went into the house and before he could say anything, Calley's mother asked the whereabouts of her daughter.

"We had an argument," he said sadly. "She left. I don't know where she went." He went over to Calley's mom and said remorsefully, reaching for her hands, "I'm sorry. I thought she would come back."

"Don't blame yourself, dear," she said. "I know my daughter. She'll be alright. I'll go find her."

"Calley's mother put on her coat and hat and thanked Mrs. Kreppe for the lovely dinner."

Milo knew instinctively what was going on and came over to his friend and wrapped his arm around his shoulders and said, "Hang in there buddy, you'll make it."

Seems like all Milo and Fuller were doing was supporting each other in time of crises.

Fuller excused himself and went to the telephone and called Calley. When she answered and heard Fuller's voice, she hung up immediately.

He knew he was in big trouble by the depth of his offense and didn't have the slightest idea how to straighten things out—or if they could ever be straightened out. He excused himself by thanking Milo's family for coming. He announced that he was going upstairs and punched Milo lightly on the shoulder as he headed toward the staircase. Milo was saddened by his best friend's torment. The advisable thing to do for the time being, was to leave Fuller alone. They could talk when he came around.

Fuller fell asleep and didn't wake up until past midnight. He laid in bed staring at the ceiling and thinking of his predicament. He relied on his favorite stratagem—hang in there—time would be on his side. His immediate problem was, he couldn't live with himself. He wished he could go back to sleep and not wake up until all was right with Calley.

✳   ✳   ✳   ✳

Calley's mother saw her daughter sitting on the steps of the front porch as she approached her house. "Come in the house, dear," she said, as she started up the steps. "You'll catch your death of cold sitting out here."

"Mom, the fresh air fells good," Calley returned.

"If you must," her mother said. "I'll fix some hot chocolate and call you when it's ready."

"Thanks, Mom."

Calley stood up and trudged into the house to be with her mother. Her eyes were red from crying. As Calley entered the kitchen, her mother walked over and put her arms around her daughter.

"Baby, I don't like seeing you like this."

"It's okay, Mom. I'll be all right," she said.

"Honey, I know a lover's quarrel when I see one. Do you want to talk about it?"

"There's nothing to talk about. I'll just have to work things out for myself," she said, squeezing her mother tightly. She laid her head against her mother's shoulder for comfort.

"When you are ready to confide in me," her mother said. "I'll be here for you as always."

"Thanks Mom," Calley said. "I love you."

✳   ✳   ✳   ✳

School was out until Monday. It was going to be a long and oppressive week-end for Fuller. He moped around his room, coming out to eat and then only to sit at the table and nibble. He would come out to go to the bathroom or to call Calley on the telephone. His mom and dad gave him a wide berth to pull himself together. He tried calling Calley but she would not talk with him. Her mom was sweet to Fuller. She said, "Give it time, dear. She will talk to you when she's ready."

He would go back to his room and agonize over his cheating mistake. He thought of the music and lyrics that touched Alma so deeply. He wept openly.

He wanted to bang his head against the wall, but knew that would only attract attention. He fell across the bed and was asleep by the time he hit the mattress.

CHAPTER 23

▼

Milo picked Delores up Sunday evening at exactly six o'clock as planned. When she opened her door, he could not believe his eyes. Her presence was so mature yet so young and fragile. She was beautiful.

"Well, are you just going to stand there or are you going to come in?" she summoned.

He snapped back from the momentary lapse that had him anchored to the floor and stepped into her apartment. "You look impeccable," he said, still half stunned by the womanhood about to accompany him on a dinner date.

"Thank you," she said, raising up on her toes to kiss him on the cheek. Her perfume infused the mystery of heaven in its bouquet. He could die now and be ensconced in the aroma of her fragrance for eternity. Everything about her was absolutely perfect.

She wrapped a scarf around her hair and he helped her slip into her coat. She reached for a small handbag. "Shall we?" she invited, offering him her arm.

He proudly took her by the arm and proceeded to escort her to his car closing her apartment door as they left. He opened and shut her car door, displaying his best manners.

"Where are we going?" she inquired curiously.

"The only place in this town worthy of a trumpet player named Star and his beautiful date," he answered. "We have reservations at the main dinning room of the Anthony Wayne Hotel." He cranked the engine and sped away from her apartment complex.

"Isn't there some place less expensive we could dine?" she suggested. Her frugal instincts prompted her to go easy on his pocketbook while trying to avoid being obligated.

No one seemed to get it. He had money coming in faster than he could spend it. He was single, the main draw for Phil Davenport's Orchestra and was going to get residuals from record sales. He parked in the hotel garage, cut the ignition and turned to face her. "Delores," he said, "there is no way I would take you any place but the best."

"But this is very expensive."

"Honey, think about it. If I didn't have the money, we couldn't be here now, could we? Look, I'm not trying to impress you with how much money I have. You know what I do. I make an excellent living and have little or no expenses. I can afford anything I want." He paused while he composed what he was about to say. Taking her hands, he held them gingerly. "Delores, I want to tell you something. I want you to listen and try to understand what it is I'm about to say and please never forget it."

What's coming now, she thought?

"I have feelings for you. You are very special in my life. I thought I had lost you last weekend and I never want to experience that feeling again." He paused, testing for a reply.

She sat quietly, reflecting on Milo's statement to her. She thought that was sweet, but inappropriate.

"Milo—I enjoy your company or I wouldn't be here."

"How do you feel towards me?" he asked, trying not to be anxious.

"I have to be honest with you. I see you as a remarkable, handsome young man with overflowing talent and a big heart. Most women dream of their knight in shining armor riding up on a white stallion to sweep them off their feet. I have those dreams too, but you must know, as long as you are my pupil, it would be insane, not to mention unethical, for me to become involved with you."

"I'm going to graduate in six months, what then?"

"Let's see how it goes."

"Fair enough," he said.

Her perfume had infected his desire to be closer to her at that exact moment. He moved his face slowly in her direction testing for a kiss. She responded by turning her head slightly away from his pursuit. She remained fixed in her position until he backed off and they found themselves locked in a standoff. He decided to go for the kiss he didn't get on the first try. Once again she turned her head reflecting the message that a kiss was out of the question. He kissed her hand instead, then exited his side of the car and went around to open her door.

He escorted her, arm in arm to the main dinning room. The Maitre'd was at the entrance when they arrived. "Good evening Mister Munroe," he said. "Your table is ready. Follow me please." Milo had requested a table near the fire place. It was a romantic setting, refining the occasion to perfection. Milo pulled the chair out for Delores, then repositioned it after she was comfortably seated. As usual, when she was alone with him, she was amazed by his self-assurance and the respect others had for him. Milo had pre-arranged for a decanter of fine wine be brought to the table for Delores and ordered an iced tea for himself. With all the consideration paid to him by the staff, he was still too young to legally partake in an alcoholic beverage. The attention he paid Delores was worthy of royalty and her poise was worthy of adoration. He was an anomaly of sorts. Even she treated him like a kid, when in reality he was mature beyond his years.

All of a sudden, like being struck by a bolt of lightening, a light bulb went off in her head. Her attitude in their age difference became clear and she saw it as self defeating to keep insisting on keeping her distance, when in fact, she really cared for the guy. She couldn't be over five years his senior. That wasn't an extreme gap in their ages. She set about to make a correction in her attitude toward the way she thought of him. She relented, conceding she was on an honest date with a popular, handsome young man. He was her student alright, but none-the-less a handsome young man. Their age difference would normalize in a couple of years. She began to question the barrier keeping them apart. If he was a young man— she was certainly a young woman. The restrictions she had to adhere to didn't seem fair. If she didn't act now, she could miss the opportunity of a lifetime. To get right with the situation, she would have to respect him as an equal outside the classroom, or risk losing him forever. She was satisfied he was a real prize and was not going to let him get away because of restricting convention.

All he wanted when they were in the car was a simple kiss and she turned him away. *What could possibly be wrong with a little kiss?* she asked herself, *What was not wrong with it? Would one kiss satisfy him or would it lead to more critical assertions on his part, and so what if it did?* She cleared her head of negative thoughts, realizing she was worrying about the wrong things.

She remembered the way the young girls at school competed for his attention. If she didn't respond to his initiative toward her, it was a safe bet she would lose out and someone else would wind up with the prize. She was out in front of all the competition and made the decision, on the spot, to keep it that way. Just not flaunt their friendship for the next six months or until he graduates.

"Milo, this is lovely. Thank you ever so much for inviting me," she said. She reached across the table and placed her hand over his. She wasn't aware she was staring. Her eyes glistened like diamonds from reflections of the flame atop the candle on their table. "You asked a question earlier and I don't remember how I answered you, but I'm going to try to answer you again, this time from the heart. Milo—I do have feelings for you," she said. With that, she stood up, walked around the table, bent over and kissed him on the lips, then returned to her chair. "There, I've said it," she said, bracing for a consequence.

Milo was startled and somewhat dazed by her sudden change of heart. He was absolutely delighted if he was reading her correctly. He stood up, walked around the table, planted a kiss on her lips and said, "Now we are even." Returning to his chair, he waited for her reaction.

Delores looked straight at Milo. "Thank you," she said. "So there is no misunderstanding, I'm proud to be here with you." Her eyes sparkled brightly over her angelic smile.

"I'm proud to be with you too," he replied, still in a state of disbelief.

A waiter interrupted and stood beside their table with pad and pencil in hand. "Are you ready to order or would you like more time?"

"I'll have what he's having," Delores said, accepting his selection from the menu to be satisfactory with her. It was her stamp of approval signifying their new beginning.

"With that settled, we'll have a rack of lamb for two."

He held up his glass of iced tea for a toast. She raised her wine glass.

"Here's to our new found friendship," he volunteered, purposely selecting the safe word friendship as having lesser domination over the alternative word, relationship. He did not wish to overpower the moment with words that could unfavorably misconstrue his desire to be moderate.

"Our new found friendship," she said.

The evening was still young when they finished dining. They left the hotel as they had entered, arm in arm. He drove to her apartment. This time she invited him in. Both were aware his visit would have a time limit since this was a school night.

"Make yourself comfortable, Sweetie," she said, while I hang up my coat. He sat at one end of her sofa. She was back in a flash. "Can I get you anything?" she asked.

"Just you," he said, extending his hand for her to sit next to him.

She sat on the sofa close to him, crossed her legs and kicked off one shoe, dangling the other from the toes of her crossed leg. "What now?" she tempted Milo, curling a strand of hair around her index finger, her eyes still glistening, this time from an inner fire and not the candle on the table.

The delicate question, *what now*, intensified his freedom of choice and the emotions flaming within him became a driving force opening the way to his cherished fantasy? She helped settle the question by offering up her lips, slowly, enticing a response then surrendering the advantage to him. His youthful eagerness ruled his passion as he wrapped her in his arms, pulling her ever closer. The dangling shoe lost it's support and fell to the floor. The warmth of her breath and the impassioned submission of her tasty lips gave entrance to his tongue, signaling surrender. Instinctively, he grabbed her upper thigh and pulled her even closer. His hand slid down her leg reaching her knee and encircled the contour tenderly while squeezing softly with a deliberate resolve. Lascivious shock waves spread throughout her submissive body. Her leg relaxed invitingly as he eased his hand up her inner thigh. She emitted a quick, vanishing shutter and aired the release of a subdued "Ugh," as she relaxed the last of her tensions in the strength of his grip. His free hand maneuvered through the top of her blouse, slowly, over the softness of her satiny skin in pursuit of the prize he could only imagine until now. His instincts led him to the exquisite rise of yielding softness and a tiny pointed nubbin which he tweaked between his thumb and forefinger, piquing from her a sudden gasp. The rest was automatic. She assisted his body weight in lowering her to a reclining position as their torsos fused together. They truly found each other's gift to the other on her sofa this night.

*　　*　　*　　*

It was ten o'clock. They lay facing each other saying witty things and giggling over the familiarity that follows intimacy. Time only mattered because they both had to be at school the next morning. She didn't want him to go and he didn't want to leave. They both agreed there would be other times so he got up and started freshening himself to leave. They were both in a disheveled state as he hurried to get ready.

She walked him to the door and they faced each other. "Please don't feel guilty or unclean in the morning," he said, feeling as though he had taken advantage of her. For the moment, he obviously hated himself, and saw no relief in sight.

"Milo," Delores said, detecting his feelings of self-loathing. She still had that sparkle in her eyes as he listened. "I enjoyed having dinner with you tonight. What happened after that, well—happened? I didn't resist because I wanted you, and knew our feelings were—mutually inspired," she assured him. "It was as much my fault as it was yours, Sweetie, so quit beating up on yourself."

Thank God, she came to his rescue. He was beginning to feel like a lech. After the comfort of several good night kisses, his faith in himself and mankind was restored, and he went home to bed.

CHAPTER 24

▼

Fuller was ready when Milo arrived to pick him up for school. He confided in his best friend concerning his problems with Calley. Someone had put him in this no-win situation and he wanted to find the culprit. It wasn't in his makeup to get physical with an adversary, but he felt in his heart he could kill the person that betrayed him.

Calley had already left when they stopped by to pick her up. It was assumed her mother had driven her to school. In any event, it was obvious she had disconnected herself from the daily ritual of riding to school with them.

Milo was committed not to kiss and tell on Delores. His experience with her was a beautiful thing and too sacred to share with anyone, including Fuller. It was obvious that he was riding on cloud nine and working hard to contain himself. When he entered homeroom he said "good morning" to Miss Hatcher with his normal tone of voice and bland facial expression so as not to arouse suspicion. She returned his greeting with the same professionalism her students came to identify her. Milo was doing fairly well receding from his high, until he saw Miss Hatcher. He started reliving the previous evening and was having trouble focusing on school business. If he was going to make it through the day productively, he was going to have to yield to self-discipline.

No one suspected Milo even knew Miss Hatcher outside the classroom. That was the beauty of their relationship. It was private, as fraternization between them was unsuspected.

Fuller was right behind Milo as they entered homeroom. He nodded a good morning to Miss Hatcher and immediately started searching for Calley. She obviously saw him enter the room and shifted her focus downward to avoid eye contact. She wouldn't acknowledge his presence. He tried desperately to attract her attention without bringing attention to himself, but she continued to ignore him.

Milo observed Coach Cagle from time to time coming in to visit Miss Hatcher. They would mumble softly back and forth and the coach would leave. Milo discerned that the coach had a crush on her and wondered how she felt about him. Many things crossed Milo's youthful mind. Had the coach gotten to her? Maybe he hadn't and her frustration was the source of his good fortune the previous night. Was the fact that she wanted him make her slutty? He ruled that one out. He wanted her and didn't consider himself slutty. Hopefully, he would beat the coach for her affections and that would give him impetus to feel like the better man. He was admiring her when she looked up from her desk and quickly surveyed the room. When she felt safe, she gave him a wink the uninitiated wouldn't recognize. As he was preoccupied with her, perhaps she was preoccupied with him Upon leaving her room, she handed him a folded note. He waited until he was alone to read it. "You have a cute tush," it said. It was signed with a capital 'D'. He swelled with engrossing pride and was set for the day.

*   *   *   *

It was a long day for Fuller. He couldn't get Calley's attention, no matter how hard he tried. Minute by minute throughout the day he was cheapened by the misery of his guilt feelings. He met Milo for lunch. Milo tried to cheer him up without success. Fuller was anxious to know how Calley found out about him and the hooker. Milo vowed to keep his eyes and ears open for his friend.

*   *   *   *

Rico and Snake had their lunch that day in Rico's convertible. The sun was shining, but a light chill filled the air. "How much money you got?" Rico asked Snake.

"Who wants to know," Snake answered brashly.

"You es-see anyone else here dumb-ass?"

"You es-smart, RRRico," Snake said. "You really es-smart, you know that? Calling me a dumb-ass." then added, seemingly irritated by Rico's comment "I ain't got no money."

"Well—it don't matter," Rico said while searching through his pockets. "I ain't got but two doelars."

"What chew need money for?" Snake queried.

"Wal—you know Es-snake—I been thinking about Fooler. As bad as we treated him, he still es-stays after school to help us with our studies. It ain't right, man. We need to do es-something to es-show our appreciation."

"You right, RRRico. You absolutely right. You got es-something in mind?"

"I don't know. You ain't got no money and I only got two doelars. We can't do much with only two doelars."

Snake's face lit up like a bathroom heater on a cold night. "I got it," he said, excitedly. "If you whant to do es-sump'um really nice, I know what we can do?"

"What you got in mind?"

"I can let him es-screw Lupe."

"He don't wan to fuck Lupe," Rico said flatly.

"You wanna do es-sump'um es-specially nice for him, don't chew? Well, laying Lupe is as nice as it gets an it won't cost us nuthin, neither."

"You really thank he'd go for dat?"

"Evabody das es-screwed Lupe goes back for more. Es-somebody likes it."

"Yuk," Rico voiced disgustedly.

"Pussy's, pussy. Nobody turns down free pussy. Besides dat little gal whose butt he es-sniffs all day ain't given him none. He could use es-some. I can tell."

"Okay," Rico said, caving. "Maybe we can make es-some brownie points. Go ahead then and fix him up with Lupe."

After lunch break Lupe saw Fuller in the hallway from a distance. She could tell by his detached gaze this wasn't a good time to accost him and switched directions from whence she was headed.

Eventually, the school day ended with the final bell. Rico and Snake were on time for their lesson with Fuller. He didn't feel like messing with them today, but was obligated because of his commitment. For the short time they had been under his guidance, both were making remarkable progress. They were treating Fuller with some measure of respect now and he was beginning to like them despite his innate sense they could never be civil toward him. He had them performing tasks in their range of achievements. They showed Fuller they liked accomplishment as he spoon fed them according to their ability to absorb. He liked achieving the impossible and their progress made him realize their antisocial attitudes were their inheritance and not a product of their mind. They were as capable as anybody, given the opportunity, to show their competence, both scholastically and socially.

These discoveries about themselves were revelations that surfaced on their own with a little guidance from Fuller. They were in the early stages of "getting it", owing to Fuller's patience and determination.

Miss Hatcher was getting ready to leave and instructed Fuller to push the desks back in place before they left. They finished the course of study for this day as Fuller had laid it out for them, moved the desks back where they belonged and the three of them left the room together. Passing the boy's rest room, Rico said he had to take a dump. Snake pulled Fuller aside. "Hey man, I want to tell you, you all right, man. I like es-studying and learning the way you help me an RRRico, right. He likes you too, I can tell. I really mean it, man. You really all right and I like you."

"Well, thank you, Snake," Fuller said, revealing his gentlemanly side once more. "I like you too, Snake—and Rico. We'll show this school what you guys can do."

"Yeah, man. We gonna' es-show em'. Listen, RRRico and me, we been talkin', you know. We wan't to do es-sump'um nice for you, man."

"Thank you Snake, but you don't owe me anything."

"Naw, naw. You don't get it, man. We wan to do es-sump'um for you, es-sump'um really es-special." He persisted. "How wud' you like to make it with Lupe?"

"WHAT!"

"Do you wan to take Lupe to bed?"

"Snake, that is disgusting!" Fuller exclaimed.

"Naw, you don't understan' man. If you whan to es-screw Lupe, I can fix it up for you. I get her fellows all the time and es-she pays me money. If I ask her, es-she will do you for nawthing."

Fuller couldn't believe his ears. He was alert to Lupe's appetite for him lately and searched the recesses of his mind for a reason. He drew a blank, except that every time they met in the hall, she propositioned him. None of this made sense after she pinned his ass to the wall and stripped him of his dignity that night at the old filling station. If he wanted Lupe, he didn't need Snake to help with an arrangement.

"What do you es-say,? You wan to es-screw Lupe?"

"No, I don't want to be with Lupe." Fuller said. "She is your woman. I'm going to pretend we never had this conversation."

"Okay, man. whatever you es-say man, but if you change your mine—"

"Okay," Fuller said, settling on a hunch. Maybe Snake's help could lead to the identity of the culprit that tipped Calley off. "Where does she take the guys you get for her?"

"Aw man, you es-should es-see it. Es-she has a nice room at the Belmont Hoe-tel. It's nice, real nice. You would love it, man."

The Belmont Hotel was the key word he was looking for. He deducted that it was Lupe that told on him to Calley. That whore he was with must have said something to Lupe and she took it to Calley out of revenge. *She must have told Lupe about the screwing I gave her, but how did she know to identify me with Lupe,* he pondered. He would just have to link Snake's story with the actual events and put it all together when he had more time to lay it out. Right now, his mind was abuzz with thoughts of Calley. Snake's arrangement with Lupe was more than he could deal with at this time.

Rico joined Fuller and Snake in the hall when he finished using the restroom and the three of them left the building together. Rico volunteered to drive Fuller home and he accepted, feeling tired and confused from Snake's latest bombshell. Climbing in the back seat, Snake grabbed Fuller by the arm. "Naw," he insisted. "I give you the best es-seat. You ride up front with RRRico."

The scent of Lupe's perfume encapsulated the entire interior of Rico's car even with the top down. Fuller breathed easier when he disembarked at his house.

He went to his room and laid down on his bed. He stared at the ceiling trying to think clearly of the events as Snake had set them out for him. *So that's it,* he thought, trying to make four out of two and what was left of Snake's frankness regarding Lupe's place of business. The entire scenario was coming together. *The missing link was how Lupe knew I had been with her partner? She was whoring downtown with the girl that gave me the ten dollar tip and that girl must have talked,* Fuller surmised. *Lupe wouldn't have anything to do with me one day and the next she was after my body and squealing on me to Calley.* If Lupe had the details of Fuller's sexual prowess, she got it from her fellow hooker and wanted to find out for herself if what she heard was true. Fuller's creaky formulae was adding up to four. It pinpointed it *was* Lupe that betrayed him. *But she had no reason to be so ruthless and cutthroat by exposing me to Calley?* He thought. But Fuller knew Lupe, she didn't need a reason. She was mean spirited, jealous and horny.

Fuller's mother woke him for supper. After eating, he tried to call Calley again. Her mother answered, ostensibly sympathetic to his cause. "She's not ready to talk yet, dear. She'll come around. I know my daughter. Just be patient."

Fuller said thank you and hung up. His most urgent need at the moment was to be around people. That's one problem he had a solution for. He got dressed and headed downtown to talk with Alma. She could be comforting in times like these.

It was Monday and a slow night at the ballroom. He looked for Alma, but she wasn't anywhere to be seen. In her place at the end of the bar was the hooker he had banged at the Belmont. They saw each other at the same time. She slid off the barstool and moved in his direction. *Oh shit,* he thought. *What did I do to deserve this?*

"Hi, stranger!" She sang out to him. "Remember me?"

"Hi," he said, devoid of enthusiasm.

"Aren't you going to offer me a seat?"

If he had to. "Have a seat," he said.

She pulled out a chair and sat down. "I'm sure glad I found you," she said. "Are you ready for another freebie?"

"Do you know Alma?" Fuller asked, ignoring her question.

"I didn't know you knew Alma," she said.

"Yeah, yeah," Fuller said. "Where is she?"

"With a trick, I suppose."

"What are you doing here," Fuller asked.

"I work for Alma," she said. "She wants me here to take up the slack during the holidays."

"Where is Alma?" he asked again.

"Like I said, she's probably with a trick. How 'bout it, honey? Wanna try your luck with me, one more time?"

"Do you know a girl named Lupe?"

"Oh, everybody knows Lupe. What-do-you-want her for when you got me?"

"No thank you, I just need to know something."

"Anything for you, darling'."

"Did you tell Lupe about the night we were together?"

"Why would you ask a question like that?" she asked, being cautious. "I didn't know she knew you and didn't think it would matter."

"You told her then, didn't you?"

"Well—I didn't tell her everything. She saw you leave the room and asked about you. She pestered me until I gave her what she wanted. Did I do something wrong?" She had a worrisome look on her face.

"If you call screwing up my life, doing something wrong, the answer is yes. Would you please leave now. I'm waiting for someone," he lied.

"Well—Okay, but there's something else I know…"

"What's that?" Fuller, queried.

"I can't tell you," she said as she got up to leave.

Awe, what the hell, he thought, *It didn't matter*. He had enough to sort through for one evening. At least he knew who squealed on him to Calley. He went backstage at intermission and hung around with Milo and the boys. When they were ready for their next set, Fuller went back to his table.

He looked to the end of the bar and the girl was gone. He surmised, she had snagged a trick. Shortly thereafter, Alma appeared. When she saw Fuller, she came over to his table.

"How's my sweetheart tonight?" she asked.

"Lousy," he said. "Shit house lousy."

"Oh honey, something's wrong. I can tell. What is it?"

"I've lost Calley," he said.

"Oh baby," she was sympathetic. "I am so sorry. I know there's nothing I can say or do to comfort you, but I feel terrible."

"It's okay Alma. It's more than a lover's quarrel, it's irreversible. I'll never win her back."

"Never say never, darling. What could you have done that was so bad for her to break up with you?" A light bulb went off in her head. "I think I've just answered my own question," she said. "You told her how you lost your virginity."

"I didn't tell her, somebody else did."

"Oh baby," Alma sympathized again. "If she loves you, she'll come around. I know she will."

"Thanks Alma, for your support, but it's *not* going to happen."

Fuller glanced up at Alma's end of the bar. The young hooker was back. When she saw him look up, she looked down, pretending not to see him sitting with Alma.

They listened to the last number, *I'll See You in My Dreams* and watched the stage revolve to the rear out of sight. The musicians disappeared one by one behind the heavy, velvet draperies. When it stopped, the lights came on and Milo emerged from backstage—"Whew, we've made another night," he said. "I'm glad this one is over."

Fuller filled in the blanks for Milo on their ride home. He said the culprit that squealed on him to Calley was Lupe. He detailed how Lupe found out about him from her hooker friend and mentioned how she had the hots for him and kept propositioning him at school. He said Lupe was whoring downtown and Snake was pimping for her, and how Snake had offered her up as a token of his and Rico's gratitude for helping them with their studies. Milo laughed out loud. "It would really be funny if it weren't so sad." Fuller agreed. Milo had taken charge of his own studies by now, using Fuller's review format with occasional help. Fuller continued to carry the load of managing Rico and Snake's intellectual progress.

*   *   *   *

Fuller spent the next few days at school trying to coax Calley to at least hear him out. She missed being with him and decided that maybe she had been too harsh by shutting him out. She had spent the last few days going to her room as soon as she reached home and crying her eyes out. Her mother tried to be helpful but was unwelcome for the first time in Calley's young life.

Calley finally gave in to Fuller's nagging to let him explain. She agreed to let him walk her home so he could give his side of the story, but still held him accountable for their predicament. She couldn't imagine anything he could say that would change things, but it was the only fair thing to do, considering how much they once meant to each other. His gloom disappeared. He put on a happy face and was temporarily relieved, but fearful of the consequences. Calley called her mother and asked not to be picked up that afternoon. The stage was set for a one on one exchange. The spotlight was on Fuller, but she had the advantage. He would offer excuses and she would decide whether or not they were relevant to his cause. His main concern was properly phrasing the account of his behavior so she could have at least a valid excuse if she would accept it.

*   *   *   *

Calley waited outside Miss Hatcher's room for Fuller as she had done so many times in the past. Fuller cut short his session with Rico and Snake with the excuse this was the holidays and they had earned a break for being so attentive.

Fuller and Calley engaged in small talk as they slow walked to the drug store. Their walk this time didn't accommodate any holding of hands or sweet talk. Upon reaching the soda fountain, they seated themselves at their favorite booth in the rear. Fuller found it hard to get a meaningful conversation started. Calley listened with a long face, making it harder for him to break the ice. They first engaged in casual chitchat which rapidly led to the moment of truth. He watched carefully for the right moment to ease the veracity of his excuse into the mix. It was an awkward moment in time. If he could apply himself in the natural and not get uptight, maybe he could present a reasonable case she could believe and forgive.

"Baby," he led with. "I have no idea how to begin, but what you are about to hear is the God's honest truth. I'm deeply sorry for what I did—I beg you to believe what I am about to tell you and—and I sincerely ask for your forgiveness.

If the shoe were on the other foot, you would be where I am; so I'm asking you to be understanding and, please—please give me another chance, honey?

Don't honey me," she spit back at him.

"In the interest of fairness I would be understanding and give you another chance."

She listened, not saying anything, but let him simmer in his own juices.

"I have this physical problem," he started, "you know—I didn't want to tell you about it 'till I knew it was safe," he said, choosing the wrong words.

"You have a venereal disease?" she inferred, indignantly.

"No baby, it's nothing like that," he said. "This is very hard to put into words. Please bear with me on this. You see—I have—well, a type of dysfunction—sexually—and if—well, we were to do it—I would not be able to finish like you're supposed to, if you know what I mean."

"No, I don't know what you mean. You're saying you are defective and that was your excuse for patronizing a whore?"

"Man, this is getting tough," Fuller thought. He needed to continue knowing this may be his last opportunity to swing her around to his thinking. "I figured it would be unfair to be intimate with you until I could prove to myself it was no longer a problem. Don't you see?"

"What does that mean? I don't understand," she challenged. "What's that got to do with you calling on a prostitute?"

"Calley—this is very hard for me to put into words, especially with you," he said as he began to perspire.

"I'm all ears," she said, finding his defense total nonsense.

"A friend recommended a remedy," he said, referring to the peppermint oil. "I was desperate to find a solution before getting together with you. I needed to prove to myself that my problem was not destructive to our relationship. A hooker propositioned me on the street and I thought this was my chance to—Jeez," he said, knowing he was digging a deeper hole for himself to fall into. "Do I have to keep this up? Can't you understand and try to believe me?"

"Hate to tell you this, Fuller, but you're going to have to do a lot better than that to regain my trust."

"What's the use?" he surrendered. "Come on, I'll walk you home."

"That won't be necessary. I can make it by myself."

His defense was so cockamamy, she felt her dignity would be compromised if she allowed him the comfort of her sympathy. She was as disappointed as he not to resolve the situation and had no one to share her feelings with—not even her mother.

Fuller headed home completely drained and discouraged. He stepped inside a Catholic Church on his way, hoping to find peace. He sat in a rear pew for a long time and wiped tears from his eyes. When he emerged, he was somewhat calmer and temporarily at peace with himself, but he still felt the sharp edge of Calley's linguistic sword twisting in his gut. He might as well take Snake up on his offer to *es*-screw Lupe. He picked up the first thoughts that came to his head even the sarcastic ones. He knew he wouldn't mess with that bitch, if she was the last female on earth. Once home, he found sleep to be his best companion. He dozed off knowing if he could survive one minute at a time, he would eventually make it past his current circumstance with Calley, hopefully with positive results.

PART III

CHAPTER 25

▼

The Holiday Season

November was history and the first fifteen days of December vanished into a busy era of Christmas anticipation. With only ten shopping days left, Fuller and Milo found themselves in the middle of the holiday spirit without having satisfied their seasonal obligation to friends and family. Fuller accompanied Milo to the jewelry store to purchase Delores' Christmas present. He settled on a magnificent blue diamond friendship ring.

Fuller was coming to grips with his new found single status. He was finally reaching the point where he could pass Calley in the hall or walk past her desk without his innards twisting in knots. There were no prospects looming for a reconciliation. Every time he thought of her, he choked up, but was in less pain as the days dragged by. These were the impending holidays and not a good time to be alone without someone special to share Christmas. Milo continued to remind Fuller there were more fish in the sea and Fuller conceded that sometime in the future he would go fishing, but for now his heart ached for Calley and his feelings had to run the course and drain from his system naturally.

Milo had taken the liberty to fill Delores in on Calley's break up with Fuller so there would be no mystery of her being absence from group gatherings. She was saddened and expressed regret.

Milo shopped for the entire band including a gift for Alma. He asked Fuller if he wanted to go in jointly for her gift, but Fuller declined. He wanted to give her something special, for her to remember him by after he split the scene for college.

Fuller was inching out of the hole he had dug for himself and was slowly getting his life back. Milo and Alma were his closest friends and when he wasn't with them, he spent his time reading and evaluating colleges.

Lupe was still accosting him with her revolting propositions. She saw the strain on Fuller and Calley's relationship and was pleased with herself as the major contributor to their breakup.

Lupe was slow to catch on, but little by little was accepting the fact she had missed her opportunity to bed down with Fuller. She had pulled the rug from under him so hard, the memories of that night in the old filling station lingered bitterly within him and Anthony Wayne High was becoming too small for the both of them.

Fuller had become accustomed to spending time with Rico and Snake after school and considered his long walks home a welcome relief from the day's destruction on his peace of mind. As he drifted homeward, he had time for reflection and space for confronting the difficulties that plagued him.

*   *   *   *

Fuller went out Saturday by himself to do his shopping. He bought his mom and dad a present together. Milo's Harmon Wa-Wa mute for his trumpet had dents in it. He elected to replace it with a complete set of new mutes. He purchased a beautifully colored crystal parrot for Alma's present. It would be a permanent keepsake for remembrance of him. He didn't wont to leave anyone out. He thought of Miss Hatcher and then remembered Rico and Snake. He purchased her a weighted crystal name plate for her desk and for his reformed friends, a briefcase each with their names stamped in gold. leaf.

The ones left he wanted to buy for were Milo's sister and her husband. He had a professionally prepared 8x10 inch copy of Milo's poster from the photographer who snapped the picture and had it put in a nice frame to do it justice.

Fuller's mom was going to prepare another dinner for Fuller's crowd Christmas Day when Milo's brother-in-law put the kibosh on her good intentions. He had made reservations at the Anthony Wayne's main dining room for seven and insisted it was his turn to do the inviting as gratitude for their Thanksgiving invitation. Milo was squeamish about Fuller's mom and dad seeing him with Delores. She was, after all, their school teacher and knew all the parents of the pupils in her class. Fuller assured Milo that his mother and father were regular people and certainly not prudish. He would have a preliminary conversation with them ahead of time so there would be no surprises. His mother's response was "that's nice, dear. She's such a lovely young lady." His dad winked his approval and gave a thumbs-up, signifying "good for Milo."

*   *   *   *

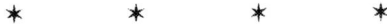

Fuller was the only member of Milo and Delores's inner circle who they trusted to keep their secret. He felt privileged to be included, but was envious of Milo for having a girlfriend like Delores. She reminded him in many way of Calley and he had trouble keeping his eyes off her. She cooked for Milo Christmas Eve and they invited Fuller.

Delores was a sight right out of a ladies magazine wearing a halter top with wraparound straps knotted in front. Her little body was cute in tight hip-hugger capri pants as she walked around her kitchen atop high heel mules.

Fuller reminded himself over and over how lucky Milo was to have such a lovely lady friend, but Milo didn't need to hear it from Fuller. He knew he had been blessed and wished something similar would happen for his buddy, Fuller.

Milo set the table and managed to slip Delores's present in her glass of iced tea. Both Milo and Fuller ate heartily and drank tea in huge quantities, hinting for Delores to drink and discover her gift. Finally she reached for her tea glass and spotted the ring before she could take a sip. She stood up, went to the kitchen sink and carefully poured the tea through her fingers until the diamond ring appeared safely in her palm. Turning around, she leaned back against the sink and slid it on the ring finger of her right hand. Then she held it up for the boys to see. "It's beautiful, darling!" She exclaimed to Milo. "Exquisite!" She took two long, rapid strides toward the table and leaped onto Milo's lap as he pushed back in time to make room for her. She passed her hand to Fuller for his inspection. Then turning back facing Milo, she wrapped her arms around his neck and planted a lengthy smooch on his lips, exclaiming, "it's beautiful, darling. Just be-u-ti-ful!" Suddenly, she restrained her enthusiasm, frowned and said sadly, "I could never accept this, baby."

"Why not?"

"It is too expensive."

"Not for you it isn't," Milo persisted. "It's my Christmas present to my girlfriend. Of course you can accept it."

"Oh, honey." Another squeeze of the arms around his neck, followed by another smack on his lips.

They exchanged Christmas presents followed by a round of thank *yous* and hugs. Time was running out on Milo. He had to leave for work. Delores stacked the dishes as she and Fuller were going to accompany Milo to the ballroom. They wanted to be on hand to toast each other a Merry Christmas at midnight. Milo divulged to Delores that every song they played that night would be a dedication to their relationship and especially to her.

Delores excused herself to get ready. She returned a few minutes later wearing a bright colored cocktail dress, becoming her dainty frame, and her signature high heels.

The ballroom was nearly full when they arrived. The diners had finished eating and the busboys were clearing the tables. Fortunately, no one was at Fuller's usual table, so he and Delores sat and waited for the music to start.

She kept admiring her ring. Fuller thought it was beautiful and befitting of Milo's lady friend. He also admired his friend's taste in women and his tenacity for staying the course to lasso his lady of choice. She looked so neat in her cocktail dress. It accentuated her natural beauty. Every now and then, Calley would cross Fuller's mind and he would have to shake her from his thoughts or let Delores see a grown man cry.

Alma came into the ballroom and took her place at the end of the bar. She saw Fuller with whom she thought was his new girlfriend and was going to slip over and introduce herself. As she approached Fuller's table, she observed a definite familiarity in Delores, but couldn't exactly place her. She decided to return to her place at the bar and avert the likelihood of an awkward situation. When Fuller saw her, he nodded and smiled, acknowledging her presence. Delores was admiring her ring at the time and didn't catch Fuller's gesticulation towards Alma.

*   *   *   *

The lights dimmed, the music started and the stage revolved to face the dance floor. The first number the orchestra played was *All of Me*. Fuller stood up and took Delores' hand. It was an invitation to dance. He helped her from her chair and they threaded themselves through the tables and other patrons to get to the dance floor. Jan Mulvahill's voice fused with the instruments, enriching her lyrics to a meaningful and sentimental inrush of collective memories, especially, *You took the part that once was my heart, so why not take all of me?* Fuller was unduly sentimental. He imagined himself with Calley as they danced. A tear dripped from the corner of his eye, but he concealed his pain by not looking directly at Delores. Milo sent a bottle of iced wine to their table while they were dancing.

When Fuller and Delores returned to their table, a waiter pointed out that Mister Munroe had complimented them with a carafe of wine. Fuller poured himself and Delores a glass of the fermented fruit juice and both held them up as a "thank you" gesture for Milo to see. He returned a wink accompanied by a nod as an acknowledgment, inferring to them, it was his pleasure. They clinked their glasses and toasted each other a Merry Christmas. Delores sipped her wine while Fuller, being inexperienced with alcohol ingestion, guzzled his. He poured himself another glass without having the slightest hint what it was about to do to him. The next slow number was the romantic *Time After Time*.

"May I have the pleasure of this dance?" Fuller asked, taking Delores's hand.

"You certainly may," Delores accepted, reflecting his jovial roll playing, not cognizant the alcohol was about to levy it's insidious toll on him.

At first Fuller's dancing was suitably responsive to the musical rhythm by normal sliding of the feet, but somewhere between normalcy and an inclining scale of silliness, he was capitulating to his first inebriation. Delores thought he was cute until she realized he was drowning beneath the sea of sobriety.

As they danced, she began to notice him invent his own tempo which was out of sync with the beat of the music. He dipped his shoulders deep to the right, then deep to the left, and his feet followed a scraggily pattern that only someone in his condition could improvise. Delores witnessed Fuller's excessive wine intake and his subsequent intoxication. He transformed from a sweet teenager, to a thing.

"Come on Fuller," Delores said. "You need to sit down. You've had a little too much to drink."

"You shank sho?" he said continuing his self configured three step—straining to tie his legs in knots. "Well I want to shay out here and dance shum-more with you, honey."

The number came to a convenient end saving Delores the prolonged embarrassment of having a drunk on her hands in the middle of the dance floor.

She managed Fuller back to their table and ordered him some black coffee. He stretched his arms out flat on the table and his eyes fixed in a glassy stare. When he looked up, he shook his head from side to side while gazing at Delores. "Man," he said. "Milo's lucky to have a chick like you. If I had met you first, would you have been my chick?"

"Come on, Fuller," she said. "We've got to get some black coffee down you."

"I jon't wan no coffee," he slurred, "and I jon't wan no black coffee. I jis wanna sit here and look at chew. Delores, you are one beautiful liddle lady an you smell so good. Boy, Milo is one lucky Sonny-Bish. I was lucky once. My lucky's name was Calley and she looked jis like you. You know that. She-uz ma gurl fren. Man, ju smell good. Gimme jour perfume—I'll dreenk it down right here without a tracer so I'll never forget how good you smell."

"Fuller, snap out of it!" Delores exclaimed. "You're attracting attention."

"Ittention! That's what ju want is ittention? Man—I'll give you ittention," he said. "Where is it? Where did all the ittention go? What were we talking about? Oh yes. We were talking about my lucky gurl fren having ittention. Did I tell you that I was in love with her? Well I was. Her name was Calley an she loved me back. Ju know that? Well she did, an' I don't have her anymore. Ain't that some shit. She flew the coop an here I am, all by myself at Christmas." His head fell and his forehead hit the tabletop with a loud thump. He was out cold.

Alma and her young assistant watched the goings on, but only left their post to go with a customer. Keeping her distance from Fuller's lady friend was the prudent thing for Alma to do, but she hurt for Fuller and wished she could go heal his agony and nurse him to sobriety.

Delores was past her embarrassment ministering to Fuller's limp drunkenness. Being familiar with his circumstance, she listened to all of his gibberish. She was also his friend. She knew he was in pain and she was troubled, seeing him this way.

The orchestra closed the dance with *I'll See You In My Dreams*. When the lights came on, Milo hurried down to Fuller's table. "I'm sorry, babe," he said to Delores taking Fuller off her hands.

"Don't feel sorry for me, honey," she said. "It is Fuller that needs your sympathy. Bless his heart."

"Bless his heart! I ought to kick his ass." Milo vented, realizing he had done the wrong thing by sending wine to their table and not taking into account the strongest thing Fuller had ever dipped into was iced tea or soda pop and maybe that glass of champagne at the Thanksgiving dance.

"Come on, Pal," he insisted as he wrapped Fuller's arm around his neck and lifted him to a standing position. "I'm going to take you bye-bye."

"Bye-bye," Fuller managed, lifting his head and waving to the people surrounding him

They took two steps and Fuller grabbed his mouth and his cheeks billowed. He tried to hold back, but gave in to a hurl that splattered the carpeted floor and drenched the top of his shoes and trousers with the Christmas Eve dinner Delores had cooked for them. Milo bolted backward trying to avoid being flecked by the nauseating splash, but was too late. His lower trousers and shoes caught an assortment of small, but stinky speckles of Fuller's vomit. Delores was lucky and missed it altogether.

A small group of janitors arrived from out of nowhere to cleanse and decontaminate Fuller's mess. Milo wrestled Fuller into the men's room and sponged down both their trousers and shoes removing the solid waste. There was nothing he could do about the prolonging stench.

Milo dropped Delores off first, out of courtesy, then proceeded to take Fuller home. Milo explained to Fuller's mom that he had a few too many glasses of wine.

"My poor baby," she said, trying to help Milo roll Fuller onto his bed while Bernard watched. "Do you think he'll be all right?" She asked as Milo removed Fuller's shoes.

"He just needs to sleep it off," Milo whispered as they tipped toed out of Fuller's room and eased the door shut behind them.

Fuller got out of bed the next morning, his two heads clanging together until they aligned themselves as one. His mother offered to fix him breakfast but he declined, saying he couldn't keep it down. She substituted a cup of strong black coffee instead.

"What time are we supposed to meet Milo and Doctor Powell for Christmas dinner, dear?" She asked.

The mention of food nearly disgorged Fuller again. "Oh God I forgot." He cradled his head in his hands and rested his elbows on the table. This was the day Milo's brother-in-law was taking his family out for Christmas dinner. The thought of food was too reminiscent of last evening. He would have to fake his way into the spirit of the occasion because right now he felt blah.

"Mom," he asked. "Do we have any alka-seltzer or tomato juice?" Someone had told him tomato juice and soda crackers were good for a hangover.

"Of course, dear, I'll fix it for you."

Fuller picked up the telephone and called Milo. "Hey man," he spouted. "I am so sorry about last night. I want to apologize."

"Not necessary," Milo assured him.

"Oh yes it is. It *is* necessary. I am *so* ashamed," he said trying to pull himself out of the hole he imagined himself to be in. "I was so obnoxious to Delores last night. I have to call and apologize to her. I've never been so ashamed or embarrassed in my life. What's her telephone number?"

"She's Okay with it, trust me."

"Trust you? That's Jewish for fuck you. Are you trying to tell me something?"

"Yes. I'm telling you she has no problem with you falling off the floor last night," Milo said, recollecting Fuller's vagary. "An apology is not necessary—Okay?"

"No, man. I've got to apologize to Delores in person. What's her telephone number, damn it?"

Milo gave him the number. "If it will make you feel any better, we can put Christmas Eve down as the day you got stink-O and make a tradition out of it."

That broke the ice and Fuller started to laugh. "Tradition—transmission—we are not doing anything to remember last night."

"You were quite a mess," Milo came back.

"What did I say to Delores?"

"Who knows," Milo said, "but believe me, if you said anything off color, she has forgiven you."

"Look buddy," Fuller persisted. "I have to call your girlfriend if you don't mind. I love her too much not to follow through and apologize for the way I acted."

"Good luck," Milo said. "Don't forget. The main dinning room at six."

"Don't you worry," Fuller said. "We'll be on time,"

After hanging up the telephone from talking with Milo, Fuller called Delores.

"Hello?" she answered sweetly.

"Miss Hatcher?"

"Yes?"

"I certainly want to apologize about my behavior last evening."

"Oh, it's you, Fuller," she said upon recognizing his voice.

"I am *so* ashamed. I know I was down right obnoxious and if I said anything to offend you, I am *so* sorry."

"Fuller, I don't know what you are talking about," she said. "I had a lovely time last evening. We'll do it again sometime."

"Thanks, Delores," he said, knowing this was her way of taking the burden off his shoulders for making an ass of himself. "I appreciate that," he said. "I know I don't deserve it."

"See you at six, then." she stated.

"At six," he said.

*   *   *   *

Doctor Powell had asked for a round table for seven so they could visit during dinner. His table was ready as the guests arrived. There was a glass of wine at each place setting, but Fuller yielded in favor of a glass of tomato juice with saltines on the side.

Milo's sister and brother-in-law were very liberal in their dealings with her sibling. Milo proved to be responsible in everything he did. His gentlemanly attitude and manners established his right of passage into adulthood and they approved of him dating Delores Hatcher, even if she was his homeroom teacher. Not only could he do a lot worse, but neither thought he could do better.

Doctor Powell clinked his glass with a utensil seeking everyone's attention as he stood up. "I'd like to make a toast," he said. "Here's to a Merry Christmas and a Happy New Year to each and every one of you."

"To a Merry Christmas and a Happy New Year," the crowd advanced in unison.

"Now to my brother-in-law, Milo and his lady, Delores. May the new year be a banner year in their young lives."

"Hear, hear," from the crowd.

"And to our good friend, Fuller Kreppe and his parents, who are with us this evening. Fuller, may your life be filled with every happiness and we ask you to stay in touch when you go off to college." Everyone cheered. Milo hollered, "he better."

He took that to mean "get on with your life and forget about Calley." He held his glass of tomato juice up and with a forced smile on his face, said, "thank you so much." He still had a few tortuous moments at the thought of Calley, but he managed to remain sturdy.

The hotel master chef had prepared a Christmas dinner on par with what the President at the White House was assumed to have. It was that special. When dinner was over, the party sat around the table visiting until it was time for Milo to go to the ballroom. Doctor Powell's guests left the dining room together and went across the lobby and through the entrance to the ballroom where three tables were pulled together near the stage and reserved in Milo's name.

Several of the band members and other employees came by to see if Fuller survived the previous night. One was the hotel detective that had asked him to leave his first night on the premises. In time, they had become friends. Fuller was more popular and well liked than he ever imagined.

Milo went backstage to make his preparation and tune up his instrument with the other band members.

Alma and her friend were on their stations at her end of the bar. Fuller would have liked to have visited Alma, but circumstances ruled against it. He was with his parents who wouldn't understand for one thing, and it was doubtful Milo's sister and brother-in-law were that liberal to allow Milo to associate with a prostitute. Delores wouldn't put up with it either. Fuller stole a side glance at Alma's assistant. She was pretty as he remembered from the night he nearly knocked her down on the sidewalk. If only she wasn't a hooker, maybe he could get interested in her. But she *was* a hooker and probably some kind of dumb ass like Lupe.

The band started to play and Milo's party took to the dance floor. They swapped partners and everyone had at least one dance with each other's significant other from the table. Fuller danced mostly with Delores except when Raymond felt obliged to do so. Fuller put on his best behavior and danced with Elaine during those occasions.

At intermission time, Milo came to the table with Phil Davenport. He made it a point to introduce Phil to Fuller's parents whom he had never met, then announced that Phil had some good news he wanted to share with everybody. They sat down as the guest prepared to listen.

"Phil," Milo said, extending an invitation for his superior to take over.

Phil lay his arms on the table, clasped his hands and thought for a moment of the best order to present the news he had for them.

"Well," he began. "As all of you know, Milo is a very talented young man. Eddie Vargus is opening a Jazz Club in New York City's, Greenwich Village, and there may be a place for Milo in his band." Everyone at the table applauded. "For those of you who are not familiar with Mister Vargus, he is a jazz guitarist. He was instrumental in putting the famous Wally Mann's Carnegie Hall Concert together. He is also a recording artist in his own right and is on his way to the top of his game. This could be a very rewarding opportunity for Milo to gain name recognition at this stage of his career. But that would require Milo moving to New York." A long subdued "Oohhh" smoked their table. "Mister Vargus has offered the job to a top flight cornetist, 'Buster' Buster. If he accepts, Milo has another option. The corporation is sending me on the road with a dance orchestra and has offered my position to Milo. If he so decides, he will headline this orchestra as Milo Star and who knows after that."

Those at the table were more supportive of this option. Seven people nearly brought the house down with applause. Delores smiled and clapped her approval toward her man. This was one of those special times she was extremely proud of Milo. So were Milo's sister and brother-in-law. Fuller also shared in Milo's glory. "Anyway," continued Phil, "he has time to make up his mind."

When it was time to leave, Milo and Phil Davenport returned backstage to get ready for the next set. The orchestra started off with their theme song as the stage revolved to face the dance floor. Phil Davenport took the microphone and announced a special treat for the fans this evening. "For the next hour, Milo's New Orleans Street Band is going to be featured, playing your favorite dixieland jazz tunes." This meant an hour of Doctor Powell's favorite musical idiom. He moved his chair to face the band stand, then leaned back, crossed his arms and was ready to enjoy the music.

"Milo is going to start this set off with Louie Armstrong's standard, *Strutin' With Some Barbeque*. Take it away Milo," Phil said as he repositioned the microphone on the stand in front of Milo and faded from the spotlight. The ballroom crowd was howling and stomping their feet as Milo's group kicked off the barbeque number. Doctor Powell was lost in the moment as his professional decorum took a back seat to the happy music and his uninhibited antics ruled as he absorbed the good time sound.

The band played *That Da-Da Strain, The Original Dixieland One Step*, and *Bourbon Street Parade* among other traditional favorites. When their time was up, the dance orchestra took over again to complete the musical complement for the evening.

CHAPTER 26

▼

The week between Christmas and New Year's was slow and boring. When Delores wasn't grading papers, she would join Fuller and take a position at what had become their usual table to listen to the music and be close to Milo. Mostly, Fuller and Delores would talk, but on occasion would take to the dance floor. Fuller, not really into dancing, had shuffled more the past few weeks than he had in his entire short lifetime. He was actually learning a few authentic dance steps from Delores. Milo would come down at intermission to be with his lady and best friend.

One evening she excused herself from Fuller to go to the powder room, Alma came by Fuller's table and hurriedly slipped him a note. She said, "I'll talk to you later." After viewing them together night after night and their interaction with Milo, she concluded the lady was there for Milo's interest and not Fuller's. The note was an invitation for Fuller to come to her New Year's Eve party at her house. He was glad because he had necessarily been ignoring her except when he could slip her a wink and a nod at opportune moments.

When Delores returned, she asked if she had missed anything. Fuller shook his head, no, then asked to be excused. As he passed the bar, he jerked his head slightly toward the lobby for Alma to meet him there.

He was partially shielded by a potted palm tree when she entered the lobby. They greeted each other with an embrace and kiss on the cheek.

"What's up stranger?" she asked, upon seeing him?

"How can I attend a party when I don't have the address?" he asked?

"Hell, we can take care of that," she said, opening her handbag and retrieving her checkbook. She ripped a blank check from the checkbook and handed it to him. "That should do it," she said. "All the info's there."

"I've missed you sweetie," she said. "You've been traveling in some mighty high cotton lately."

"I've missed you too, Alma," he said. "I'll make it up to you New Year's Eve, I promise. See you then." He returned to the ballroom to be with Delores.

That was a happy moment for both Fuller and Alma. Their short meeting had cleared the air, if there was any air to be cleared and they were again comfortable that their friendship was rock solid and surviving the seasonal festivities.

*   *   *   *

Milo and Fuller were visiting Delores at her apartment the afternoon of New Year's Eve.

Her telephone rang. She picked up the receiver to Charles Cagle, the P.E. Coach on the other end.

"I haven't seen much of you lately," he said, with the sound of someone setting a trap.

"You know," she said, "the holidays and getting ready for Christmas and everything—"

"Well here's your chance to make it up to me, honey. I have reservations at the 'Top Hat' tonight. Wha-da-you say,?" The Top Hat was a dive with a flashy neon marquee hanging out front and a curb cluttered with trash. It catered to the good time crowd and had to extinguish at least one tumultuous brawl every evening.

"C.C.," Delores said firmly. "There is something I have been meaning to tell you. I should have told you sooner, but haven't had the chance. I'm seeing someone else."

"What are you saying?" he asked, startled. "You dumping me for some other guy?"

"There is nothing to dump," she informed him. "We are good friends, that is all, and shall remain so."

"Aw come on, baby. You can break it this once, with that other guy. I saw you first."

"I'm afraid not," she said, demonstrating the integrity of her feelings for Milo. "I can't see you anymore, C.C., I'm sorry."

"I see," he said. "I'm not good enough for you, is that it?"

"I didn't say that," she returned. "Those are your words, not mine."

"Wahl, if that's the way you feel about me, s c a–r u e you." His words acutely reviled Delores. She wasn't accustomed to such verbal abuse. "I won't have any trouble finding someone to flange up with ME,baby" he continued, before slamming the receiver down cutting her off.

Delores looked at Milo and Fuller. "I'm glad that is taken care of," she said.

The guys could tell what was going on and listened to her explanation before giving each other a high five. Milo was glad he wouldn't have to see this guy's puss in her classroom anymore. He opened his arms and Delores came flying into them. Her lower legs hinged tightly upward at the knees as she squeezed her arms around his neck. She was happy that she was free of the coach. Delores was so relieved. She looked tenderly into Milo's eyes."I love you," she said. "I really do. I love you honey." She followed her assurance with a, lengthy, meaningful kiss.

*   *   *   *

Fuller took a temporary hiatus from the New Year's Eve blow out at the ballroom so he could attend Alma's New Year's Eve party.

"Wish her a Happy New Year for me," Milo said.

"Anything else, Master?" Fuller asked.

"No. Just tell her to keep her hands off you."

"Get out!" Fuller exclaimed. "It's you she's after."

Fuller followed Milo to Delores's apartment to wish her a Happy New Year.

She was nearly finished applying her makeup, when they arrived. She had made a little pitcher of virgin eggnog to toast the New Year. When she opened the door to let them in, they saw in her an unbelievable ornament of subtle culture and refinement. Milo was so proud of her and content with himself for choosing her as his steady. She poured three small snifters of eggnog and they toasted the New Year. Turning to Fuller, she said "Milo tells me you are not going to be with us this evening."

"Just for a short time," he said.

She walked over and gave him a light peck on the lips. "Happy New Year, dear," she said.

Fuller felt her "light peck" all the way down through his toes. "Happy New Year to you, Lady, Really to both of you," said Fuller as he put the empty snifter down and left for Alma's party.

*   *   *   *

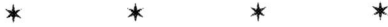

Fuller thought Alma's place looked familiar. He rang the door bell and a room full of people yelled a reverberating "come on in, the door's open." The symphony of echoes penetrated the door. It felt like the booming sound dislodged the wax from his eardrums. He opened the door to Alma making her way through a crowded, smoke-filled room to greet him. She gave him a big hug and kissed him on the cheek. "Happy New Year, honey," she said.

Happy New Year to you and a belated Christmas," he said, handing his gift to her. She opened it then and there and saw this piece of colored crystal shaped like a parrot. She could see it was fairly expensive. "Oh honey, you shouldn't have."

"Nothing's too good for you, Alma," Fuller said.

"Come on in and I'll introduce you around."

He walked into the living room and almost straight into Lupe. Alma wrapped her arm around Lupe's shoulder. "Fuller," she said, "I would like for you to meet my daughter Lupe." He remembered why the house looked so familiar. It was here he parted company with Lupe the night of the semi-affair at the old filling station. Fuller distinguished the opposing features in the frame structure of mother and daughter. There was as much difference as night and day. Lupe must resemble her father, he decided. She was short and frumpy while her mother was a statuesque thirty something with a pretty face. He remembered the hooker that night at the ballroom saying "there was something else that she couldn't tell him." This, he concluded, is what she was alluding to.

"Mister Kreppe and I know each other," Lupe said, cutting her mother short and hoping to gain some impetus with Fuller since this unimaginable circumstance brought them together. "We are in the same home room."

"I didn't know that. Well that's wonderful, dear" Alma said. "I'm glad you two know each other. You show Fuller around while I go check the oven and get more punch ready." Then it dawned on Alma. Putting two and two together, she remembered the lady always sitting at Fuller's table at the ballroom. She was Miss Hatcher, Lupe's home room teacher. *Shit!*, She thought. *Milo's dating his school teacher.*

Alma pulled Fuller aside and asked if she was correct in assuming Milo was dating Miss Hatcher.

This was an awkward moment for Fuller. Whatever he said, he needed to speak normally and be discrete. "Alma, I've got to be honest with you. Miss Hatcher is Milo's sister's best friend. You see—Milo is on probation and she's keeping an eye on him for his sister while she works the night shift, at least until his probation is over."

"Oh, I see," Alma whispered, anticipating a scoop. "What's he on probation for?"

"Something to do with yielding right-of-way, contempt of court or some such shit," Fuller said, purposefully uncertain to avoid being caught in a trap down the line.

"Really? When will his probation be up?"

"Sometime after graduation," he answered. "Please do not tell anyone, including Lupe. If this gets out, it might damage Milo's reputation and keep him from graduating." Fuller hated not being truthful with Alma, but he was dedicated to protect Milo and Delores at all cost. He concluded if Milo made it until the end of the school year, it would be too late for gossip aimed at him and Delores to hurt them in any way. Hopefully, any charges the school board could consider against Delores would be nullified if her secret with Fuller was discovered.

She assured him that Milo's secret was safe with her and that "mums the word."

He didn't believe he was capable of making such a dumb excuse; but what the hell, if it worked for just a few more months, Milo and Delores would be home free. He wondered how many more lies he would have to tell to validate this one? He was wasting his time here and would rather be at the ballroom sitting with Delores, enjoying the music. There he would be among friends instead of being caught in this morass of porcupine needles, Alma excluded.

Lupe honed in on Fuller after circulating amongst her friends. She held out her hand for shaking. "Let's call a truce. What do you say?" she besought.

Fuller looked at her with disbelief and made no attempt to take her hand. "There's no need for a truce," he said. "You're the only one with a problem. I'm not at war with you or anyone else. I don't play that shit, but I do make it a point to stay away from you."

"Okay buster, if that's the way you want it," she said spitefully.

Just then, Snake came in from the kitchen. When he saw Fuller, he rushed over and grabbed him. "Hey, everbody! This here's my best friend, Mister Fooler."

Somebody yelled, "I thought Rico was you best friend?"

"Him too. If anybody mess wid dis guy, he's gonna have to answer to me an RRRico first. You know what I'm saying?"

Rico appeared from the kitchen. "Hey, Amigo," he yelled, when he saw Fuller. "Happy New Year."

"Yeah! Yeah! An a Happy New year," mouthed Snake, remembering why they were there.

Fuller was basking in more negative enjoyment than he could comfortably ingest at the moment. *Gee,* he thought. *What the hell am I doing here?* He remembered why he was there; Alma had invited him.

His association with this crowd had a smothering effect on him except for Alma. Next to Milo, she was his best friend and he knew her heart.

Snake pulled him aside and offered to "fix him" up with any girl at the party. Lupe kept her distance feeling poochy lipped with hurt feelings. All the while she kept giving Fuller the evil eye. He was ill at ease and felt like going over and kicking her in the ass.

The hooker Fuller had his affair with, walked in from the kitchen area stuffing her mouth with cookies. She spotted Fuller across the room. Approaching him from the rear, she capped her sticky fingers over his eyes.

"Guess who, baby," she spoke.

"I give up," he said.

"Don't you want to guess?"

"The Virgin Mary?" Fuller answered facetiously.

"Silly boy," she said, dropping her hands. "It's me and I'm not a virgin and my name ain't Mary," she bragged.

He turned around and was disenchanted at the sight of her. She offered him food and drink and another chance to be with her, but he declined and broke away politely with the excuse to search for Rico. When he was satisfied he was free of her, he forgot about Rico and started mingling with the crowd.

When he decided he'd been around long enough to depart without hurting Alma's feelings, he found her and announced he had to leave so he could get up early and go with his dad. It was another untruth, of course He had no plans with his dad, but he had to get the hell out of there and back into civilization or risk going bonkers. He thanked her for inviting him and assured her he had had a grand time.

Grand time, my ass, he thought, as he arranged himself comfortably in the driver's seat of his father's car. He returned to the ballroom in time for the New Year's celebration. Was he ever glad to see Delores? She gave him a pointed hat and a noise maker. At exactly midnight the band played "Auld Lang Syne" and balloons of different colors rained from the ceiling, intermixed with confetti. The guests blew their tin horns and rattled their noise makers in concert with each other. He and Delores gave each other a Happy New Year's kiss and the cheers from the audience prompted a thirty minute encore from the orchestra. When the lights finally came on, Milo joined them.

"Happy New Year," He saluted Delores with a hug and a kiss and Fuller with a handshake.

"Let's go by the diner for some coffee," Fuller suggested. "I have a news flash."

Milo followed Fuller to the all night diner with Delores snuggled close by his side.

"What's up, pal?" Milo asked when they were seated in a booth.

"Alma knows you two are dating," Fuller informed them.

"Who is Alma?" Delores insisted.

"Hang onto your hat," Fuller alerted Delores. "She's your prize student's mother."

"You and Milo are my prize students," Delores winged it. You must be speaking of some one else,"

"Lupe Alonzo." Fuller said.

"Let me get this straight," Milo asked. "Lupe is Alma's daughter?"

"That's what I'm saying."

"Who'd a thunk it?" Milo joked, then he started to laugh. "I would have never guessed it," he said, cranking up the tempo of his response to Fuller's scoop.

Delores put it together. Alma looked familiar to her the first day she saw her at the ballroom. *Of course, that is whom they are speaking of,* she thought. "What if she causes a scandal about us?" Delores asked Milo.

"We are down to five months left in school," Fuller said. "If we can keep you guys camouflaged until then, you'll have it made." He went into detail about the lie he told Alma and informed them Lupe knew nothing about their relationship and her mother promised to keep it secret from her. He added, "I trust Alma to keep her word."

Milo trusted her also and assured Delores their secret was safe with Alma. Then he congratulated Fuller for telling the biggest lie of the century and reminded Delores to keep her guard up and remember her part in this charade.

She wouldn't be amused if she was forced to tell a lie, but on the other hand, five months was a short span of time in the context of their future together. She could do it.

CHAPTER 27

▼

Fuller and Milo were coming into the home stretch of their senior year. The hours turned into days, the days into weeks and the weeks gave way to months until there were only two short ones left before graduation. Fuller remained loyal to his neophyte scholars, Rico and Snake. That was the major trait Miss Hatcher admired in Fuller. No one else she could think of was capable of raising their tedious levels of understanding to the point of their present day achievements, without giving up in disgust. He stuck it out and pulled it off. They were probably going to make it, if just by the skin of their teeth.

Rico and Snake were by now treating Fuller as if he had hung the moon. They even jumped a handful of school yard punks for calling him dumb ass and making reference to him being full-o-crap and bragging about it. They prevailed and threw each other a high five, each time thereafter, at the mere mention of the incident.

The senior prom was on the horizon and those who weren't going steady were scrambling to land the flavor of the month as their date for the occasion. Fuller didn't have a date and if he went at all, it would be to see who Calley went with. As with a death wish, he was bent on torturing himself with Calley's affairs that didn't concern him. He supposed he could leave at any time and head for the ballroom should he become bored or depressed at the sight of Calley with another guy. Milo had no plans to attend and was glad of it. He would rather be leading his orchestra at the ballroom which would be advanced to him by the time of the prom. Delores was obligated to be at the prom as a custodian because of her position on the faculty.

*   *   *   *

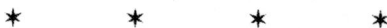

The English teacher, Mrs. Rhodamy, had given her class a last semester assignment. They were instructed to write a minimal 1,500 word, *original* allegory. She emphasized originality and asked it be turned in three weeks prior to graduation. She added, "the pupil with the most original story will have the privilege of coming up front and reading it before the class."

"There is always someone fucking with you," Milo complained to Fuller. He thought they were *past all that essay writing crap*. Milo was adamant. "She can take that allegheny shit or whatever the hell she called it and stick it up her ass."

"That's my boy, Milo," Fuller clowned. "Give em' hell."

"Shit!" Milo nailed the assignment emphatically. "There is no way I am going to write a 15,000 page anything." He had moved up from typical bitching to a tirade.

"It's 1,500 words, honey," Fuller emphasized, "not pages."

"This is the fucking straw that broke the camel's back," Milo bitched again indignantly. "I quit," referring to high school in general and being around teenagers in particular. Then added, "And to think I was almost through with this fucking mess."

"Don't be so hasty, Harry James," Fuller admonished. "If it's originality, the teacher wants, it's originality she'll get."

"Why? What do you mean?"

"I mean, go toot your horn, Mister Armstrong and let me handle this. I can do 1500 words in my sleep."

"Are you suggesting you would write my allogony for me?" Milo razzed Fuller with dramatic roll playing.

"You know damn well that's what I'm suggesting," Fuller answered.

"But that's illegal. I could be called on the carpet for cheating" Milo came back, facetiously, still being theatrical,"and you could be called up as an accessory."

"Yea, I know," Fuller said, joining Milo's *bull shit* "One stipulation, though."

"What's that?"

"You have to copy it in your own handwriting so you'll know the story in case you get quizzed."

"But isn't that also illegal?"

"Why don't you ask somebody that gives a shit?" Fuller said.

"Thanks, pal," said Milo. "Your word is good enough for me. You know I'd do the same for you."

"I know," said Fuller, "when Mrs. Rhodamy kisses an alligator ass. You go on about your business and leave the rest to me. I've got too much invested in you for you to give up now. We probably need to keep this from Delores."

"We need to do that," Milo agreed.

*   *   *   *

Fuller introduced Rico and Snake to the definition of an allegory and instructed them to write at least a nine-page story each, which should reach the 1,500 word minimum requirement. They needed an example to the meaning of the word, allegory. Fuller tried over and over to get the meaning across to them. He said, "Look, the United States flag is a symbol of our country. A policeman is a symbol of authority. This high school is a symbol of education and so forth. An allegory," he explained, "is an expression or instance of symbolism." After drawing many verbalized pictures, he finally got the message across to them.

Mrs. Rhodany slipped this allegory in on the class after they thought they were through with assignments. This hurt Rico and Snake more than anyone else. Fuller assured them they could do it. He would check their allegorys to insure they were written well, hopefully for a passing grade. He would see they had plenty of time to make any necessary corrections. Fuller had the feeling this was not entirely in line with the dos and don'ts of the school district's policies, but what the hell, these guys were his charges and he was given the responsibility to push them through the school system. If anyone had doubts, just ask Mrs. Hatcher. She was a school official and entrusted Rico and Snake to Fuller with instructions to help them out of their rut and onto the high ground. This, he had accomplished; school policy or otherwise. He confided in Rico and Snake, making them promise to keep their mouths shut, regarding the extent of his help through the allegories. This confidentiality endeared Fuller more to his two out-of-step characters.

Fuller then proceeded to write two nine-page stories over the weekend, one for Milo and one for himself. When he gave Milo his allegory to read, Milo read through it carefully and died laughing from start to finish. "Man," he said to Fuller, "this is some weird shit. Where'd you come up with this?"

"You heard Mrs. Rhodamy say the key word here is originality," Fuller said. "Tell me, that's not original."

"Why don't you do it over again using a mutated woman as the mother. You could put her tits between her legs and let the baby suck her off when she was hungry. Now that's originality."

"You're crazy, man," Fuller commented. "You want your paper to be accepted, don't you?"

"I'm not so sure," Milo said.

Fuller laughed out loud and threatened, "Let's show it to Delores and get her opinion."

"Now you're trying to get me in trouble."

"Not really," Fuller said. "I just want your head on straight so we can use what we've got. It's more subtle that way and time will not run out on us."

"Subtle my ass. It's not as original as mine."

"Go with the story as it is, damn it," Fuller ordered. "You'll win the prize."

"Yeah, right. I'll either get thrown out of school on my ass or win the *Pulitzer* prize for foolishness." They broke into a mild laughter at first that gained intensity by gradual increase until they were roaring so hard their giggle boxes broke. They wound up coughing, sighing and hiccupping every time the story Fuller referred to as Milo's allegheny revitalized their giddiness. They had a hard time breaking away from the hysteria brought on by uncontrollable laughter. They moved around the floor in odd patterns, bumping into each other and throwing their heads back in self-sustaining guffaws. They wound up, face to face, supporting each other, stiffed armed with their hands gripping each others shoulders and tears streaming down their cheeks. Each time they calmed down to a normal straight face, one would crack up and the other, unable to contain himself, would shatter his own peace with uproarious, tearful convulsions. Finally, after many false starts at simmering down, their outlandish laughing attacks eased off to sore ribs and fatigue.

"Yeah, and just think, you'll get to read it in front of the whole damn class," Fuller reminded Milo.

"I don't think so," Milo said, cracking up again into a side splitting testimony to Fuller's genius. He pushed on his ribs to minimize his pain.

"You can do it, Gabriel. It'll give you fame on another level besides tootin' your horn."

"Just what I need," Milo said. They started up again and wore themselves out from the habitual hysterics of the now painful hilarity.

*   *   *   *

Miss Hatcher sat in the faculty meeting where decisions were being made concerning the senior prom. Mrs. Holt, a fat lady high school principal with a three-hair mole on her chin, nominated the Mad Anthony Wayne Country Club as the place the prom should be held and recommended a popular band to play for the occasion. The country club was named after the famous Revolutionary War General, and a fitting place to pass the graduates, from their celebration of young adulthood into *World class winners like General Wayne*. The faculty members considered it wise to yield to Mrs. Holt's endorsements and voted for the country club and the recommended band. With these important items settled, preparations for the prom began. Some students volunteered for assignments to help make the auditorium ready for the big dance.

C.C. was trying to get Miss Hatcher to go with him. The last time they spoke on the telephone, his rudeness provided Delores with the leverage to deny him the privilege of ever dating her again. She turned him down flat.

He started parking across the street from her apartment to keep an eye on her activities. He thought he saw her leave attached to the arm of someone who looked very familiar. As they advanced, it became clear *that* someone was one of her pupils. He wasn't going to let her get away with this disregard of propriety. Consequently he reported her to Mrs. Holt.

Subsequently Miss Hatcher was called into the principal's office.

Mrs. Holt was sitting stiffly at her desk with her fingers locked together when Miss Hatcher entered.

"Please have a seat," Mrs Holt said to Miss Hatcher.

Miss Hatcher looked to the right of Mrs. Holt's desk for a chair and her eyes met with those of C.C. Cagle. The expression on his face resembled what she surmised to be the *shit eatin' grin* she had heard mentioned in other people's conversation.

She elected to sit across the room, having no idea why she was there, but certain it had something to do with C.C. Cagle and his bent for revenge.

"Miss Hatcher," the principal was noncommittal—"Mister Cagle has levied a grievance against you. In the interest of fairness, I wanted you here to face your accuser. Mister Cagle, please begin."

"Wahl—" he drawled. "I've always tried to do the right thing."

Bull shit, Miss Hatcher thought. Her vulgarity was influenced by Milo and Fuller's sophomoric profanity and conformed to the social acceptance of modern society, otherwise she was too proper to even think it.

"I'm not here to cause trouble," Cagle said. "I'm just acting on my responsibility as a faculty member to report any breech of propriety I happen to come across."

Oh boy, Miss Hatcher thought. *What's he up to now?*

"And that is—" Mrs. Holt allowed, the hairs on her chin mold twitching.

"Well, like I say, I'm not here to cause trouble, but I was driving by Miss Hatcher's apartment the other day and saw her walking down the sidewalk in the company of one of her students. I don't believe I know his name."

"Miss Hatcher?" Mrs. Holt faced her direction. "What do you say for yourself?"

"It is very simple," Miss Hatcher replied, implementing Fuller's excuse to Lupe's mother. "If he is speaking of Milo Munroe—his sister is my best friend and she has asked me to watch over him on the evenings she works so he won't abuse his probation."

"He is on probation?" Mrs. Holt questioned, surprised, "and you are baby sitting. Have I got this right?"

"Something like that," Miss Hatcher answered. "His sister and I help each other out."

"Do you know why he is on probation?"

"He had an altercation or something—Er—I don't know exactly," She avoided being specific like Fuller was with Alma in the event she had to give more thought to answer this charge at another time.

"I see," said the principal. "Do you have anything further to say, Mister Cagle?"

He wasn't going to let her off this easy. He knew what he saw, but what else incriminating was there to say without sounding vindictive and forfeiting another chance to nail her buns to the chalk board? "Not for the moment," he hesitated, trying to sort through her excuse. When it became apparent he was stymied, the meeting came to an abrupt finish with Mrs. Holt thanking them both for coming.

Delores couldn't wait to tell Milo and Fuller how she had won big over her former suitor. She had her chance that evening when the three of them were together. She told them of the risk she took in the principal's office earlier that day. They were as proud of her as she was of herself and they shared a three-way high five. Telling a white lie saved her ass this day and may continue to do so in the future. It didn't feel bad either. She struggled with the ethics of how she handled the situation and asked herself, *Would it have been better to have told the truth and lose her job?* Prevarication was contrary to everything she believed and every moral issue she tried to instill in her pupils since she began teaching. Right or wrong, the benefit of lying, in this instance, was without question, the only thing to do if she wanted to keep her job. She tried to imagine anyone else in this situation telling the truth and surviving unscathed. She couldn't.

*   *   *   *

The entertainment section of the WAYNESFORD DAILY HERALD featured a half page splash on the orchestra at the Anthony Wayne Hotel, now under the Baton of MILO STAR and his Golden Trumpet. There was a large picture of Milo with a baton in one hand and his horn in the other, fronting his new orchestra. His face was turned toward the camera. He was sporting a broad smile that featured a chiseled image like a permanent fixture from birth that never left his face.

*   *   *   *

His secret association with the orchestra was out of the bag. When he walked the halls at school, the students and faculty both stared, mumbled to each other and got out of his way. He felt the privilege of being awed by others, but wasn't fond of being avoided like he had the plague. He was caught between the two realities and would have liked the introspection to know which was being thrust upon him at any given time. The truth of the matter smacked him across the forehead. It didn't matter. Either was a no win situation.

*   *   *   *

Cagle saw the spread in the Herald and decided this might be his chance to catch Delores in an indefensible lie. He started watching her activities after school hoping to corroborate his initial argument before the principal.

Delores, knowing Cagle, was automatically put on notice that he may raise his ugly head and tag her at anytime. Her choices were to quit seeing Milo until he graduated or take her chances and risk the consequences. The choice was easy to make. She was not going to give up seeing Milo for anybody. As a safety net, if this charge filed against her by C.C. were to get nasty, she could always quit teaching for a while and go back to Purdue to get her masters degree. She decided to stick by her original justification of protecting Milo from probation violations and let the chips fall where they may. She called an emergency meeting with Milo and they met at a diner in the vicinity of the hotel. Their favorite place in any public facility was to find a table or booth distanced from other patrons. She explained Cagle's possible interference with her and Milo seeing each other and asked Milo what they should do?

Milo thought a moment, then said, "Let me confront the silly bastard and take him out with a karate chop."

"Be serious," she said.

"I am serious," he returned with a tinge of sarcasm in his voice.

"We are not going to do anything like that," she admonished. "You are better than that. I've decided to stick by Fuller's story. What do you think?"

He looked into the natural sparkle of her eyes and said, "You are so beautiful, I think I'm dreaming. Pinch me," he said.

"Get serious," Delores said, discomforted by Milo's flippancy.

"I am serious," Milo argued. "I've never been affected by anyone in my life as I am by you."

"That's sweet, darling," she wrinkled her nose cutely and leaned forward giving him a light peck on the lips.

A flash bulb brightened the area and they looked up in time to see C.C. tucking a Polaroid camera inside his coat. "Let's see you get out of this one," he barked sarcastically as he bolted toward the door.

Milo started after him, but Delores held him back. "Let him go," she said. "If he makes something out of this and my excuse won't hold up, our worries will be over. Besides, I've thought about it, honey; If he gets me fired, I'll get my masters degree and teach somewhere else or maybe become a principal and have him working for me."

CHAPTER 28

▼

The student body was excited over tomorrow's big night at the country club. Preparation for the prom was advancing at full speed. C.C. Cagle brought his instant photograph of Miss Hatcher's peck on Milo's lips into the principal's office and registered a formal complaint with Mrs. Holt. He flung it on her desk with a snap of his wrist and said, "See, I told you."

Mrs. Holt picked it up, studied it for a moment, then said, "My, my. This can be serious. What do you think we should do?"

"Wahl—" Mister Cagle said. "I don't want to cause anyone no trouble, but the punishment should fit the crime. You know, as an example to the rest of us, but I don't want to be the one to say it." He was trying to frame his complaint as a reflection of his Mister-Nice-Guy character while suggesting that the suitable thing for the school board to do was to throw the book at her. He was trying to have it both ways.

Mrs. Holt asked him, "Aren't you and Miss Hatcher more than just good friends?"

"Oh, yes. We are very close," he said.

"I see," Mrs. Holt said. She saw jealousy intermixed in his motive for filing against Miss Hatcher. "Why would you file against a friend?" she wanted to know.

"You see, Mrs. Holt, right's right and wrong's wrong. I'm just trying to do the right thing for the school's honor. In other words, just doing my duty."

"Well," Mrs. Holt said, lifting from her chair. "We will take this matter under advisement and get back to you. Thank you, Mister Cagle for your loyalty to the school and concern for social graces." There was a cynical tone in her voice as she spoke.

*   *   *   *

The next morning during Miss Hatcher's free period, a runner from the principal's office informed her Mrs. Holt would like to see her in her office right away. She figured the jig was up and readied herself for the worse. The principal kept her eye out for Miss Hatcher and when she saw her coming, motioned her into the office.

"Good morning, Mrs. Holt."

"Morning, Miss Hatcher," the principal said. "Please have a seat."

"I saw Milo Munroe's picture in yesterday's newspaper. Did you happen to see it?"

"Yes, I saw it," Miss Hatcher answered.

"Isn't that just wonderful?" Mrs. Holt said. "One of our students doing something so progressive. He is such a lovely young man. I think he will go a long way," she said, "don't you?"

Miss Hatcher was momentarily relieved, but suspicious of what might follow the niceties.

Before she could answer, Mrs. Holt continued."Miss Hatcher, lets get right to the point. The reason I sent for you—"

Here it comes, Miss Hatcher thought.

Mrs. Holt was getting ready to lower the boom on Miss Hatcher when the telephone rang. "This is Mrs. Holt, the principal speaking," she answered. "How may I help you?…I see…I see…I see…You will have to do better than that," she said. "Tonight's the night of the senior prom. We have an agreement and I'm going to hold you to it…Well I don't care, you are responsible to provide a substitute if you can't hold up to your end of the agreement…I don't know why you are bothering me with this in the first place. You are the one with the problem— You are legally bound by contract…Well, if that's your attitude, I will just have to turn it over to the school board and let them dispose of it. No! We won't be needing your services in the future." She hung the telephone up in disgust.

She had just finished speaking with a representative from the talent agency that booked the band for the prom. They informed her, with regrets, the band contracted for, was quarantined with the mumps and would not be attending this evening's school function. He also stated it was highly unlikely a substitute band could be booked on such short notice, again, with regrets, but was asked to keep them in mind for future entertainment needs.

What started out to be a downward spiral to Miss Hatcher's position on the faculty actually neutralized her standing with Mrs Holt. Mrs. Holt was also neutralized from a position of power to one of near hysteria. Her chin whiskers, like antenna, were reaching out for rescue signals. Miss Hatcher sat there and watched while Mrs. Holt simmered.

The principal frittered with articles on her desktop attempting to regain self-control following the crisis that developed from the telephone call she had just exited. She had decided to dismiss Miss Hatcher for the moment and confront her with Mister Cagle's grievance at a more convenient time. Then, as though being splashed in the face with cold water, it came to her. Orchestra leader Milo Munroe was Miss Hatcher's student and who knows what else from Mister Cagle's photograph now in her possession. She was faced with the prospect of pleading with Miss Hatcher to use her influence over Mister Munroe to persuade him to provide music and rescue prom night.

"Miss Hatcher," Mrs. Holt said sweetly. "You know the senior prom is tonight?"

"Yes, I know," Miss Hatcher replied.

"A major problem has developed regarding the prom. I think we need your assistance."

"Anything," said Miss Hatcher.

"Do you think Mister Munroe, or is it Star?"

"Munroe."

"The band we had contracted for tonight is quarantined with the mumps and we don't have any music for the prom. That wouldn't make for a memorable prom night for our boys and girls now, would it?"

"I'm sure it wouldn't," she said.

"Let's see," said the principal, pretending to be looking through a batch of papers for something relevant to prom night. She flicked Cagle's latest complaint with the Polaroid picture of Miss Hatcher and Milo kissing onto her desk in a way that Miss Hatcher would be sure to see it.

"Why is it you can never find anything when you want it?" She was using her feigned search as an excuse until she was certain Miss Hatcher had seen Cagle's grievance.

When she was satisfied Miss Hatcher had sufficiently digested the grievance, she reached for it and said, "What is this?" She picked it up and observed it as though seeing it for the first time. "This is ludicrous," she said, referring to the grievance in general. She wadded it up being careful not to crease the picture and threw it in the waste basket." Mister Cagle knows you were acting on Mister Munroe's sister's behalf," she said. She was hoping Miss Hatcher got the message. *If you scratch my back, I'll scratch yours.*

Miss Hatcher just sat there waiting for what was coming next.

"Miss Hatcher—" Mrs. Holt hesitated, "I'm forced to call on you for help. Do you think there is anyway Mr. Munroe, would let us use his orchestra for the prom tonight?"

Miss Hatcher was shocked. She was being bribed outright by the principal of the high school. She got the message loud and clear. The school needed her help and paved the way to receive it by discarding Cagle 's grievance against her. The only problem was, Milo was committed to the hotel and this might prove to be a situation beyond his control.

"Only he can make that decision, Mrs. Holt. Let me talk to Mister Munroe and see what he can do. I will get back with you," she said.

"Let me remind you, we are running short on time," the principal warned.

"I know," Miss Hatcher said, getting up to leave the office.

"Thank you so much, Miss Hatcher, for your diligence in helping our school through one of the year's most serious crisis," the principal said.

Miss Hatcher had just been harpooned into an obligation she had to deliver on, or else. The Polaroid photograph was still in the principal's waste basket.

She stopped by the student desk to get Milo's schedule and sent a runner to have him report to her room immediately.

"What's up, Miss Hatcher?" Milo winked, as he entered her classroom.

"Come sit down," she said. "I have some good news and some bad news. The good news first. We will never have to worry about Cagle again if we can accommodate the bad news."

"And the bad news is—"

She went into detail about the band with the mumps.

Milo laughed aloud. "Maybe if we all had the mumps, we could really stir up some prom night jitters."

"Milo, please," she tried to appeal to his better judgement. "This is our chance to be free of the coach's intimidation. Lets not foul it up. Pleeease."

He thought for a moment how to avoid the crisis. "Okay," he said. "If it's up to me to rescue Old Anthony Wayne High, I can put something together, but only because you asked me."

"But aren't you required to be at the ballroom tonight?"

"Here's what I know I can do," Milo said, assuming he had the solution to the school's predicament. "I need my rhythm section," he said, "but I'll pull a man from each section of the orchestra and call the union for a piano, bass and drummer and *voila*, Ol' Anthony Wayne High will have their band."

"Sweetheart," she said as her eyes twinkled in his direction, "you never cease to amaze me."

"I'm an amazing fellow," he said.

"You'd better return to your class before I put you on report," she feigned authority over him. It sounded official, but it was tied to her reverence for her Milo. On the way out, he blew a kiss in her direction.

✳   ✳   ✳   ✳

She returned to the principal's office with the good news. "We girls gotta stick together," Mrs. Holt said as her way of thanking Miss Hatcher and tacitly assuring her secret with Mister Munroe was safe.

✳   ✳   ✳   ✳

Milo wasted no time getting in touch with his brother-in-law, Doctor Powell. "Hey Ray—Milo. Your dream has just come true."

"How much?"

"Nothing like that," Milo said. "How would you like to lead a band tonight?"

"Why do you ask? I'll do it." He thought a moment, then said, "Wait a minute. I'm a doctor, not a band leader."

"Just stand there and wave a stick. That's all there is to it," Milo said. "I'll fill the guys in on the gig. They'll know what to do."

Milo reported to his brother-in-law over the telephone of the happenings at school. Then he went to the principal's office. He asked Mrs. Holt for, and received permission to take rest of the day off to get the band together and coordinated. He would headline the orchestra at the ballroom while Doctor Powell led the band at the prom for a lark. With Milo at the ballroom, C.C. would have nothing suspicious to append to Miss Hatcher.

*　　　*　　　*　　　*

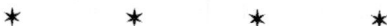

The students were starting to fill the hall at the Mad Anthony Wayne Country Club. The girls were pretty in their new dresses and the boys handsome in their rented tuxedos. The hors d'oeuvres table was surrounded by early arrivals.

Rico and Snake arrived on the scene wearing tuxedos from the twenty's era with tiny moth holes showing, but neatly pressed. Their trousers were hiked up over white socks. They were a sight, provoking snickers amongst some of the better dressed students. There were no outright derogatory comments or laughs that would turn the festive occasion into a free-for-all.

The band was on stage setting up and tuning their instruments. They were slated to start at eight o'clock. Milo had reached an understanding with the union musicians for Doctor Powell's collaboration in the evening's charade. No one questioned if his participation violated any union codes, nor did anyone know specifically what the codes were. The fellows from the ballroom orchestra were already acquainted with the doctor and knew that he was Milo's brother-in-law. They were tuned and ready to begin on time.

Mrs. Holt took to the microphone on stage and asked if she could have everyone's attention for a moment. "I would like to welcome everyone to this year's Anthony Wayne High School Prom Night. Let's hear it for the Generals," she signified, alluding to their team nickname. Applause! And more applause! "Are we having a good time?" More applause, this time with rambunctious affirmatives. "As some of you may not be aware, our regularly scheduled band was quarantined with the mumps and couldn't join us here tonight." A mixture of disappointment and funny gestures rumbled through the hall. "We have Miss Hatcher to thank for coming to our rescue." More applause. "As most of you know by now, her homeroom student, Mister Milo Munroe, leads an orchestra at the ballroom of a downtown hotel. Miss Hatcher was kind enough to persuade Mister Munroe to arrange for the band we have here tonight." There was applause from the students on the floor and bows from members of the band standing on stage. "Next, students, it is very important to refrain from bringing alcoholic beverages on the premises. Conduct of this nature will not be tolerated. Remember we are here to have a good time and to culminate twelve years of hard work and accomplishments with this celebration. What we do here tonight will reflect on every aspect of our lives tomorrow. Now without further adieu, I turn the activities over to Doctor Raymond Powell and his wonderful band."

Before he could finish raising his baton, the band started without him, playing their first number. He looked over his shoulder at the dancers and smiled as he remembered the expressions of Phil Davenport and began waving his baton in time with the music.

Snake and Lupe were dancing together as were Rico and his date. Calley was there with a pimply faced kid that, by comparison, complemented Fuller's average looks. Miss Hatcher was on the side lines with other members of the faculty viewing the activities. Cagle approached her to let bygones be bygones and requested she dance with him. She refused. He found Mrs. Holt and asked how she was coming with his grievance against Miss Hatcher. She informed him, it was on her agenda. She didn't say when, but even she knew that after the upcoming graduation, it would be a moot point. She had already trashed his only proof, the Polaroid picture. Without that, Miss Hatcher's excuse of monitoring Milo's probation, would prevail.

Fuller arrived halfway through the dance period. He stood on the sidelines and looked around. He noticed various attendees taking sips from whiskey flasks which were in direct violation to the principal's admonition. Lupe came to him and said, "This is your last chance, fellow. You'd better grab it while it's still hot." He ignored her and walked away. Finally his eye caught Calley on the dance floor with her date. He made his way through the crowd and tapped her date on the shoulder to cut in. The partner looked at Calley and she nodded, indicating that it was okay.

"How have you been?," Fuller asked as they rocked back and forth in a stationary side step.

"Fine, and you?"

"I'm okay, I guess."

"That's good, real good," she said. "How is your mother?"

"Oh, she's doing well, thank you, and yours?"

"Fine, she's doing just fine."

"Well, I guess you are enjoying yourself," he ventured.

"Oh yes," she answered. "Very much so."

"I assume you are going to college after graduation." he continued.

"Yes," she said. "I've been accepted at City College. What are your plans?"

"I'm enrolled at State U. as Nostradomus Kreppe. My dad likes me using my first name and I like it too." Both Fuller and Calley looked innocently shy at one another and chuckled.

You've earned it," she said, managing a smile.

Then their meeting careened downward. The vibes were not there. They needed more than conversation to return to the closeness they once shared. Time stopped momentarily and the magic they were searching for wouldn't spark. The music stopped and he led her outside the hall onto the veranda where they could be alone and continue probing for a workable solution. They were cordial to each other, but couldn't penetrate the depth of cordiality required to reach the compassion each sought from the other. Both became discouraged and frustrated by the impasse. Fuller prayed that she would find a way to accept his excuse and she prayed he would try again to come up with a less absurd defense. She was unable to forgive for the sake of forgiving. Neither prayer would be answered this night. The chasm in their relationship was too wide to bridge on the spur of the moment. Both wanted a little more time, but the evening was gaining past their hunger to reinstate their love. When time failed to yield the aspired results, Fuller reluctantly returned Calley to her date.

On his way out, he saw Rico and Snake at the punch bowl and decided to go hang out with them. Just as he reached the area they were standing, another guy showed up and asserted, "Well, what-do-you-know? It's Mister Dumb—" Before he could get the last word out, Rico grabbed him under one elbow and Snake under the other. They lifted him a couple of inches off the floor and proceeded to escort him out the side door. Fuller shook his head in amazement that the denigrating insults originated by Rico and Snake, were being vigorously upended by them on his behalf. He had won Rico and Snake over by his tenacity to help them graduate and they were just showing their appreciation and respect. He sauntered over to greet Miss Hatcher who had been keeping an eye on him and Calley. She could tell it didn't go well, by the dejected look on his face.

"I'm sorry," she said, feeling disappointment for him.

"It's okay" he said. "I tried. I think I'll head to the ballroom."

As he turned to leave, she grabbed his arm. "I'd go with you if I could," she said, reflecting her state of boredom. She wanted to be near Milo, but it was her duty to stay there as custodian.

"I understand," Fuller uttered, then left the prom and headed toward the ballroom where he could be with his friends.

CHAPTER 29

▼

Rico and Snake had given Fuller their allegories to inspect. He marked them up appropriately in hopes of getting them a passing grade. They proudly turned their papers in on the due date. Milo waited until everyone else had turned in their paper then approached the teacher's desk and turned his in.

A week and a half later, Mrs. Rhodamy passed her graded papers back to her students. Rico and Snake passed by the skin of their teeth. She handed Milo his and said "This is truly amazing, Mister Munroe—truly amazing." It was marked with an A plus. She returned to the front of the class and faced the students. "Mister Munroe," she continued, "you drew the black bean for originality. It is important to note that this story was nearly discarded without benefit of being graded because of it's content. After consulting with our principal, Mrs. Holt and other members of the faculty, it was decided that your allegory would be an acceptable exercise or study amongst young graduating adults. The value and validity of your allegory is questionable. You class, can make of it what you will. We wouldn't want to infringe on Mister Munroe's rights of free speech, now would we? Without further adieu, I present Mister Milo Munroe and his original allegory, 'A Thalidomide Story'. Let's give Mister Munroe a hand as we ask him to please come forward and read his allegory to the class?"

"Goddamn you son-of-a-bitch," Milo whispered to Fuller. "Thanks a lot?"

Fuller replied, "don't say I didn't warn you."

Milo slowly erected his frame from the side of his desk and strolled contemplatively toward the front of the room. Would he read his offering as a sad story or a funny one. He decided on being noncommital and straight forward. He turned around facing the class. He stood very erect and loosened his necktie.

"This is a story you should pay close attention to," he began, getting started on a neutral note. "The title is, *A Thalidomide Story* by Milo Munroe. The effects of some approved drugs can be very harmful," he began, "even dangerous. Take the drug Thalidomide, for example; it was usually prescribed as a sedative or hypnotic. It was prescribed by physicians with the most well meaning and noble intentions. Sometimes it was prescribed to young women in pregnancy who needed its benefit. Some women taking this drug in early pregnancy gave birth to babies with extreme malformations. Little Annie Hawkin's mother had taken Thalidomide when she was pregnant with little Annie. Annie was born with the most peculiar malformation ever recorded in the annals of medical history. She was born without nipples." The class snickered and looked around at each other for reaction. "The front of her biceps showed signs of little round birthmarks that grew to resemble nipples by the time she reached the tender age of nine. They were inverted and popped out only when she tensed her muscle. Releasing the tension caused them to snap back into her biceps." The snicker was louder this time. "To cover this oddity, she was forced to wear blouses with elbow length sleeves. As Annie grew past puberty, it became obvious she was not going to have any breasts. She became withdrawn and self-conscious."

"The boys were beginning to notice the transformation taking place as the girls developed. They also noticed that Annie's chest remained flat and they teased her. In Annie's youthful mind, since her chest was flat as a pancake, she thought of herself as a freak of nature in light of her female peer group. She was never going to be noticed by the boys and was doomed to a life of loneliness and frustration."

"Then one day, she noticed when she tensed her biceps, the nipple would pop out followed by a small mass of softness that resembled a breast. She was excited by this new manifestation and noticed when the muscle was relaxed, the new found peripherals disappeared back into her upper arm. Her biceps took on a proportionate size as they grew and resembled the appearance to that of a strong man. Annie's mother bought her a brassiere and a pair of falsies so that she could appear normal and regain her self-confidence."

The students in Mrs. Rhodamy's room were crying with laughter and stomping their feet, by now. Mrs. Rhodamy asked the class to "calm down and show some respect for Mister Munroe's allegory."

He continued. "Needless to say, she was happy with her new look except for the size of her upper arms." The entire class was giggling, sniffling, and once in a while broke into outright hyperactive laughter, as Milo kept reading. "One day," he continued, "she was approached by a boy in the school cafeteria."

"Is anyone sitting here?" he asked, motioning his tray toward the seat next to her. She was delighted that with all the empty places, he chose to sit with her.

"No," she said. "No one is sitting there."

"Good," he said, placing his tray on the table beside her. "Then I'll have lunch with you. My name is Nature Boy."

Annie smiled. "That's an unusual name."

"My real name is Franklin, but my mother calls me Nature Boy because I eat healthy food. You know the old cliché, you are what you eat."

Milo kept reading. "They became friends and started dating, to her mother's delight. Annie was excited by anything he said that exposed his true feelings regarding their friendship. Her excitement was overshadowed by the fear of his eventual and most certain revelation that she was breastless. What then? He had complemented her on several occasions regarding the softness to the touch of her upper arm. When touched, she stiffened quickly and made a low, audible, involuntary sigh." This was one of the moments that had the students stomping their feet the loudest and roaring with uncontrollable convulsions of laughter. People passing Mrs. Rhodamy's room slowed to a snail's pace hoping to satisfy their curiosity on the happenings going on inside. Mrs. Rhodamy began to doubt the wisdom of allowing Milo the range to read his allegory.

Milo compared the parallel in the story Fuller had written about Annie to Fuller's own life experiences. While they were different realities, they were unique and nonetheless physical afflictions. He felt sorry for his friend, Fuller. Fuller still carried the weight in his subconscious of a physical handicap that never truly existed and that is probably why he wrote a story of a disorder stranger than fiction.

"Annie began," Milo continued, "to suspect for the first time the bulbous tissue residing between the skin of her upper arm and the muscles of her biceps were the breast she never had. She now had the option of being offended when someone touched her upper arm or of offering her consent if she chose to allow it."

Mrs. Rhodamy capped her hand over her brow, horrified with disbelief at what she was hearing. She had crossed out several parts of Milo's allegory containing improper suggestions or statements. This was one of them. Milo read right past her markups as though they were not there.

The entire wing of the school was being annoyed by the sounds emanating from Mrs. Rhodamy's classroom. The word began to spread that something big was going on in there.

"Annie was slowly taking on the persona of a normal...

—and Nature Boy said he didn't care, he loved her the way she was. They eventually graduated. He proposed marriage and she accepted. They were married in a church ceremony with a best man, bridesmaids and a church full of well wishers. In other words, they had a normal wedding. They had a reception equal to any either had ever attended. In four months, a child was on the way. In another nine months, a normal baby girl was born to Annie and Nature Boy. She soon discovered, as her husband had been trying to instill in her, that looks were deceiving. It's the kind of person one is inside that governs beauty. She also discovered that as long as the breast within her biceps functioned properly, the location on her body was unimportant. Nature Boy professed to Annie that he had been a breast-fed baby and wanted their baby to receive its nutrition from her mother's milk, the natural, old fashion way. Annie, Nature Boy and their new baby girl comprised a happy family and no one else's opinion really mattered. She happily accepted the distinction of being unique within the human race and had put the unhappiness she had borne as a child behind her."

"When she went out in public, she carried her infant daughter across her arms with the baby's head resting in the joint of her elbow. When the baby was hungry, she would turn her head, Mommie would flex her biceps and baby would take to her favorite milk bottle. The final result was a self-respecting rebuttal to the present-day custom of banning breast feeding in public. Annie got away with it, without opposition. To date, she wasn't aware of anyone enjoying the liberty that was naturally hers because of a trick mother nature had played on her at birth. The End."

The classroom exploded with applause, bravos and shrill whistles. With that, Milo was elevated among Mrs.Rhodamy's class to another tier of celebrity, likened to his existing status of orchestra leader. The boys crowded around, slapping him on the back with compliments and the girls hoped he would notice them favorably. Mrs. Rhodamy was in a panic to regain order in her classroom. When it was over and Milo and Fuller were in the hall, they enjoyed another spasmodic round of levity.

Miss Hatcher was part of the faculty that approved this story as acceptable reading for Mrs. Rhodany's class of mature seniors. She knew this didn't come from Milo. It's origin had to be concocted by Fuller. She wasn't about to do anything to get Milo in trouble so she accepted it as a step forward in Milo's experience as a pre-high school graduate and let it go at that.

CHAPTER 30

▼

Driving home, after picking up his cap and gown, Fuller let his thoughts drift into the next day; the day of graduation. *After tomorrow, it will all be over*, he conceded. Concerns of Calley tried wedging themselves into Fuller's consciousness, but he had lastly developed an expert level of neutrality in this regard and was capable of keeping her impalpable presents suppressed. His mother met him in the hall when he entered the house and took his mortarboard and gown to hang in the closet.

"I've just made a fresh pot of tea, dear, if you'd like some," she tempted Fuller.

"Thanks, Mom," he said. "I'd like that."

"Let's go into the kitchen, I have something to tell you."

After taking their places at the kitchen table, Maggie poured the tea.

"I called Chicago, today," she said leisurely.

"Who's in Chicago," Fuller wanted to know, measuring the seasoning for his tea.

"You know, Tyrone's mother. You remember Tyrone?"

"Of course, Mom. He was my best friend, remember? It's only been a year. What did she have to say?"

"Tyrone answered the phone—"

"Then what did he say?"

"I told him you were graduating high school tomorrow and he was happy for you. He's driving down in the morning to be with you."

"That's great, Mom; really great. I'll be happy to see him."

*   *   *   *

Elaine greeted Milo with similar news when he arrived home. Their mother was driving down for the graduation ceremony from Chicago. Milo was ecstatic hearing his mother was going to get to see him graduate high school and join the celebration. She would be proud that he made it through high school without her prodding. He wanted to surprise her with his diploma before breaking the news that he led his own orchestra. If she had known he was gainfully employed while attending school, she would have worried herself sick wondering if he was playing hooky instead of taking his education seriously. As it was, Elaine would receive their mother's kudos for seeing that he made it through the school system. Milo had no argument with that, but wanted his brother-in-law in on the credit, if there were enough to go around. Of course, Fuller's ingenuity was the steam that drove the engine responsible for Milo's scholarly success, but that was best left with him and Fuller. The bottom line was, he would be happy to see his mother, graduate high school on time, and command the most popular dance orchestra in Waynesford, Indiana. Add Delores to the mix and Milo became the most complete individual in his universe.

*   *   *   *

Fuller was the only natural selection for class valedictorian and he was ultimately chosen for the honor. He wrote his speech in an hour and took another hour to firm it up and practice his articulation on his father.

Graduation was over the horizon and only a few hours away. The members of the Kreppe family were each getting ready to leave for the festivities when the door chimes sounded.

"Honey," Fuller's mother called to him. "See who's at the door. Your Father and I are getting dressed.

Answering the door, Fuller was greeted by Tyrone. His mother and father were standing beside him. His parents joined him in coming to celebrate Fuller's graduation exercises.

"You old son-of-a-gun," Fuller mouthed as he grabbed Ty's extended hand, yanking him across the threshold into the house. "Boy, am I glad to see you."

"Watch who you callin' boy, honky," Tyrone chided, then flashed his headlight grin. They laughed and hugged, then backed away to look at each other. They declared how neither had changed, except maybe for filling out some.

Tyrone's mother cleared her throat to get Fuller's attention. "Ahem, aren't you going to invite us in?"

"God, I'm sorry," Fuller apologized. Turning to face Tyrone's mother and father, he invited them into the house.

"You'd better give me a hug," Tyrone's mother demanded of Fuller. "I knew you when you were in training pants and used to changed your diapers. I watched you grow up from a little nothin' to where you is today."

"I wouldn't forget you," Fuller yielded as he hugged Ty's mother. He took her husband's hand and shook it, saying, "Please have a seat. Mom and Dad will be out in a moment and you can freshen up before we leave for the ceremony."

Mister and Mrs. Kreppe appeared shortly from the rear of the house. The reunion was a happy one and Mrs. Kreppe served refreshments while waiting for the time scheduled to depart for the graduation exercises.

"What have you been doing with yourself?" Bernard asked Tyrone.

"You haven't heard—Why, I work for the city of Chicago," Tyrone said, revealing his pearly whites and thrusting his chest forward.

"That's respectable," Bernard complimented.

"Tell Bernard what it is you do for the city of Chicago, boy," Tyrone's father pushed, verbally.

"I'm a garbage man," Tyrone responded, maintaining his luminous smile at Mister Kreppe.

"Talk about dreams coming true," Fuller remarked.

"Yeah, I finally made it." Tyrone chuckled. "I stand on the back of the garbage truck and whistle for the driver to move on to the next can."

*   *   *   *

At the Powell residence, another reunion was taking place. Milo and Elaine's mother had arrived in time for the festivities. It was a syrupy get together. Tears of joy streamed down Elaine and her mother's faces. Minette apologized for not driving down Thanksgiving or Christmas. "The weather, you know and my arthritis." Milo was just happy to see his mother without getting misty.

"Stand back, Milo. Let me look at you," his mother asked of him. "My, how you've grown in just a year. You've turned into such a handsome young man."

"I love you too, Mom," Milo teased, happy they were all together for this once in a lifetime occasion. He was also happy to be at this place in time instead of making excuses for why he dropped out of school, which was his mother's worst nightmare when she let him move south to live with his sister. She will never know how close he came to throwing in the towel, save for Fuller's grace.

His mother noticed an attractive lady standing in the doorway waiting to be introduced. She was small, but magnificent atop three inch heels.

"I'm Elaine's and Milo's mother. And you are—"

"I am Delores Hatcher, Mrs. Munroe, Milo's date. I am so happy to meet you," Delores declared, introducing herself.

"Excuse me, Mom. I didn't mean to be rude," Milo said, putting his arm around Delores's shoulder. "Delores is a special friend."

Mrs. Munroe freshened up from her trip and after having coffee and catching up on family gossip, it was nearing time to leave. No one had mentioned Milo's orchestra to her. They wanted her to be surprised. She pulled Elaine aside. "Isn't she a little old for Milo?" she asked referring to Delores.

"She's five years his senior," Elaine answered without hesitation. "When you get to know her, you'll love her. She's been good for Milo."

*   *   *   *

The high school auditorium was a noisy place as the final touches were being applied for the evening gala. The stage was still in the process of having the audio tested and a final check of the lighting. Students were milling around the assembly hall searching for their preset seating arrangements when the Kreppe family arrived with their guests. They looked for Milo and his family who were also looking for them. Milo and Fuller spotted each other about the same time. The families converged in the hall behind the main entrance to the building and knitted their way through the introductions before finding a block of seats large enough for their crowd. "I'm finally glad to meet you Fuller," Minette Munroe said. "Now I can see a face when Milo speaks of you."

The program began on time. A silence settled over the guests as a member of the faculty introduced Mrs. Holt. As she stood in front of the podium, the lights dimmed and a spotlight focused on the principal's face. It streamed downward, spreading across her large bosom and concentrating on the full roundness of her distended stomach, catching the attention intended for her face. An involuntary facial twitch distracted the hairs on her chin mold.

"Ladies and Gentlemen," Mrs. Holt began. She went through the line of dignitaries, thanking them for their presence this evening, then proceeded to address the assembly. "We are here tonight…and now, from Miss Hatcher's homeroom, it is my distinct pleasure to introduce to you, this year's graduating class valedictorian, Mister Fuller Kreppe." The usual applause with the exception of Rico and Snake. They hooted and howled like caged circus animals as their testimony to Fuller's credentials.

Fuller took the podium and thanked Mrs. Holt, the faculty members, student body and, sidestepping decorum, said "especially Ricardo Castro and Jesus Morales."

The student body resounded their approval of Fuller's acknowledgment of the school's two infamous hell raisers. "We are here tonight to accept diplomas authorizing us to migrate into our great society as disciplined ladies and gentlemen, ready to accept the responsibilities and rewards awaiting us. We have prepared long and hard for this day, beginning twelve years ago. We are...and the love we have for each other and our alma mater will sustain us throughout our lifetime. In closing, I would like to congratulate each of you as you cross this stage to receive your diploma. The glory is yours for keeping the faith and not giving up on yourselves during the bad times, and knowing your personal victory was waiting for you in this final moment. Thank you, very much."

More applause and animal noises from Rico and Snake.

Mrs. Kreppe was proud of her son. Tyrone's mother reached over and squeezed her hand while nodding approval. She looked to Tyrone, sitting on her other side and said, "See, I told you not to drop out of school, boy."

Everyone receiving a diploma was applauded as they crossed the stage. When Rico and Snake came through the line, they gave Fuller a high sign of appreciation which he proudly returned. Their faces were ablaze with alligator grins, knowing they wouldn't have made it if Fuller hadn't extended the educational straw they clung to, to survive. Anyone else would have let them drown in their own ocean of difficulties. Their success was a bit different and opposite from the single finger sign Snake used to shoot regularly at Fuller. The mood this time was appropriate.

Fuller watched with a heavy heart as Calley walked through the line. Calley's mother clicked pictures of her receiving her diploma. Alma came up front to snap a picture of Lupe receiving hers. She also took pictures of Fuller and Milo when they crossed the stage. When Milo received his diploma, his recognition as a renowned orchestra leader and purveyor of the Thalidomide Story brought the auditorium to a new instance of screams and whistles. His mother was delighted that her son seemed to be so popular. She leaned over to Elaine and asked, "Isn't that Delores sitting on the stage?"

"Yes, Mom. She's a member of the faculty."

Several negative thoughts crossed Mrs. Munroe's mind regarding Milo's special friend, but she was wise not to go there for the time being, at least until she
knew more of the circumstances surrounding their friendship. She was happy to
see Milo's friend, Fuller, was the class valedictorian.

When the ceremony was finally over and the crowds mixed together congratu-
lating each other, Fuller went looking for Rico and Snake to offer his personal
congratulations. He found them wondering through the crowd, prideful of
attaining equality by virtue of their diplomas. A sublime, unanticipated moment
gripped the three of them as the reality set in that high school was really over and
it was time for them to move on. Fuller smiled at both of his former tormentors.
They snapped to each other in a spontaneous, three-way hug.

"I'm going to miss you Latino smart asses," Fuller said fondly. "You'd better
stay in touch or I'm going to have you picked up on charges of being yourselves."

"Ha!" Rico came back, holding back the dampness in his eyes. Machismo tears
were not allowed, but were on the verge of betraying his self respect. "Hey—
Guess what?" He offered, pushing Fuller back and breaking his fixation of pending sadness at the thought of separation from Fuller. "What do you es-see when
you look at us, me and Es-snake?"

"I see the two biggest fuck-ups that ever graced Anthony Wayne High?"

"No, no. Besides that" Rico said, trying to be serious while suppressing a
laugh. "Take another look. We are the newest recruits in the United Es-states
Marines, me and Es-snake," he announced.

"Yeah, United Es-states Marines," echoed Snake. "We leave Monday morning
for boot camp in San Diego, California."

Fuller stepped back to observe the two *come from behinds* he had molded into
high school graduates. His mood angled him into a corner of serene contempla-
tion. He observed how far they had progressed as socially acceptable friends
instead of the unstable nonconformists they were when the three of them were
spun together, nine months ago, as rivals in the same high school. The impact
transcended his reflective ambience with a tinge of personal sadness. He was careful not to let gloom infringe on his achievement of reconstructing these guys. He
knew he was probably going to ease away from them in the real world, as nature
wove its indefinite patterns of change. Rico and Snake sensed it too. They sensed
an uncoupling of the emotional strands that bonded the three of them together
so strangely.

There was this crazy moment of admiration between Fuller and his former
nemeses. As it passed, an involuntary impulse drew the three of them back

together in another three-way hug. They stood there patting each other repeatedly on the back.

"I'm proud of you guys," Fuller said. "Go show the marines what you've got."

"We love you Fooler, and dat don't make us queer, neither. We really do love you, man." Rico repeated with an emotionally shaken voice.

"RRRico's right. We love you, man," Snake echoed Rico's sentiment. "We never gonna forget dat it was you dat made the difference for us to graduate. We owe averything we are today to you, Amigo. We owe you big time."

"Por nada (for nothing)," Fuller said in Spanish.

Now that Milo had received his diploma, he and Delores were free of pending threats from Charles Cagle. By the grace of Mrs. Holt, Cagle's time had run out. Milo excused himself to find a telephone and call the ballroom. He made seating arrangements for twelve near the stage and ordered a continuous array of hors d'oeuvres be served to his guest. The extra seat was for Calley. He then searched and found her in the mass of humanity. Milo invited her to his party. She thanked him and politely excused herself.

When he returned, he invited Fuller's family and friends to join the party with his family and Delores at the ballroom. The disclosure that she was going to a party was casually accepted by Milo's mother. She saw it as one of those affairs where the young folks discarded the old timers to an obscure corner of the room, leaving them to sit and be entertained but not seen. She had no idea she was about to witness the stardom her son has achieved since leaving Chicago.

They were to meet Fuller's group at the ballroom where Milo was to take charge of his baton, now under the direction of his number two man.

Milo's mother wanted to know more about his car but refrained from asking questions for fear of dampening the thriving ambience.

After parking in the Anthony Wayne garage, Milo excused himself and entered the rear door via the musician's lounge to be with the orchestra.

"Where did Milo go?" Mrs. Munroe asked Elaine.

"That's part of the surprise," Elaine told her mother.

"What surprise, dear?"

"You'll see," Elaine said.

They entered the ballroom through the lobby. Doctor Powell lead them to their reserved, elongated table. Milo had arranged for a brief intermission to allow his party to get seated. The intent was for him to be on stage leading his orchestra when it revolved to face the audience. He wanted his mother to be surprised by his success. Elaine sat on one side of her mother and Delores on the other.

Mrs. Monroe was obviously uneasy, turning from side to side, looking for Milo. "Where did he go?" she asked Elaine again.

"He'll be along in a minute, Mom."

The lights dimmed and the music started as the stage began its slow spin toward the dance floor. Elaine was hinting at how good the music sounded, then how nice the band members looked in their jackets.

Her mother agreed, but didn't take the hint. Finally, she did a double take and turned to Elaine. "Why that looks like—it is!" She exclaimed. "Elaine, that's your brother up there. What's going on here? Is this some kind of joke?"

"No, Mom, it's no joke."

The theme song ended. Milo turned to face the audience, acknowledging his mother's presence, and pointing downward to her behind a huge grin. Then speaking through the microphone, said, "Welcome to another session with the Milo Star Orchestra—"etc, "and we invite everyone to dance and have a fun evening. Our first number is an oldie. I'd like to dedicate it to my mother who is here in the audience; *More than you know*".

Mrs. Munroe turned to face Elaine. "Did you know about this?" she asked.

"He's good at it, isn't he," Elaine answered.

"But his name isn't Star," she said.

"I know, Mom. Listen to the music."

In the middle of another dance number, contrasting sounds from an assortment of instruments began emanating from the lobby; softly at first, but growing louder as they advanced toward the ballroom. Milo was becoming agitated until he recognized the intentionally disorganized sounds of *What a friend we have in Jesus* invading his dance floor. He knew it had to be—it was, it was Joey Crabtree, Pete Scalibib, Cully Tujaque, Isadore Rosenbloom and last but certainly not least, Charlie the Queer. Joey was blowing his trombone out of cadence and Pete fingered his saxophone with a tacky sound. Cully played his trumpet like a beginner. They remembered the song was Milo's favorite when he was little. Their adaptation was wild and disorderly, bordering on sacrilege, as they marched toward the stage. Izzy and Charlie the Queer didn't have an instrument. Izzy was laughing out loud with his arms outstretched as he neared the stage to greet Milo. Charlie the Queer sashayed behind Izzy, smiling at everyone and waving with his fingertips to the men in the audience that struck his fancy.

Milo raised his baton and brought the current number to an abrupt finish. He reached for the microphone and said to the audience, "Excuse me. These are old friends of mine from Chicago." Then he jumped off the stage and into the arms of his five roistering friends. A five round hugging session ensued gleefully. He looked at Izzy who was suspiciously jovial. "Where is your instrument?" Milo asked Izzy.

"Milo—baby—You know I can't play anything but the radio."

"Then why aren't you singing," Milo jumped down Izzy's throat, figuratively.

Izzy opened his arms again, gripping Milo's shoulders. "You know I can't sing about Jesus. I'm a Jew, for Christ's sake."

Milo threw his arms around Izzy as far as they would go, saying, "God I'm glad to see you nuts. Come up on the stage."

Milo stood behind the microphone. "Ladies and Gentlemen," he announced. "May I have your attention for a moment. Please excuse me while I calm down from this incredible surprise. Cully Tujaque, here, is my mentor." Milo's emotions betrayed him as a tear welled in each eye. Flashbacks of his father giving him his trumpet and Uncle Cully's promise to teach him to play it, manifested as he spoke. "He taught me to play the trumpet when I was too young to do anything else but be a nuisance. Thank you, Uncle Cully for putting up with me all those many years." The audience applauded. "Cully Tujaque plays first trumpet for the Chicago Symphony." More applause.

Milo turned and motioned for Pete and Joey to join him at the mike. "Joey Crabtree leads my deceased father's orchestra in Chicago and Pete here, plays in that orchestra. More applause. Joey gave me my first professional job, and let's not forget Izzy and Charlie. Move over here, guys," he said, making room for the two characters that followed the musicians. "Izzy here hired me as a regular in his Chicago Night Club and Charlie here takes care of the needs of the boys in Joey's band." The audience applauded Izzy and Charlie. Izzy faced the guest with a sunshine smile, and spreading his arms out from his sides like angel wings in flight, bowed majestically. He eased over to the microphone. "The kid used to play in my sleazy South side strip club," Izzy chortled in his normally strained, damp voice while expressing good humor and illuminating his already broad smile. While Izzy spoke to the audience, Charlie surveyed the crowd with his smiley giddiness and continued waving with his fingertips, this time to the general audience instead of certain men that attracted his attention. The audience laughed with their applause. Milo was embarrassed by Izzy's harangue in front of his mother because he had purposely avoided the legality of playing while underaged in places that served alcoholic beverages and danced half naked women on stage. Instead, he invited the three musicians to sit in with his orchestra. Izzy and Charlie the Queer went to join Milo's family at their table. Joey, Pete and Cully recognized Milo's mother, sister and brother-in-law and acknowledged their presence from the stage. It magnified the notability of those sitting at the table and they reveled in the recognition from Milo's old friends. Minette turned to Elaine and said, "I didn't know he played in those places." Saying nothing, Elaine just smiled at her mother.

It turned out to be an exciting evening. It ended with more questions on Mrs. Munroe's mind than were forthcoming answers. She remembered Elaine saying that Delores had been good for Milo. After observing his achievements, she had to agreed with Elaine. Delores would have to share credit somewhere in the making of the man Milo had become. Milo's trumpet solos were sentimental and reminiscent of his father's playing; beautifully expressed, trapping his mother in the duality of sadness and happiness at the same time. She privately absorbed the moment of nostalgia. Everyone experienced the magic the party generated. Before it was over, Minette danced at least once with the different men at their table. Fuller joined in the merriment and danced with all the women. The evening was an occasion to remember.

When it was over, Mrs. Munroe turned to Delores and observed her beautiful smile and sparkling eyes. They had evaded her until now. She knew instinctively at that moment, Delores was right for her son. She found herself staring into Delores' captivating eyes and when the feeling of being caught flashed her back to reality, she took Delores' hand and said emphatically, "I like you."

CHAPTER 31

▼

Ten weeks had past since graduation and Milo was leaving from a meeting with his business manager when he saw Calley waiting at the bus stop. He approached from behind and tapped her shoulder. "Hello stranger," he said.

She turned around to see Milo as the culprit invading her space. "Milo!" She screamed. "Gee, it's good to see you. How have you been?" she asked as they hugged each other.

"The same ol', same ol'," he said. "How have you been?"

"I've been doing swell. You know, under the circumstances. How is Miss Hatcher?"

"Delores? Oh she's doing fine, thank you. She will be happy to know we bumped into each other. Where are you headed?" Milo asked.

"I've done a little shopping," she answered. "I guess I'm ready to catch the bus and go home."

"Catch the bus?"

"Yes," her pleasantry gravitated to neutrality. "That's the way I travel these days."

"Not on this day, sweetheart. I'm going to give you a lift." Milo insisted. "Tell you what?" he said, "We haven't seen each other in quite a spell. What do you say we have lunch, then I'll take you home?"

"Thank you, Milo. I'd like that."

The Anthony Wayne Hotel was around the corner. He purposely selected the main hotel dining room. It would give her pause to think of her time there with Fuller. The timing was perfect, if he could get her to broach the subject.

The Maitre d' greeted them. "Good morning, Mister Munroe. Your usual table, sir?"

"Yes, please," Milo replied.

He held the chair for Calley, then sat across the table from her. After placing their order, they engaged in idle conversation. He gave her leeway to bring up the subject of Fuller. She didn't. He knew it was incumbent upon him to mention Fuller if he was going to be discussed at all. His endeavor to be tactful was shaky and uncertain at best. "What do you hear from Fuller?" he asked, trying not to be nervous.

"I don't," she said. "We're not in touch."

"That's too bad," he said. "We miss being with you and Fuller. Maybe some-day we can all be together again."

"I guess it's a little late for that," she said. "We need to get on with our sepa-rate lives. You understand."

"I do. I surely do," Milo said. "I wish you both the very best."

They didn't say much after that. Finishing their lunch, Milo reached across the table and covered her hands with his. "Calley," he remarked, keeping the tone of his voice steady and clear. "I love you, babe and Fuller loves you. I know he misses you terribly."

Tears welled up in Calley's eyes. "Oh Milo, I don't know what's right any-more," she sobbed. "I do miss Fuller, but it's gone too far. I don't know whether I did the right thing or not by shutting him out, but he left me no other choice."

"Believe me, Calley. The situation between you and Fuller is a case of good intentions gone bad."

"I wish it was that simple, Milo. When Lupe told me about him and the pros-titute," she said, assuming he knew, "I was so hurt. You just don't know. Later, when we discussed it, his excuse was so humiliating and absurd, only a fool would have believed him. It's like a bad dream come true. I guess you know the story?"

"Yes, Calley, I know the story—There's something you should know and I'm not quite sure how to tell you, but be patient and allow me to get it out. Okay?"

She looked down at her lap timidly and nodded okay.

If it was Fuller's story he was alluding to, she had heard it all before. She was willing to listen one more time and tune for missing signals that would give her pause to exonerate Fuller.

"Fuller loves you, honey, and he beats himself up on a daily basis. What I'm about to tell you, is going to sound strange, I know, but what you find humiliat-ing and absurd is the honest to God's truth."

Yep, she thought, *it's the same ol' story.*

"What he did with that woman was to prove to himself that he was worthy of you. Calley, does that make sense?"

"Nothing makes sense anymore," she said.

"Calley, Fuller grew into manhood thinking he had a sexual dysfunction and…" He told her the entire story, from the doctor visit to their breakup.

She knew Milo was credible but how could she believe such an insane rerun of the same old story? Then she wondered if this was a fabricated tale to regain her trust, or one of those things you throw against the wall and hope it sticks. She wanted to believe something, anything reasonable, that would put an end to both her and Fuller's yearning for each other. She was looking for a break in the ice, but this was the second verse to the same old story and still lacked the likelihood required to set them free.

"I don't know, Milo. I put so much trust in Fuller and the way he let me down was so damaging. I'm so hurt that he went to a prostitute, instead of confiding in me." She became somber as she spoke. "I would have helped him work through any problem, whatever it was. You know that."

"Calley, you have every right to feel the way you do and believe me, I do understand."

"Thank you Milo, I appreciate that," she said.

"What would it take for you to forgive Fuller?"

"There lies the problem; I don't know. I doubt he would take me back."

"Fuller feels like half a person. I know he will take you back. How about it Calley. What would it take for you to forgive Fuller?"

"I would like to forgive Fuller, but to answer your question truthfully, I really don't know."

They had established some dialog on the subject of Fuller and that was a good sign. She was at least listening. "Don't hold him under forever," Milo said, "he'll drown in a sea of bitterness—and don't let pride stand in your way, either. This may be your last chance, darling."

"Pride has nothing to do with it," Calley said, wishing it was that simple. "It's more of a case of trust and self respect."

"Calley, what if I can prove to you that everything Fuller has told you is the truth? Would that make a difference?"

"How could you do that?" she asked. "I've heard it all before."

"The doctor Fuller went to is not far from here. Would you believe him if he corroborates Fuller's story?"

"I don't know," she said, confused and doubtful. "I would like to," she added, not confident she meant what she had just said.

Milo took Calley at her word and wasn't going to let this moment slip by the wayside. "Let's go," he said, rising from his chair and taking Calley by the arm. "He told me the doc that examined him. He's in the same hospital building Ray's office is in." Milo signed the check and they left the Anthony Wayne Hotel together.

They entered the doctor's anteroom and asked to be worked in. When their name was called, the nurse deposited them in a treatment room, saying "the doctor will be with you shortly," and shut the door. The short wait soon transformed into tiny dissections of accumulated time. Finally the doctor came in and introduced himself. "I'm Doctor Mason," he said. Milo introduced Calley first, then himself, followed by "My brother-in-law is Doctor Raymond Powell. His office is in this building."

"I know Doctor Powell," the doctor said. "What can I do for you?"

"Doctor Mason," Milo started off. "I have a friend that's one of your patients. His name is Fuller Kreppe. He came to visit you last year with a symptom he thought was some kind of sexual dysfunction. The reason we are here today—Calley is his girlfriend. They have a drastic misunderstanding regarding the purpose of his visit—"

"Let me stop you there, Mister Munroe. You have to know that anything said between Mister Kreppe and myself is privileged information. I'm not allowed to discuss his visit with you."

"I fully understand," Milo said. "I was hoping you could give Calley some much needed assurance that might help heal the rift between her and her boyfriend, without getting involved in his reason for coming to you."

"Tell me Mister Munroe, how do you suggest I give this assurance without getting involved in Mister Kreppe's record."

Milo was afraid of being shunted toward a dead end by professional standards, but he kept trying. "There are two lives at stake here, doctor. Since I'm paying for an office visit, I want to discuss my sexual deficiency with you and I'd like Calley to remain in the room."

"I see," said the doctor. "You look familiar. Do I know you from somewhere?"

"My orchestra plays at the ballroom in the Anthony Wayne Hotel."

"Yes, yes, I remember now," said the doctor. "You played at our Medical Convention last month. My wife and I visit your ballroom quite frequently. We enjoy your music very much, young man. Er, what did you say your friend's name was?"

"Fuller Kreppe," Milo answered, then spelled it out. "K-r-e-p-p-e."

The doctor excused himself and left the treatment room. After a short absence, he returned and sat on his examination table. "I remember Mister Kreppe," he said. "Now what is it I can do for you?"

"Doctor, I have this problem during sexual intercourse. Everything seems to work okay, but I can't make it happen."

"You mean ejaculate," the doctor interjected.

"Exactly," Milo said as if they were getting somewhere. "Is there something wrong with me?"

Calley's eyes popped wide open.

The doctor said, "There is a precedent for your condition, young fellow. My advice is to hang in there. In time, it should correct itself, however, I can tell you this much. I had a patient once with a similar symptom. I told him exactly what I'm telling you, but I could tell from his disappointment that he didn't believe me. Don't you make the same mistake?"

"Thanks, Doc," Milo said as he directed Calley from the treatment room. He paid for the office visit on their way out.

From the time the doctor came back and they left his office, Calley was lost in the confusion as to what transpired, everything happened so fast. Milo clarified her confusion by the doctor's assessment of his condition, combined with a previous patient's disbelief of his diagnosis. He finally got the message across to Calley the doctor had done them a favor without crossing the privilege line. The previous patient the doctor was referring to had to be Fuller. Like he said, this patient didn't believe him.

"You see, Calley, Fuller was searching for a solution, not lip service. That's why he went to the prostitute."

Milo laid out all the facts to Calley, including the peppermint oil. "I'm not comfortable talking to you about this as I am sure you would just as soon not listen, but if we are ever going to get you guys back together, you're going to have to understand the reality of the situation. It's the only way you can free yourself up to forgive Fuller. What I've told you Calley, is the truth and the entire story. There's nothing more to add. Don't miss this opportunity, honey. What do you say?"

"I do believe you," she said, "and I'm beginning to understand. Do you think Fuller can ever forgive me?"

"He has a big heart," Milo said. "I'm sure he's hoping *you'll* forgive *him*."

"Oh, Milo—I've been so wrong and I've treated him so badly."

"What if he has a new girlfriend?"

"We will have to face that when we come to it."

"Milo, please take me to him."

"I can't," Milo said. "He's at State University for his orientation. He starts classes next week."

"Ohhhh," she showed disappointment. "How can we ever get together?"

"As soon as he gets settled, I'll get you his address and phone number."

"Promise you won't forget," she begged of Milo.

"Not a chance," he said.

"I've been so stupid," she said, debasing herself. "I should have trusted Fuller. I put both of us through so much hell."

"Don't be too hard on yourself, baby" Milo said. "It wasn't an easy story to believe." Milo drove Calley home. When they arrived, he walked her to the door. She was wiping tears from her eyes.

"Keep your chin up, honey," Milo said. "Everything is going to turn out all right. You'll see." He kissed her on the cheek and left.

*　　　*　　　*　　　*

Calley begged her mother to allow her to switch from City College to State University. Her mother was reluctant at first, but was happy her daughter's endeavor was to make up with Fuller. Luckily, she was barely under the wire to make this semester when she applied at the University for admittance. In a few days she got a letter of acceptance. She arrived at the university the day classes were to begin. Calley's mother helped her move into her dormitory and they met her roommate. Her parting words to Calley were "Goodbye, darling and don't forget to write."

Calley said "Goodbye, Mom. I love you. Don't forget to send money."

Her mother smiled as she closed the door behind her.

*　　　*　　　*　　　*

Calley wasted no time in putting her things away. She said goodbye to her roommate and hurried out to search the campus for Fuller's dormitory. When she found it, it was early. She sat on a concrete bench outside and waited for Fuller. She was afraid if he saw her first, he may try to avoid her by going in the back door, or go in the back door because it was more convenient, missing her all together. It was a long and dubious wait. She was ready to give up and return to her dorm in defeat when she saw a figure a block away she thought she recognized. As he came closer, she knew it was Fuller. She stood up and waited for him to come closer. His face appeared strained with preoccupation and didn't seem to belong to the Fuller she knew. He nearly passed her by without recognizing her. When he looked over and saw Calley standing there, he stopped dead in his tracks.

"Calley—is that you?" He was doubtful and utterly surprised with disbelief.

"It's me, Fuller," she said, trying to smile, not knowing what to expect. She was frozen in her footsteps, her palms sweaty. "I'm enrolled here at State," she informed him, anxiously.

He was speechless for a long moment, then asked, "Are you here to see me?"

"Yes—YES! Oh, Fuller," she cried, taking a step in his direction. "How could I have been so—stupid?" Her purse slipped from her hands and fell to the ground. She raised her arms in anticipation of receiving him close to her.

To him, her presence, bordered on surrealism. She was the last person in this world he expected to see. His books fell from limp arms as he took a step forward. Then, as if drawn together by magnets, their bodies snapped together, in a binding embrace; neither saying anything. They just stood there and sniffled with tears in their eyes. Her mind went blank. She was overcome with joy having him close to her again.

It was several minutes before he realized the rift between them was over and they were together once more. The hopelessness of ever seeing her again disappeared and the void it left was filled by the warmth of her presence. He stepped back to have another look and satisfy himself that the person standing before him was really Calley. She was fearful he wouldn't accept her and was happy when he smiled his approval of her being there. She knew then she had another chance with Fuller as they stood there facing each other.

Tears were streaming down both their faces. They eased closer to each other until their lips met. The resulting kiss was long, intense and sincere. They stood there locked in a secure embrace. It was at this point they both knew they had survived their senior year. They had moved up from the halls of a local high school to those of the ivory towers and maturity.

With maturity came a completeness of two hearts filled with joy. He erased from his mind and soul the thing that had caused them so much misery. He was finally exonerated of the shame for having exceeded their boundary by him cheating on Calley with another woman, no matter what the circumstance. When all seemed hopeless, he was blessed with a rare second chance. He knew if there were any truth to heaven being here on earth, it had to be now, at this very moment, with Calley held tightly in his arms.

❧

0-595-31097-4

Printed in the United States
19888LVS00005B/121-177